The Undertaking

Audrey Magee

W F HOWES LTD

This large print edition published in 2014 by
W F Howes Ltd
Unit 4, Rearsby Business Park, Gaddesby Lane,
Rearsby, Leicester LE7 4YH

1 3 5 7 9 10 8 6 4 2

First published in the United Kingdom in 2014
by Atlantic Books Ltd.

A CIP catalogue record for this book is available
from the British Library

ISBN 978 1 47125 837 4

Typeset by Palimpsest Book Production Limited,
Falkirk, Stirlingshire
Printed and bound by
www.printondemand-worldwide.com of Peterborough, England

The Undertaking

For Johnny

CHAPTER 1

He dragged barbed wire away from the post, clearing a space on the parched earth, and took the photograph from the pocket of his tunic. He pressed the picture against the post and held it in place with string, covering the woman's hair and neck, but not her face. He could still see that, still see her sullen eyes and sulking lips. He tied a knot, and spat at the ground. She would have to do.

He lay down to soak up the last of the summer sun, indifferent to the swirling dust and grit, wanting only to rest, to experience the momentary nothingness of waiting. But he sat up again. The ground was too hard, the sun too hot. He lit a cigarette and stared into the shimmering heat until he located a rotund figure, its arms and legs working furiously, but generating little speed. The man arrived eventually, grumbling and panting, sweat dribbling onto the white of his clerical collar.

'Why are you so bloody far away?' he said.

'I wanted privacy.'

'Well, you've got that. Is everything ready?'

'Yes.'

'Let's get on with it, then,' said the chaplain. 'We should make it just in time.'

He drew a pencil and piece of crumpled paper from his pocket.

'Who is the groom, Private?'

'I am.'

'And your name?'

'Peter Faber.'

'And the witnesses?' said the chaplain.

'Over there,' said Faber, pointing at three men curled up in sleep.

The chaplain walked over and kicked at them. 'They're drunk.'

Faber blew rings of smoke at the blue sky.

'Are you drunk too, Faber?'

'Not yet.'

The chaplain kicked harder. The men moved, grudgingly.

'Right, we're doing this now. Put your cigarette out, Faber. Stand up. Show a little respect.'

Faber stubbed the cigarette into the soil, pressed his long, narrow hands against the earth and slowly got to his feet.

'Hair out of your eyes, man,' said the chaplain. 'Who is it you're marrying?'

'Katharina Spinell.'

'Is that her there? In the photograph?'

'As far as I know.'

'As far as you know?'

'I've never met her.'

'But you want to marry her?'

'Yes, Sir.'

'You're keen.'

'To escape this stinking hellhole.'

The priest wrote briefly, and returned the pen and paper to his pocket.

'We can begin,' he said. 'Your helmet, Faber?'

'That's it. On the ground. Next to the photograph.'

'Gather round, men,' said the priest. 'Right hands on the helmet.'

They squatted in a small circle around the dirty, dented helmet, knees and elbows tumbling into each other.

'Groom first.'

Faber placed his hand on the metal, but quickly took it off again.

'It's too bloody hot.'

'Get on with it,' said the chaplain. 'It's a minute to twelve at home.'

Faber pulled his sleeve over his hand.

'The flesh of your hand, Faber. Not the sleeve.'

The priest picked up a fistful of earth and scattered it over the helmet.

'There.'

'Thank you.'

Faber replaced his hand, and the other men followed. The chaplain spoke, and within minutes Faber was married to a woman in Berlin he had never met. A thousand miles away, at exactly the same moment, she took part in a similar ceremony witnessed by her father and mother; her part in a war pact that ensured honeymoon leave for him and a widow's pension for her in the event of his death.

'That's it,' said the chaplain. 'You're now a married man.'

Each of the men shook his hand.

'I need a drink,' said Faber.

He picked up his helmet, but left the photograph and walked back to camp.

CHAPTER 2

He stared, for longer than was polite, and then spoke.

'I'm Peter Faber.'

'I know. I recognize you from your photograph.'

'You're Katharina?'

She nodded and he shook her hand, surprised by the softness of her flesh, by the tumble of dark hair over her shoulders. She tugged at him.

'My hand,' she said. 'May I have it back?'

'I'm sorry.'

He dropped it and stepped back onto the pavement, to stand beside his pack and gun. She stayed where she was, her hip leaning into the half-opened door.

'Was it a long journey, Mr Faber?'

'Yes. Yes, it was. Very.'

She raised her hand against the sun and stared at him.

'How long are you staying?'

'Ten days.'

She pulled back the door.

'You should come in.'

He picked up his kit and stepped into the dark, windowless hall. She put her hand over her nose and mouth. He stank. She moved away from him and set off up the stairs.

'We're on the second floor.'

'Who's we?'

'My parents.'

'I didn't know you lived with them.'

'I'm not paid enough to live by myself.'

'I suppose not. What do you do?'

'Oh yes, I forgot.'

He followed her up the frayed linoleum steps, watching each plump buttock as it shifted her skirt from side to side. She looked back at him.

'Do you need any help?'

'I'm fine,' he said.

'They're looking forward to meeting you.'

She pushed open the door to the apartment. He slid the pack off his shoulder.

'Let me take it,' she said.

'It's too heavy.'

'I'll manage.'

She dragged the bag to a room behind the door, and returned for his rifle.

'I'll hang on to that,' he said.

'You're in Berlin now.'

'I prefer having it with me.'

He followed her along a narrow corridor to a small kitchen shimmering with condensation. Her parents got to their feet and saluted, each movement brisk with enthusiasm.

'I'm Günther Spinell,' said the man. 'Katharina's father.'

Faber shook his hand.

'We are extremely proud to have a second soldier in our family.'

Faber looked down at the table. Four places were set, the crockery mismatched and chipped.

'My son is to the north of you, Mr Faber. Somewhere outside Moscow.'

'The poor sod.'

'Johannes is a very brave man, Mr Faber.'

Katharina's mother, her greying hair tightly curled, pointed to a chair.

'Do sit down, Mr Faber.'

He unhooked his helmet, ammunition pouches and bread bag from his belts, and heaped them on a narrow counter beside the cooker. He sat down and scratched his back against the wood.

'Are you comfortable?'

'I'm fine.'

'Did you have a good journey?' said Mrs Spinell.

'Nights in the train were cold.'

'You don't have a winter coat? No gloves?'

'Not yet.'

'Do you think Johannes has any?'

'I don't know.'

Mrs Spinell took a handkerchief from her sleeve and held it over her mouth and nose. She coughed, and cleared her throat.

'Open the window, Katharina.'

He watched her push at the glass and lean out,

her bottom sticking back into the room. She remained there, breathing the cold October air. He stared at her broad, fleshy hips.

'Mr Ewald is stacking his crates,' she said.

Faber heard wood slapping against wood.

'That's our grocer, Mr Faber,' said her father. 'A remarkably loyal man.'

'He's finishing early,' said Mrs Spinell.

'There wasn't much today,' said Katharina.

She turned back into the room.

'Come on, Mother. We should make coffee.'

Faber lit a cigarette. Mrs Spinell placed an ashtray on the table. It was shaped as a swastika.

'It belongs to Johannes, Mr Faber, but you can use it.'

The two women, without talking, set to work.

'Have you been to Berlin before, Mr Faber?' asked Mr Spinell.

'No.'

'Katharina will show you the city later.'

Mrs Spinell poured coffee and Katharina slid a slice of cake onto his plate.

'It's lemon.'

'Thank you.'

He lifted the coffee to his nose, put it down and took up the cake. He let out a little sigh. They laughed.

'I'm sorry,' he said. 'It's been a long time.'

'Go ahead,' said Mrs Spinell. 'Eat.'

He slipped the sponge into his mouth and chased it with the coffee, a rush of sweet and bitter. He did it again. They laughed again.

'It's so good, Mrs Spinell.'

'It's real coffee,' said Mr Spinell. 'From Dr Weinart, a friend of mine.'

'And a neighbour gave us the eggs for the cake,' said Mrs Spinell. 'As a wedding present.'

'She's a communist,' said Mr Spinell.

'Mrs Sachs is a good person, Günther.'

'That's how they disguise themselves, Esther. That neighbourly sharing.'

Katharina sipped at her coffee, but nudged her cake towards Faber.

'You have it. You want it more than I do.'

He ate her cake and a third slice, then sat back into his chair and lit another cigarette.

'What do you teach, Mr Faber?'

'Elementary, Mrs Spinell.'

'Do you have a job?'

'Yes. At the school I attended as a boy.'

'Are they keeping it for you?'

'Yes.'

'But a teacher's salary is not much,' said Mrs Spinell. 'Can you provide properly for my daughter?'

He felt their eyes on him. And then her father sniggered.

'Katharina's mother worries a lot,' he said.

'I am only trying to protect our daughter, Günther,' she said. 'To save her from what I had to go through at the end of the last war.'

'Not now, Esther,' said Mr Spinell.

'Yes now. I had to scavenge for food, Mr Faber, rummage through bins to stop my children crying

9

from hunger. Johannes howled and howled. He's still hungry, I'm sure of it.'

'Johannes is fine, Mother.'

'You don't understand, Katharina. And won't until it's your children suffering at the end of this war.'

'It'll be different this time, Esther,' said Mr Spinell. 'Everyone is afraid of us now. Victory will be swift.'

'But he'll still only be a teacher,' said Mrs Spinell.

The sweating walls, hard chair and chipped crockery suddenly irritated Faber. He sat forward.

'My father has been a teacher all his life, and has provided perfectly well for us,' he said.

'But will that be enough?'

'It has been enough for my mother.'

'Is she a modest woman?'

'She is like any other woman, Mrs Spinell, who has dedicated her life to her husband and children.'

'You can expect the same of Katharina,' said Mr Spinell. 'She will make a fine wife. And a fine mother.'

'To be that she needs a husband with a good job, Günther.'

'Teaching in our new world will be a very respected profession, Esther. Now, young man, tell us about the front. About Kiev.'

Faber lit a third cigarette, dragging the smoke deep into his lungs, silently absorbing its kick before slowly, evenly, releasing it into the room. He flicked the ash and cleared his throat.

'The Russians are tenacious, Mr Spinell, but useless against our modern weaponry.'

'It will all be ours by Christmas,' said Mr Spinell. 'Only three hundred kilometres from Moscow – we are invincible.'

'We are doing well.'

'I am very proud of you, and of all German soldiers,' said Mr Spinell.

Faber inhaled again and nodded his head as he blew smoke towards the ceiling.

'Thank you, Mr Spinell.'

'When this war is over, we will have enough space, food, water and oil to last for centuries. You and my daughter can take all the land you need.'

'Will we do that?' said Katharina.

'What?'

'Take land? Move to the east and set up home there?'

He stared at her. He was sweating, even though the weather was cool.

'Russia is poor, filthy and full of peasants living in houses made of mud. I'm here because I can't stand the place.'

'They will work for you,' said Mr Spinell. 'You can tear down their huts, clean up the landscape and build a beautiful German house. Imagine, your own farm.'

'I know nothing about farming.'

'There will be training. After the war, young men will be taught how to become farmers, how to grow food for Germany.'

'I am happy to serve my country, but once the war is over I will return to Darmstadt to resume my life as a teacher.'

'You could do other things. Earn more money.'

'I like being a teacher.'

'You seem such a capable man.'

'I am a capable teacher.'

'But there are so many other things to do, especially in Berlin. You can always teach when you are older, after you have made your money.'

Faber ground his cigarette into the ashtray and looked slowly around the room.

'As you have done, Mr Spinell.'

Katharina began to clear the dishes.

'Let me show you the city,' she said. 'Before it's too dark.'

'My fortunes are about to change, Mr Faber. And yours could too.'

'I am happy with my life, Mr Spinell.'

'Let me introduce you to Dr Weinart. He is a man of great integrity and connections.'

Faber stood.

'I'll think about it.'

He picked up his rifle.

'You should leave that here,' said Katharina.

'I prefer to have it with me.'

'It's better left at home. We're going to the park.'

'I'll take it with me.'

He moved towards the door.

'You could at least wait for me,' she said. 'I have to get my coat.'

He left without her, going down the stairs and onto the street where the grocer was dismantling the stall at the front of his shop. The two men nodded at each other. Faber bounced up and down on his toes and rubbed at the sleeves of his tunic, buffeting his arms against the chilling wind. Katharina arrived on the doorstep, buttoning a coat too short for her skirt.

'Should I go back to fetch you my brother's coat?'

'I'll be fine.'

'You look cold.'

'I said I'd be fine.'

She walked past him, away into a city he did not know.

'Where are we going, Katharina?'

'To the park. The lake.'

'You could at least wait for me.'

'Why? You didn't bother waiting for me.'

He stopped, a slight curve in his shoulders.

'I'm sorry. I just needed to get away.'

'My parents have that effect.'

'It was intense. More than I had expected.'

'It always is.'

'How do you manage?'

'Years of practice. They mean well. And they like you.'

'Your mother hates me.'

'She doesn't. She just wants the best for me.'

'And I'm not good enough?'

'I'm her only daughter.'

'And she thought you could do better than a teacher.'

'Something like that.'

'What was she hoping for? A doctor? A lawyer? They don't marry bank clerks.'

'I don't suppose they do, Mr Faber.'

She walked ahead of him again. He caught up with her.

'I'm sorry, Katharina.'

'The bureau gave us details about you and four other men, including a doctor's fat son.'

'And your mother wanted him?'

'Exactly.'

Faber laughed.

'And instead she got a useless lanky schoolteacher.'

'So it seems.'

'So, where is he? The doctor's fat son. Is he here? In Berlin?'

'No. On the Russian front somewhere.'

'He's not fat any more then.'

They both laughed, and he offered her his arm. She took it.

'And your father? What does he think?'

'He approved of you. From the beginning.'

'So why does he want to turn me into a farmer?'

'He gets ideas. But you should see Weinart. It can't do any harm.'

'I said I'd think about it.'

She tugged his arm and he shortened his stride to keep pace with her. He took a deep breath and

rolled from the heel to the toe of each foot, ⟩
the hard pavement, the distance from R⟩
felt her press into him.

'Actually, my father likes you.'

'How can you possibly tell?'

'You're a soldier, fighting on the front. That is enough for him.'

'He made that clear, I suppose. And you? What do you think?'

'I haven't decided yet.'

'Should I try to persuade you?'

'You could try.'

He put his hands on her shoulders and steered her backwards, into the doorway of a shop that was already closed. He kissed her. She pushed him away and moved back onto the pavement, her right hand over her mouth, overwhelmed by his stench.

'Your buckles were sticking into me,' she said.

He smiled at her.

'You're a funny woman. Come on. Let's see this park.'

She took his arm again. They walked through the gates to a bench overlooking a lake. Three boys were using the last of the day's light to push boats around the lake with long sticks.

'It's good to sit among trees again. Russia's forests are huge and dark. Frightening. I hate them.'

'Is there anything you like about Russia?'

'I was in Belgium before and it was civilized, comfortable. The people were like us. But Russia is different. Hard and hostile.'

'It'll soon be over.'

'It's such a big country. It seems to go on for ever.'

'All the better for us.'

'I suppose so.'

He kissed her again and she let him, briefly.

'I thought it was against the rules for soldiers to kiss in public,' she said.

'I'm sure they'd forgive a man on his honeymoon.'

He stared at the lake, at the water lapping at the boys' feet. She put her head on his shoulder, her face away from him.

'Why did you marry?' she said.

'I wanted leave. And you?'

'My mother said it would be a good idea. A bit of security, I suppose. The title of wife. Other girls are doing it.'

'Why did you choose me?'

She smiled.

'I don't know. I liked your picture. Your hands, especially.'

He flipped them over and back.

'What is there to like about my hands?'

'I don't know,' she said.

She touched his thumb.

'They're strong. Sinewy. I like that.'

'Ah yes, I remember. You don't like fat.'

They both laughed and he kissed her again.

'You're prettier than I thought. Your hair and eyes. Your smile. Why didn't you smile in the photograph?'

'Mother said I shouldn't. That it might put men off.'

'You'll have to stop listening to your mother.'

'If I had, you wouldn't be here.'

He opened her coat and ran his hands over her breasts.

'You're much prettier than I expected.'

'So you keep saying. What had you expected?'

'Somebody duller.'

'Why would you marry somebody dull?'

'God knows.'

They laughed and she stood up.

'We should go,' she said.

They passed the boys' abandoned sticks.

'What do your parents think of our marriage?' she said.

'I haven't told them yet.'

'Will they approve?'

'I doubt it. They don't know you.'

'Nor do you.'

'No, but I will.'

'Will you, Mr Faber? You sound very sure of yourself.'

She took his arm.

'We should hurry. Mother will be waiting for you.'

Mrs Spinell stood at the end of the corridor waving her arm, directing Faber to the bathroom. The bath was already full.

'Please use the toothpaste and soap sparingly,' she said. 'They're hard to come by.'

'I will.'

'Leave your clothes in there.'

'Thank you.'

He smiled at Katharina, closed the door and began to undress, dried Russian soil falling to the floor as he removed layer after layer of clothing stiff with sweat. He looked in the mirror, at his tanned face and torso, at his white legs and red feet, blistered and chafed by months of marching over hard Russian earth.

He stepped into the hot water and submerged his head, wallowing in the warmth and quietness, in his distance from the other soldiers. He splashed water over his chest, relieved to be away from the noise, the chaos, the explosions, the buzzing of flies, the rattle of machine guns, from the voice of Katharina's father making plans for the rest of his life. He didn't need another father. Another set of parents.

He bent his knees and dropped his head under the water again. Away from the maggots crawling from corpses, from the sickly sweet stench of death. Cocooned in water. In stillness. In nothingness. He wanted to stay, but came up for air, took the flannel and soap from the end of the bath, and scrubbed himself until the water turned brown.

Mrs Spinell had left clothes, a razor, toothbrush and paste on a stool by the sink. He dragged the dull blade through his stubble and scrubbed at his teeth, so neglected that the foam turned from light pink to red. The trousers were too short, but the shirt fit well enough. He hesitated at the sweater with swastikas on each sleeve but pulled it on anyway, grateful for the warmth of the thickly knitted wool.

Mrs Spinell hurried from the kitchen as he opened the bathroom door.

'It feels good to be clean again,' he said.

He saw her looking at the floor.

'Could you at least empty the bath?' she said.

'Of course.'

'Your food is ready.'

'I'm afraid that I used all the soap.'

'And the toothpaste?'

'There was only a small amount anyway.'

Katharina and Mr Spinell were already at the table. A single black pot sat between them, steam seeping from an ill-fitting lid.

'Sit down,' said Mr Spinell. 'Eat with us.'

Mrs Spinell piled stewed vegetables onto her husband's plate and selected three pieces of meat to place on top of the mound. She gave the same to Faber, but only two to herself and Katharina. Faber ate in silence, chewing at the gristly beef offcuts, mopping the watery sauce with grey bread. He sat back from his meal, months of hunger still to be sated.

CHAPTER 3

Mrs Spinell slipped a brown paper bag into the pocket of her daughter's faded blue apron.

'You'll need that.'

'What is it?'

'Powder.'

'For what?'

'He has lice.'

'What? How can you tell?'

Katharina turned from the sink to look at Faber, who sat beside her father scrutinizing Johannes' trophies and badges. He scratched his scalp, briefly but aggressively, still holding the thread of conversation. She whispered to her mother.

'He doesn't even know he's doing it.'

'The bath must have roused them,' said Mrs Spinell. 'That's some husband you chose.'

Katharina wiped down the sink, although it was already clean.

'You'll have to treat him, Katharina.'

'But I hardly know him.'

'You're his wife, Katharina. Do it or you'll get them too. We all will.'

'It's too disgusting.'

'They might be all over him. You'll have to ask.'

Katharina folded the tea towel and took down the crockery required for breakfast.

'Leave that, Katharina. You have to do this.'

'I don't want to do it. Any of it.'

'It's too late for that now, Katharina.'

Katharina rubbed her hands down the length of her apron and lingered as she hung it from its hook.

'We should sort out your things, Peter.'

'Your brother has done very well, Katharina.'

'He was a star of the youth movement. He won everything.'

'And you?'

'I won nothing. I either tripped or came last.'

He smiled at her and followed her to the large bedroom used by her parents until that morning. Katharina had removed their possessions and cleaned the room, the walls, floor and bed, turning the space into her own, marking it with vases of rose buds on either side of the bed. She opened the door and inhaled sharply.

'God, this place stinks,' she said.

'It's my pack,' said Faber. 'I'm sorry.'

The lights still out, she opened the two large windows and looked down onto the street, drained of movement and light by the curfew.

'My mother thinks you have lice.'

'She's probably right. Everybody does.'

'How can you come here with lice in your hair?'

21

'I didn't know I had them. It's second nature to scratch in Russia. Have you ever had them?'

'We are sometimes a little hungry in Berlin, but never dirty.'

'I didn't mean it like that.'

Katharina looked at him. At the man she had chosen.

'We need to sort you out,' she said. 'Close the shutters and curtains, but leave the windows open. Then we can turn on the light.'

Faber sat on the chair she had positioned below the bulb hanging from the ceiling. She lifted a clump of hair. Dozens of parasites were crawling across his scalp.

'It's disgusting.'

'Will you ever kiss me again?'

'I haven't yet.'

She stepped back from him and sprinkled the powder over his head, its caustic cloud falling onto his face, into his eyes. She ignored his complaints.

'Do you have them anywhere else? In your armpits?'

'Not that I am aware of. I didn't notice any in the bath.'

She took a narrow-toothed comb from her mother's dressing table and used it to drag the powder through his hair, her throat burned by the bile rising from her stomach. She went back to the window and waited for the insects to die and then picked them out, dropping them into the dressing table dish she used to hold her hairpins.

'I'm sorry, Katharina.'

She went to the bathroom, bumping the door against her mother who was on her hands and knees mopping the muddied floor with a cloth. Katharina stepped over her and scraped the lice into the toilet.

'You've got your hands full with that one, Katharina.'

She flushed, scrubbed furiously at the comb and dish, and then at her hands.

'He said that he had none under his arms.'

'What about his groin?'

'I didn't ask.'

'Maybe you should.'

'I don't know that I can.'

'I'll soak his uniform in the bath. You can do his pack. They'll be in there too.'

'We'll need more powder.'

'I'll look for some in the morning.'

Katharina stared at herself in the mirror, certain that her skin had aged since his arrival.

'I hope you're not right, Mother. About the doctor's son.'

She ran her fingers across her now pale lips, but decided against adding more lipstick.

'I'd better go back to him.'

'I suppose you had.'

'Goodnight, Mother.'

'Goodnight, Katharina.'

He rose to his feet as she walked in, clicked his heels and bowed.

'My dear new wife, will you ever forgive me?'

'I doubt it.'

He ran his fingers across her forehead, flattening the deep furrows.

'I'm not as awful as you think,' he said.

'Aren't you?'

She moved away from him, back towards the window.

'What were you expecting, Katharina? Casanova? You picked me from a bloody catalogue.'

'And it was obviously a lousy choice.'

'Thank you.'

'You arrived here covered in lice and stinking so badly that I thought I would vomit. What was I expecting? Somebody who had bothered to wash.'

'I didn't want to leave the train, Katharina.'

'What?'

'I was supposed to get off in Poland, at the cleansing station, but I was afraid that they would send me back. That I wouldn't get home. So, I stayed on the train. And nobody noticed.'

'I bloody did.'

He laughed, and covered his face with his hands.

'I'm sorry, Katharina. I just had to get away from there.'

She sat down on the end of the bed.

'I'm sorry, Peter. I didn't expect it to be this difficult. This awkward.'

'What had you expected?'

She smiled.

'I don't know. Flowers. Chocolates. Not head lice.'

He sat down beside her. She moved away.

'I don't want to catch them.'

'You nearly killed me with the powder, so I doubt that any of them has survived.'

She laughed.

'You're beautiful when you laugh.'

'Not just pretty?'

'No. Beautiful. How many men did you write to?'

'Just to you. Did you write to other women?'

'No.'

He reached for her hand and she let him take it.

'When was your photograph taken?' she said.

'Just before I left for Russia.'

'It's a nice photograph.'

'Nicer than me in the flesh.'

'I don't know. Just different.'

'How?'

'Your face is different. Kinder, maybe.'

'So you're disappointed?'

'I don't know yet.'

'It's a hard place, Katharina.'

'I can smell that.'

They lay across the bed that she had made up that day, working with her mother, an embarrassed silence between the women as they tucked and folded the sheets. She moved her hair away from his.

'What's it like on the front?' she said. 'Johannes tells us very little in his letters.'

'Let's talk about something else.'

'Like what?'

'Like you as a little girl.'

'I lost all the races. There is nothing more. That's all I was – the girl who came last in everything. Except sewing and cooking – I was always good at those. What about you? What were you good at?'

But he was asleep. A light snore rose from him. She prodded him.

'There are pyjamas under the pillow for you.'

He put them on, his back to her.

'I'm sorry, Katharina. I'm exhausted.'

'It's fine.'

He kissed her on the cheek, this man in her brother's pyjamas, and fell back to sleep. She sat at the dressing table to brush her hair, to look at herself, this woman married to a man she did not know. She pulled on a long nightdress and climbed in beside him.

CHAPTER 4

Shortly before dawn, Faber woke, sweating and panting, his body no longer accustomed to comfort and warmth. He threw off the covers and lay still, quietening his breath, absorbing the coolness of the dark air.

Katharina lay beside him, still asleep. He turned away from her and put his feet on the floor. He would leave, slip away to his parents' living room of soft chairs and matching crockery. He stood up but then slumped back down again. Her mother had his uniform. He slapped his head onto the pillow. Katharina woke.

'Are you all right?' she said.

'I'm fine. Go back to sleep.'

'Are all those lice dead?'

He laughed.

'They're well murdered.'

'I'm glad.'

She moved across the bed towards him, and set her hand on his chest.

'It's all a little odd, isn't it?' she said.

'We didn't start well, did we?'

'No.'

'So what do we do now?'

'I don't know.'

He sat up.

'I'm hungry, Katharina.'

'I'll go and see what there is.'

He lit a cigarette and looked through the dawn light at the room, at the sagging curtains and the cheap, functional dressing table. His parents' furniture was old and ornate, passed from one generation to the next.

She returned with a hot drink and bread.

'It's not the real coffee. Father must have taken it to his room. He's very protective of anything given by Dr Weinart.'

'Who is Dr Weinart?'

'I'm not really sure. I know they were together in the last war. I haven't met him.'

Faber drank.

'My God, Katharina. It's disgusting.'

'They say that if you think of it as coffee, then it tastes like coffee.'

'I'm not that bloody mad. Not yet anyway. We get better than this on the front.'

'I suppose that's a good thing. You need it more than we do.'

'It is until I get leave.'

He set down the cup and plate and pulled her to him.

'So, you were telling me what you were like as a girl.'

'Yes, and I was so interesting that you fell asleep.'

He nuzzled his face into her hair.

'I am so sorry, Katharina Spinell. I will not fall asleep again. Now, tell me what were you like?'

'I don't know. I was always good, but my mother adores my brother.'

He dropped his head onto the pillow and snored. She laughed and slapped him on the arm.

'You're so unfair to me,' she said.

He kissed her.

'So you were a daddy's girl?'

'I suppose so. And you?'

'I was never a daddy's girl.'

They laughed, and he kissed her on the cheeks and lips, moving to her neck.

'And you, Peter Faber?'

'All I have done is march. Left right, left right. Youth movement, war, pack on my back – it's all I have done so far in my life.'

She kissed his lips, his cheeks.

'You must have done something else,' she said.

He slipped his hand under her nightdress.

'Let me see if there is anything else I can remember.'

He ran his hands over her bottom, stomach and breasts.

'I'm remembering,' he said.

She opened the buttons of her brother's pyjamas and fingered his chest.

'We need to fatten you up a bit, Mr Faber.'

He took off the pyjamas and pushed up her nightdress.

'You do that, Katharina Spinell. Turn me into a doctor's fat son.'

They giggled and she parted her legs.

'Next time I'll bring you flowers and chocolates,' he said.

'I only like dark chocolate. And white flowers.'

'You're a very fussy woman, Mrs Faber.'

'I'm very particular, Mr Faber.'

When it was fully bright outside, she pulled a robe over her nakedness and went to the kitchen.

'Katharina, you should dress for breakfast,' said Mrs Spinell.

'I'm not staying.'

'You have to eat breakfast.'

'I'll take food back to Peter.'

'Sit down and have yours first.'

'No, I'll take mine too. Is there any ham?'

'Hopefully later today.'

Her father put down his newspaper.

'Be a good girl, Katharina, and do as your mother asks.'

She moved towards the hob.

'How did you sleep, Mother?'

'Not very well. Your bed is very small.'

'I've been saying that for years. It's a child's bed, Mother.'

'You're still my child, Katharina.'

'For God's sake, Mother.'

Mr Spinell rustled the newspaper.

'Fetch Peter and have breakfast with us,' said Mr Spinell.

'He would rather eat in the room, Father.'

'Your mother has set the table for you both.'

'I'll take the tray.'

She hummed to discourage further interference, loaded coffee, cheese and bread onto the tray and went back to the room. Faber was waiting for her, smiling, tugging at her robe as she set down the tray, sliding it off her as she poured coffee. Dr Weinart's coffee. He buried himself in her.

He sat again on the chair under the light and she, humming, picked lice from his hair.

'I should cut it,' she said.

'Are you any good?'

'Would you notice?'

She cut the fringe dangling from his receding hairline, and sheared the back of his head with her father's clippers. She wiped the loose hairs from his neck and face, kissed him and left the room. She returned with a basin of steaming water.

'You will want for nothing,' he said.

'All I want is to be away from my parents.'

'I'll buy a big house with a garden.'

'How, as a teacher?'

'I'll find a way.'

She knelt in front of him, lifted and lowered his right foot, then his left, into the water, splashing his shins and calves, rubbing her hands over his

31

ankles and heels, over his bruises and calluses, squeezing and releasing the flesh of each toe until she could feel the weight of his fatigue. She dried each foot and led him to bed, tucking him between the still-damp sheets. She went back to the kitchen.

'He's exhausted,' she said.

'I'm sure.'

'What's wrong, Mother?'

'Nothing.'

'Fine, then.'

Mrs Spinell stabbed at a potato with her rusting peeler.

'This is not a hotel, Katharina.'

'I'm aware of that.'

'Fine, then.'

'Fine, what?'

'A little more decorum and respect for your parents would be appreciated.'

'Yes, Mother.'

'Dinner will be at six, Katharina.'

'Yes, Mother.'

At dinner, they held hands beneath the table, tangled feet and answered any questions put to them. When it was over, he undressed her under the bedroom light and gently unpicked the pins from her hair, watching as each lock fell the length of her unblemished back.

The following evening, after dinner, Mr Spinell insisted that Faber accompany him to the city centre.

'Dr Weinart will be there.'

'But we had plans, Father.'

'Peter needs to meet the doctor before he goes back, Katharina.'

Faber took her brother's coat, but walked a little behind her father through silent, shuttered streets. Mr Spinell halted in front of the opera house, its damage almost fully repaired.

'You see, Faber, we are invincible. Anything they bomb, we fix.'

They walked down steps into a fuggy warmth of men. Faber stood at the edge of the crowd, envying its drunkenness. Mr Spinell disappeared for some time and returned with four tankards of beer.

'Get stuck in, Faber.'

They toasted Katharina, and Faber was soon surrounded by men in brown uniform, all older than he, lauding his efforts at Kiev.

'You remind us of ourselves,' said Mr Spinell, 'only we want you to do better. To hammer them all this time.'

'I can't do any worse.'

They laughed, raised their glasses and drank. Dr Weinart joined them.

'Your father-in-law has told me all about you, Mr Faber. It's an honourable thing you have done.'

'What is?'

'Marrying Miss Spinell. Securing the future of our nation.'

'We are very happy, Dr Weinart.'

'Of course you are.'

The doctor sipped from his small glass of beer.

'You have chosen a good family, Mr Faber. Mr Spinell works very hard for me, and I hugely appreciate his support.'

'I'm glad.'

'So the next thing, Mr Faber, is to find you some work. Good, useful work.'

'Like what?'

'What are your interests?'

'I'm a teacher.'

'I know that, just like your father.'

'And my grandfather.'

'A fine tradition, but you can break free if you want to.'

'What do you mean?'

'Decide for yourself. It is your life, Mr Faber. Not your father's. Or your grandfather's.'

Faber drew from his tankard.

'Have you anything in mind?'

'Berlin will soon be the centre of the world, Mr Faber.'

'Indeed it will, Dr Weinart,' said Mr Spinell.

'We will need to educate our new empire, to communicate to our new citizens what it is to be a true German.'

'So not farming?'

Dr Weinart laughed.

'You don't look like a farmer to me.'

'Mr Spinell thought that I could be turned into one.'

'I doubt it.'

'I still hold out hope, Dr Weinart.'

They all laughed.

'Will I be well paid?'

'You'll be looked after.'

'Enough for a house and garden?'

'We take good care of our own, Mr Faber.'

The speeches began and Faber moved away to stand by the wall. Dr Weinart, his black uniform impeccably pressed, came and stood beside him.

'You need some more time with us, Faber. I'll have your leave extended.'

'You can do that?'

'I'll get you another week. Ten days, maybe, so that you can come out with us. Let me buy more beer.'

Faber toasted Dr Weinart, drank and joined in the singing, and the shouting.

CHAPTER 5

They took the train to the Darmstadt house hidden from the road by a dense laurel hedge. His mother rushed at him, hugging him and chiding him for the surprise. She straightened her skirt and hair when she caught sight of Katharina.

'Excuse me, I'm Peter's mother. I had no idea that he was home.'

'Mother, this is my wife, Katharina Spinell.'

Mrs Faber snorted.

'Is this a joke, Peter?'

'No.'

'You'd better come in. I'll make some coffee. Your father will be home soon.'

'Good.'

'We'll use the living room.'

She went before them, hurrying to open the curtains.

'It's a beautiful room,' said Katharina.

'Thank you.'

'My mother keeps the curtains drawn to protect the furniture from the sun.'

'And the books, Peter,' said his mother.

'It works,' said Katharina. 'Everything's perfect.'

'Like a museum,' said Faber.

'You're being rude,' said his mother.

'Don't think of doing this in our house, Katharina. I want the sun in every room.'

Faber looked around. Nothing had changed. It never did. He led Katharina to the sofa, sat her down, kissed her, and followed his mother into the kitchen.

'You should have told us, Peter. Warned us.'

'It was all very sudden, Mother.'

She stood on the tips of her toes to take down the fine china.

'But who is she? How do you know her?'

'I met her through a marriage bureau.'

'What? Have you gone mad, Peter?'

'It meant I got leave. To come home. To be here.'

'And you married for that? A complete stranger?'

'I really like her.'

'Oh, thank God. Your father's home.'

His father put his satchel on the counter as he always did, and hugged his son. Mrs Faber talked quietly to her husband.

'It's a stunt, Peter,' he said. 'A Nazi breeding stunt.'

'It's a deal, Father. Nothing more. And it's worked out. You'll really like her.'

Mr Faber picked up the tray and carried it into the living room, followed by Mrs Faber holding the coffee pot and their son carrying a plate of still-warm shortbread. Katharina stood as they walked in, saluted, and reached out her hand. His parents shook it, but sat down before their guest.

'Katharina lives in Berlin,' he said. 'I think that I'll move there after the war.'

Mr Faber's two large, soft hands rose to his face, hovered momentarily in front of his eyes, but moved on through his hair.

'Your job is here, Peter. Your life. Your career. What would you do in Berlin?'

'Katharina's father will help find me a job. He has contacts. Good political ones.'

'You don't need the help of politicians to be a good teacher, Peter,' said Mr Faber.

'I might not teach any more. Not conventionally, anyway.'

Mr Faber's derisive laugh startled even his wife.

'All teaching is conventional, Peter. That's how it works.'

'It'll be different from classroom teaching. I'll be teaching the nation.'

'About what?'

'I don't know. Germany. Its future.'

His father sat back into his chair, silent as he drank his coffee.

'Excuse me, young lady – I'm sorry I don't even know your name,' said Mr Faber.

'Katharina. Katharina Spinell.'

'Miss Spinell, my son—'

'Mrs Faber, Father. Mrs Faber.'

'Katharina. My son appears to have lost his way.

38

It can happen. War can challenge the mind as vigorously as it can the body.'

'I don't think that applies here, Father.'

'Since he was a child, Peter has wanted to be a teacher, to work in the same school as his father and grandfather.'

'That has all changed now,' said Peter, kissing his wife's hand.

'I don't see why. Did something happen, Peter?'

'I'm married, Father. I have a different life ahead.'

'I married, Peter, and it changed nothing.'

'My wife is very beautiful.'

'And your mother wasn't?'

The train back was almost empty, so she stretched across the seat and placed her head on his lap. He draped his coat over her and stroked her hair until she fell asleep. When they reached Berlin, he nuzzled at her ear, whispering her awake.

Her mother had kept dinner for them, potato and vegetable soup, which they ate in the kitchen until her father came home.

'Where's your mother?'

'Bed.'

'Fine. You may go, too, Katharina. I need your husband tonight.'

'What for?' said Katharina.

'Dr Weinart wants him.'

★   ★   ★

39

Faber jumped into the back of a truck filled with men in brown uniform. They passed a uniform to him. It was too short, but he pulled it on anyway and sat as silently as the other men. The truck stopped at the top of a wide tree-lined street and the men got out, the doctor emerging from the front cab. He shook Faber's hand.

'Thank you for joining us, Mr Faber.'

'Thank you.'

'You take that house over there. Number seventy-one.'

'What do I do with it?'

'Just get in.'

Faber went, knocked at the door and pushed the doorbell. He received no reply, and returned to Dr Weinart.

'There's nobody home.'

'They're in there, Faber.'

'Yes, Sir.'

He lifted the brass knocker and slammed it heavily against the door. He shouted through the keyhole, but the house inside remained still.

'Maybe they've gone out, Dr Weinart.'

'There's nowhere for them to go, Faber.'

'We could come back later.'

The doctor snorted.

'Get in there, Faber.'

'How?'

'Jesus Christ, you're a soldier, aren't you?'

'Not this kind of soldier.'

'Move, or I'll ship you out with those fucking Jews.'

40

The doctor blew his whistle. Six men carrying a telegraph pole charged the width of the street and battered at the door until it splintered, cracked and finally imploded. Faber stepped over the debris and hurried up the stairs after the doctor and his father-in-law.

'Do as I do, Faber,' said Mr Spinell. 'And make sure the doctor sees you doing it.'

They found them, two old men, three women and four children behind a false wall under the stairs. Faber put his gun to their backs and marched them into a truck parked under darkened street lamps.

The following nights, he smashed soup tureens and china clocks, irritated that he had to leave Katharina to drag snivelling children from attics and cellars. He shouted and screamed at them, struck their legs and backs with the butt of his gun, slapped them across the face when they took too long moving down the stairs, more comfortable with howls of hatred than pleas for mercy.

Katharina was always waiting for him afterwards, always warm. On the seventh day, as the sun rose, he took a wide band of wedding gold from an old woman. Later he slipped it on his wife's finger.

'I need you, Katharina.'

They built a routine for themselves, the young married couple; they spent mornings in bed, and afternoons in the park, always on the same bench overlooking the lake.

'I think that we should have four children,' he said.

'Two boys and two girls.'

'But no traditional names. Or family names. We're starting everything again, Katharina. Doing it our way.'

He spent nights with Dr Weinart, moving across Berlin, while she stayed home, humming, singing, twisting the wedding band on her finger.

CHAPTER 6

He folded her brother's pyjamas and tucked them under the pillow, his back to Katharina as she pinned up her hair.

'Do you promise me you'll come back?' she said.

'Of course I will.'

'How can I be sure?'

He pulled on his socks and boots, and went to her.

'You stink,' she said.

'Your mother likes disinfectant.'

'Leaving as you arrived.'

He kissed her.

'I'll be back, Katharina. Just wait for me.'

'I'll be here. In this room. This bed.'

They went to the kitchen and sat down to breakfast with her parents.

'He'll be back sooner than you think, Katharina,' said her father. 'There's not long left in this.'

Mrs Spinell gave him a package of brown paper and white string.

'It should keep you going for a bit.'

'Thank you.'

'Give some to Johannes if you see him.'

'I will, Mrs Spinell. I'll look out for him.'

The train station teemed with men in uniform. Katharina pressed against her husband.

'You're shivering, Peter.'

'I hate going back there, Katharina. The noise. The smells. I hate it all.'

'It won't be for long, my love.'

She buried herself into his chest and wrapped her arms around him.

'You'll be all right, Peter.'

The younger men, the new recruits in fresh uniforms, marched around the station, singing.

'Bloody fools,' said Faber.

'They're excited, Peter.'

'About what? Dying.'

'It's not that bad.'

'You're not there.'

'You're doing very well. It'll soon be over. One last push.'

'You don't know what you're talking about, Katharina.'

She stepped away from him and turned to the crowd, to the men playing cards in huddles on the ground.

'I'm sorry,' he said. 'I don't want to go.'

He hugged her, and held her, stroking her hair, until his unit was called.

'It's time,' she said.

He kissed her.

'I will be back. You understand that, don't you, Katharina?'

'Yes.'

'You understand that no matter what happens I will come back to you.'

'I know that, my love.'

'I need you here for me, Katharina. I need to know you're waiting for me.'

'I'll be here, Peter. I promise.'

'I'll be back. No matter what.'

He hugged her tightly, as though trying to absorb her.

'You should go,' she said. 'Get a seat.'

The train ground its wheels into the metal track, inching forward until it gathered pace and carried him out of the station, away into the morning light. The other women left, went back to their homes and children, but Katharina lingered in the dusky anonymity of the station, warding off the moment when she would return to being a daughter. She sat on a bench, silent among the men, until the cold wind whipping at her legs made it too uncomfortable to stay. She began the walk home, but stopped at a café, remaining for as long as she could, for as long as seemed decent for a woman on her own.

Her mother hurtled towards her as she opened the door.

'Where have you been?'

'At the station, with Peter.'

'But his train left hours ago. Anyway, it doesn't matter. You're here now. Hurry up, pack your things. We're leaving.'

Mrs Spinell picked up a bundle of clothes from the floor.

'What do you mean?'

'We have to leave here. Pack. Quickly.'

'Mother, stop. I have no idea what is going on.'

She dropped the clothes and put her hands on her daughter's shoulders.

'Katharina, it has finally happened.'

'What has?'

'The apartment. We have a new apartment! A huge one. With its own living room! And three double bedrooms!'

'That's marvellous. But I can't go.'

'What do you mean? You hate your bedroom, and the smallness of this place.'

'I promised Peter that I would wait for him. Here.'

'For God's sake, write to him. Give him the new address. And Johannes too.'

'But this was his home, our home. I'll wait here, move into your room.'

'Don't be ridiculous.'

'I'm not ridiculous. I'll live here by myself until Peter comes back.'

'And how will you live? Pay the rent? Anyway, somebody else will be coming here.'

'Who?'

'Oh God, Katharina. I don't know. It doesn't matter.'

'It matters to me.'

'Stop it, Katharina. Just pack. We have to move today. It's our big chance.'

She turned her back on her mother and walked into her parents' bedroom. The bed had been stripped. She ran back into the hall.

'Where are the sheets? Where did you put the sheets?'

'In the bath. I was washing them when your father came with the news.'

Katharina raced down the hall, her coat slipping from her shoulders as she fell to her knees in front of the bath. She picked at the folds of sheet that rose above the water, at the coils of black, wiry hair floating on the surface, then plunged her arms into the bath, soaking her clothes in the traces of their time together. She lifted the sheets to her face, and rubbed them across her lips, cheeks, forehead and eyes, soaking her skin with what remained of him.

Mrs Spinell walked by the bathroom door.

'Katharina, what are you doing?'

'Washing the sheets.'

'Oh, leave them. The Jews have much better sheets than those.'

Katharina dropped her hands and arms back into the water.

'You're soaked, Katharina. You'll catch cold. Just leave them.'

'I'm taking them.'

'Do as you please. But we have to leave today. Before somebody else gets it.'

'So you keep saying.'

She rinsed the sheets in cold, clean water, squeezed and folded them, and left them on the side of the bath. She went to find her father, who was packing Johannes' medals and trophies.

'So you've heard the news,' he said.

'How did it happen?'

'Dr Weinart organized it. It's on the other side of the city, on the second floor and very big, with lots of furniture to dust. It should keep your mother happy.'

Katharina tapped her toe against the door into her brother's room.

'He got away, then?'

'Yes.'

'He'll be back. Sooner than you think.'

'I hope so,' she said.

'He's a good young man. There'll be space in the apartment for him until we find you somewhere of your own.'

'I'd rather stay here, to wait for him.'

'It's not practical, Katharina. They wouldn't let me keep two apartments. Anyway, you'll change your mind when you see this place.'

Katharina fell silent.

'I'd better go and pack,' she said.

'Good girl.'

She closed her bedroom door and pushed against it, locking out her parents. She was twenty-two years of age. A married woman. When would they accept that and stop calling her girl? He had to

48

come back to take her away from them, because she couldn't bear it any longer. Being their daughter. The good girl.

She packed her things quickly, easily, into a small suitcase, covering everything with the wet, dripping sheets taken from the side of the bath. She placed the case by the hall door and returned to her mother in the kitchen.

'What are we taking from here?' asked Katharina. 'Plates? Cutlery? Saucepans?'

'Only saucepans. The rest they leave behind. They are allowed only one suitcase. What remains is for us.'

'Where have they gone?'

'I don't know. East, I think. Out, anyway. Here, take this.'

She handed over Johannes' favourite mug, dark brown with a heavily moustached man etched into its side.

'He would never forgive us if we left it behind. And take his ashtray too.'

The hall filled quickly with boxes and suitcases.

'I think we're ready,' said Mrs Spinell. 'Mr Ewald is lending us his cart.'

'Will you miss it, Mother?'

'No. Not a bit.'

They stacked the grocer's cart and pushed it until the streets grew quieter and wider.

'The trees are beautiful,' said Katharina. 'They're huge.'

Mr Spinell stopped the cart behind a car, in front

of two enormous and elaborately carved wooden doors.

'Is this it?' said Mrs Spinell. 'It can't be.'

'It is, my love.'

They stepped into a large hall, its ceiling heavy with white sculpted plaster. Mr Spinell rubbed his shoes against the back of his legs and stepped onto the red patterned carpet covering the staircase. The women followed. Katharina squealed at its softness; her mother bent down to touch the rails and rods.

'Solid brass, Günther.'

They climbed, three abreast, to the second floor, uncertain whether to turn left or right.

'The key is in the door,' said Mr Spinell.

'I can see it,' said Katharina. 'We're on the right.'

She turned the key and they entered a square hallway with a gilt-edged mirror and a white marble bust. Two glass doors led to the living room with polished wooden floors, a grand piano, sofas, rugs, paintings and alcoves lined with leather-bound books.

'It's beautiful,' said Katharina.

'Finally,' said Mrs Spinell. 'A proper home.'

The two women threw off their shoes and rushed around the apartment, laughing as they opened doors onto enormous bedrooms and balconies. The kitchen drawers were stacked with equipment for slicing and beating, and cupboards filled with starched linen sheets, tablecloths, napkins, and huge soft towels, still perfectly white.

'They had everything,' said Katharina.

'While we had nothing,' said Mrs Spinell.

They converged again on the living room, telling Mr Spinell about the bathtub big enough for two, but he was focused on the alcoves, cursing loudly and throwing books onto the floor.

'Rubbish, rubbish. These will have to go before we can sleep a night in this house.'

Katharina chose the bedroom furthest from the kitchen, with a balcony overlooking the small but richly planted courtyard. She opened the large mahogany wardrobe and tried on the silk dresses and linen skirts, but none would fit. The shoes were also too small, so she settled for some cardigans, shawls and a long fur coat with matching hat that she wore into the living room.

'Any jewellery?' asked Mr Spinell.

'No,' said Katharina. 'Not that I can see.'

'Bloody thieves, the lot of them. They swallow it, you know. To hide it from us.'

He piled his arms with books and headed for the front door.

'Take your things off the cart. I need it,' he said.

He dumped the books into the cart, their covers splaying as they fell.

'Wait here. I'll fetch the rest. Make sure nobody takes any of them. They're corrosive. Every one of them.'

He disappeared back up the stairs, and returned with more books and the marble bust.

51

'Not the statue, Günther,' said Mrs Spinell. 'It suits the hall.'

'It's Mendelssohn, Esther.'

Katharina carried her suitcase to her room and unpacked, draping the wet sheets across the balcony and hanging her dull, limp clothes alongside the fur coat. On her way to the linen cupboard, she caught sight of her mother in a red, woollen dress.

'You look lovely, Mother.'

'But it's Jewish. I can't possibly wear it.'

'Take it. It suits you.'

'I don't know.'

'You deserve it.'

'Do you think so?'

She looked at herself in the mirror again. And smiled.

'I suppose I do. But I'll wash it first. And disinfect it.'

When Mr Spinell returned, the three of them sat at the polished dining room table.

'It's our turn now,' said Mrs Spinell. 'Our turn at the good life.'

'I think I'll take piano lessons,' said Katharina.

'A fine idea,' said her father. 'It's about time we had a musician in the family.'

CHAPTER 7

Faber found them picking over the remains of a tractor, its bullet-pocked bonnet folded back to allow them to scrutinize what was left of the engine. He bellowed at them.

'Get back! That's Russian property.'

Weiss turned, his rifle already cocked.

'You bastard, Faber.'

He dropped his weapon.

'So, how was she?'

'Better than expected. You should try it.'

'I have all the woman I need here, without the burden of a wife.'

'It was no burden.'

'It will be.'

They all laughed, slapped him on the back and shook his hand. Faustmann passed around his cigarettes.

'You've been gone a long time, Faber,' he said.

'Did you miss me, Faustmann? They extended my leave.'

'Why?'

'I was working in Berlin.'

'Doing what?'

'Working with my father-in-law. Nothing much. What are you doing with the tractor?'

'Building a shower,' said Weiss.

'Still at that?' said Faber.

'We've regulated the flow, but not the temperature,' said Weiss. 'Sit, sir, and tell us about this woman.'

Faber climbed into the cold metal seat that curved to the shape of his bottom, his legs either side of the broken steering shaft. Weiss, Faustmann and Kraft sat on the rear mudguards.

'How is my mother, Faber?' said Kraft.

Faber exhaled slowly, relishing their curiosity.

'She looked after me well, boys. That's all I can tell you.'

'Oh, come on,' said Weiss. 'We need more than that.'

'It's private, Weiss.'

'It was never private before.'

'Well, it is now.'

'Oh, come on. We're starved of all sensation.'

'You look pretty healthy to me.'

'What about Berlin?' said Faustmann. 'Is there much damage?'

'Some to houses, but people are getting by. The food is dull, though. Heavily rationed.'

'It's been good here,' said Weiss. 'Lots to eat and lots to buy.'

'And what about Darmstadt?' asked Kraft. 'How is my mother?'

'I never got to see her, Kraft. But I posted your letters.'

'Bloody hell, Faber. You said you would.'

'I'm sorry. I ran out of time.'

'You've been gone for three weeks. You got extra time.'

'It went by very quickly.'

'But you promised.'

'I'm sorry, Kraft.'

'You're fucking useless, Faber.'

Kraft slid down the mudguard and walked away. Faber cleared his throat and spat at the ground.

'I was busy with my wife.'

'You did promise,' said Faustmann.

'I know.'

'He thinks she's dying,' said Weiss.

'I only saw my own mother for a couple of hours.'

'She's not dying.'

'Jesus Christ, I just didn't go home much. That's all there is to it.'

'But you could have,' said Faustmann. 'Even for a day.'

'I didn't have a day to spare.'

'An afternoon, then,' said Weiss. 'You could have taken your wife, just to check on everyone.'

'I took her for one afternoon. That's all the time there was.'

'You had three weeks!'

'It was busy.'

'My parents were looking forward to seeing you,' said Weiss.

'I barely saw my own, Weiss. Anyway, it was my leave. Kraft should have organized his own.'

'Like you did?' said Faustmann.

'Yes, Faustmann. Like I did.'

Faber finished his cigarette, dropped it to the tractor floor and ground it into the metal with the toe of his boot. He lit another.

'They must be disappointed,' said Weiss.

'Who?'

'Your parents. Your father, especially. His teacher son.'

'Damn it, Weiss, leave me alone. I've already done my penance.'

'What do you mean?'

'I never collected my mother's food parcel. I was bloody starving on the train.'

'Nothing from your wife?' said Faustmann.

'Scraps from a mother-in-law who has a son of her own.'

Weiss laughed.

'Serves you right for putting your dick first.'

'Let's hope she was worth it,' said Faustmann.

'She's much more beautiful than her photograph. The one you saw.'

'I can't remember it,' said Weiss.

'She'll send another. I'll show you then.'

They fell silent and stared west, at the sun sinking into the horizon. Weiss shivered.

'It's cold,' he said. 'We should go back.'

'What about the shower?' said Faber.

'Fuck the shower. We're moving out in a couple of days, anyway.'

'How do you know?'

'That's the talk.'

'Have you reported to Kraus yet?' said Faustmann.

'No.'

'You should.'

He found Kraus cleaning shoes in the doorway of the house he had taken as his own. Faber saluted.

'Ah, the honeymooner is back.'

'Yes, Sergeant.'

'You were a long time away. Longer than expected. How did you manage that?'

'My father-in-law has connections, Sir.'

'I see. Well, you're back with us now, Faber. Eat and rest. We'll be moving out in a couple of days.'

'How much longer will it take, Sir?'

'What?'

'The war?'

'A week? A year? Ask your father-in-law.'

'He says Christmas.'

'Go and eat, Faber.'

He joined the line behind Gunkel, a butcher from Darmstadt, and Fuchs, the oldest among them and once a pupil of Faber's father.

'I don't smell much fat,' said Gunkel. 'They must be pleased with us.'

'We're heroes,' said Faber.

'They're feeding us to be ready for a Russian winter,' said Fuchs.

'But it's almost over,' said Faber.

'Things are moving too slowly around Moscow,' said Fuchs.

'Berlin thinks that it's almost all over,' said Faber.

'The boys up north don't see it like that.'

'You're such a bloody pessimist, Fuchs.'

Stockhoff, the cook, dug his ladle deep into the pot and drew up a large portion of meaty stew. A second soldier handed out two pieces of bread, both buttered, both fresh. Faber sat beside Weiss. He gestured at the butter, and at the sauce and meat.

'Maybe Fuchs is right.'

'He's usually reliable. The radio operators talk to him.'

'But I promised Katharina I would be back by Christmas.'

'You promised Kraft you'd visit his mother.'

'This is different.'

'And what happens then?'

'When?'

'When this is over? When you go back?'

'Her father said he would find me a job after the war. A good one.'

'Doing what?'

'Teaching, training.'

'In Berlin?'

'Yes. And around Germany. Around our new empire.'

'I thought you'd be in Darmstadt all your life. Continue the great Faber teaching tradition.'

'Things change.'

'So I gather.'

Faber chewed his meat.

58

'It's good. Better than anything I had in Berlin.'

'You should have stayed here then.'

'Any news on winter clothing?'

'Who knows? Kraus said soon.'

'He said that before I left.'

Faber drank from his water canister, sluicing down the meat stuck in his teeth.

'Is Fuchs still coughing?' he said.

'Yep.'

'I hate that noise. Every bloody morning.'

'He can't help it.'

'How has Faustmann been?'

'Fine. Same as ever.'

'Are you sure?'

'What do you mean?'

'Can we trust him?'

'Faustmann? What are you on about?'

'Well, he speaks Russian.'

'Jesus, Faber, I speak French.'

'That's different. We're at war in Russia and he speaks the language of our enemy.'

'You never gave a shit when I spoke French in Belgium.'

'That's different.'

'Only if you want it to be.'

'It's not that simple.'

'Make it as complicated as you like, Faber. I'm going to get more food.'

The following morning, they wandered by the river and through Kiev, ending up at the market, the soldiers picking over jewellery, picture frames, coats, scarves and ties, the peasant sellers dressed in high-heeled shoes, fur stoles and long white leather boots. One woman used a silver clutch bag as her till.

'Where did it all come from?' said Faber.

'It's Jewish,' said Weiss. 'They don't need it any more.'

'They'll take whatever you offer,' said Faustmann. 'It's all an unexpected harvest for them.'

Faber bought a silver bracelet for Katharina, and a silk scarf with swirls of a green that matched her eyes. He bought some apples and pears too, and some coarse vodka and bread, then went down to the river with Weiss, Kraft and Faustmann. It was midday and the sun was warm. They sat on a beach and picnicked close to a bridge bent and twisted by the retreating Russians. Faber stared at the expanse of the river.

'Is there any end to this country?'

'We're only on the edge of it,' said Faustmann.

'My wife's father had some notion that I should move here after the war.'

'What for?' said Kraft.

'To farm and grow food for Germany.'

'There'll be empty plates in Berlin if they send you,' said Weiss.

They laughed and lay down, relishing the warmth until the sun gave way to the late autumn winds.

CHAPTER 8

At five, Kraus bellowed them awake.

'Up! Out! Let's go! There's a war to win.'

Faber groaned.

'I thought we had one more day.'

'Change of plan, Faber. Up.'

'I wanted to write to my wife today.'

'You should have written yesterday, Faber. Up.'

He rolled onto his hip, sat up, scratched under each armpit and pulled on the rest of his clothes. He packed his rucksack, ate hot porridge, drank cold coffee and fell into line alongside buildings still in darkness, the blue, grey and pale yellow of their stone yet to be picked out by the day's light. Kraus ran up and down, counting, checking and shouting.

'Right men, march.'

Faber quietly swore at the sergeant. He didn't want to go. Nor did he want to stay.

'So where are we off to?'

'East,' said Weiss.

'I gathered that, Weiss.'

'I heard talk of Poltava first, then Kharkov or towards Rostov,' said Fuchs. 'We'll know when we're there.'

61

'Another grand plan,' said Weiss. 'How far is it?'

'About two hundred miles to Poltava and three hundred to Kharkov. Rostov is too far to think about.'

Lace curtains twitched as they walked through the streets towards the river, hidden eyes tracking them as they passed.

'When did the others leave?' said Faber.

'Most infantry last week.'

'Why are we so late?'

'The whole army was waiting for you, Faber,' said Weiss.

Fuchs laughed.

'You took a bit of a risk,' he said. 'Marrying a stranger like that.'

'I suppose I did. But it worked out.'

'What's her family like? Her parents?'

'They were kind to me.'

'And her father?'

'Not easy to get used to. But a good man. Committed.'

'To what?'

'The cause. The party. I had a couple of drinks with him, and some friends of his. They have some good ideas, especially this doctor I met.'

'About what?' said Fuchs.

'Germany's place in the world. Our future. The doctor pieced it all together very eloquently.'

'And you were impressed?'

'Very.'

Fuchs lit a cigarette, inhaled and coughed.

'You shouldn't be smoking, Fuchs.'

'I know that. What do your parents think?'

'Of what?'

'Your marriage, your wife's new family. They must be very different from yours.'

Faber spat at the earth.

'They've met her.'

'And what do they think?'

'They like her.'

'Have they met her parents?'

'No.'

'Any plans for them all to meet?'

'No. God, Fuchs, you're like an old woman with your cough and your questions. It's done now, anyway.'

They reached the open plains, where Reinisch, their lieutenant, picked up the pace, forcing a march across ruts left by the tanks. Faber adjusted his pack and gun, and lengthened his stride, his legs settling back into their soldier rhythm. War had made him fit. Katharina had healed his feet. The sun rose, his shadow stretched behind him, and they began to sing.

They set up camp before darkness, Faber sharing with Weiss as usual. At midnight, Kraus shook their tent.

'You're on, lads. Faustmann and Kraft take over at two. Berlin time. No messing. No smoking.'

He pulled on his boots and crawled out after Weiss. The air was cold. He slapped his hands together and stamped his feet.

'You're supposed to be quiet, Faber.'

'I forgot.'

Faber walked north, to a corner of the camp shrouded in darkness and silence. He took out a cigarette, cupped it in his hands to light it and inhaled its warmth. He checked his watch. Ten minutes after midnight. He wriggled his fingers, slapped his hands, walked a few paces and hunkered down. One hour and fifty minutes. One hour and forty-nine. He stared at the steppe, willing something to happen. Anything at all. Anything that might distract from the darkness around him. He hated the dark. A twig snapped. Then nothing. More silence. More darkness. He lit another cigarette and reached for Katharina, his mind resting in her body until his shift was over, until he could climb back into his tent and sleep.

In the morning the rains came, thick, heavy sheets that turned the road to liquid mud. Word came down the line that tanks, trucks and half-tracks were stuck ahead. Weiss laughed.

'The great blitzkrieg,' he said. 'Thwarted by a drop of Russian rain.'

'That would cheer up your lot, Faustmann,' said Faber.

'What do you mean?'

'Your Russian friends.'

'What?'

'You speak the language so you must be pretty pleased to see us in this mess.'

'Jesus, Faber,' said Fuchs.

'My lot, as you call it, is with Germany,' said Faustmann. 'Have you failed to notice which uniform I'm wearing?'

'It's hard to tell through the mud,' said Weiss.

'It looks Russian to me,' said Faber.

'Come on, Faber,' said Fuchs. 'You're walking with me.'

Faber hurried to keep pace with Fuchs' fury.

'Don't bring that here, Faber,' he said.

'What?'

'Her father's politics. Keep it for Berlin.'

'I wasn't doing anything.'

'Have the courage to bloody admit it.'

'Admit what?'

'When did you become such an idiot, Faber?'

Reinisch ordered them to dig vehicles out of the mud some ten miles south of the main road.

'What size?' said Weiss.

'Just jeeps and trucks,' said Kraus. 'No heavy weaponry. Only task force.'

'Thank God for that,' said Faber.

Stockhoff distributed rations.

'I'll make you beef stew when you catch up with us,' he said.

They found forty men in six vehicles, three jeeps and three trucks, the wheels so deeply embedded that only the tops of tyres were visible. Faber sat on the nearest jeep.

'It'll take a week to dig this out,' he said.

'Your fat arse is sinking it further,' said Weiss.

Faber looked at the task force men with their black collar tabs. He had seen some of them in Kiev, rounding up Jews. They nodded at him. He nodded back and set down his pack and rifle. He began digging. But the vehicles remained stuck. They pitched tents, felled trees and, after days of labour in the rain and mud, finally released the vehicles and fell to the earth, their bodies shattered by fatigue.

'We are allowed a few days' rest,' said Kraus.

Faber looked around, at the mud and trees.

'Where exactly?'

'Those lads were supposed to do a village about five miles south of here. The road is too bad, so we can have it.'

'Is it worth it?' said Fuchs.

'They're sure it's untouched.'

'Jews or Partisans?' said Gunkel.

'Aren't they the same thing?' said Faber.

It was night when they reached the village, the rain banished by dry, cold air from the north and a flicker of something at their faces that might have been snow.

'Everybody out,' shouted Kraus.

The whitewashed houses were still and in darkness.

'You'd better translate, Faustmann.'

'Yes, Sir.'

His bass voice boomed and, one by one, the

doors of about twenty houses creaked open. The villagers, holding lanterns, stood in the doorways, old women huddling into old men, young children into their mothers.

'Faustmann, tell them to leave immediately.'

He spoke again and an old woman, wrapped in coats and scarves, yelled back at him. She slapped her chest, coughed and spat at the ground. She pointed at it with her light. Green phlegm.

'She says that she is too ill to sleep outside, that she has nowhere else to go.'

'Nor do we,' said Kraus. 'Unless she knows of some hotel we can book into.'

The soldiers laughed.

'Throw them all out, Faustmann. Tell them that they can come back in a couple of days, when we have gone.'

The old woman spat again towards Faustmann and went back into her house. She shut the door. A young child, a boy, started to cry; his distress spread to the other children, then to the women. An old man stepped forward, into the middle of the village, its centre marked by a bench under a cherry tree.

'We need to get some things,' he said. 'From our homes.'

'Five minutes,' said Kraus.

The villagers disappeared and re-emerged wearing blankets over their coats and hats, the sick old woman in even more clothing. The old man pulled a rickety wooden trolley, also covered with a blanket. Kraus stamped on the trolley and lifted the cover.

'The food stays,' he said.

The old man started to cry.

'But we will starve. The children need food.'

Kraus lifted his gun and shoved it into the man's stomach.

'No food.'

They shuffled past, about seventy of them, out into the winter. Faber took the old woman's house, its single room still warm, smoke escaping from the metal flue attached to a stove of baked earth. Kraft slipped off his pack and began poking at the embers, scraping away the damp ash that had been thrown over the flames as the soldiers arrived.

'How do you cook on this thing?' said Weiss.

'God knows,' said Kraft. 'But we can boil water.'

Kraft hummed as he unpacked the coffee that his mother sent every month, then the pot. Faber, Weiss and Faustmann sat beside him, waiting for their share, their boots and coats scattered around the room. There were two large beds and a neat row of sheepskin slippers by the door, small and large. The walls were lined with yellowed newspaper, layer upon layer of insulation that reeked of poverty.

'It's a pit,' said Faber. 'How could anyone live here?'

'At least it's warm,' said Faustmann.

'Your ancestors probably came from this kind of hovel.'

'All our ancestors came from this kind of hovel, Faber.'

Kraft bounced to his feet.

'Is there any food?'

They rummaged through chests and wardrobes but found nothing until Weiss threw back a rug, uncovering a hatch that led to a small cellar neatly lined with shelves of bread, salted ham, flour, oats, corn, seeds, nuts and jars of fruit and vegetables, boiled, pickled and poached. And vodka. Crude and home-made.

Faber slept well, warm in a bed beside Weiss. In the morning, they went to find more food. Weiss carried a bucket, determined to find milk.

'Do you know how to do this?' said Faber.

'I've seen my uncle do it.'

They kicked at the snow, which had settled thinly on the ground, and headed towards a large barn at the other end of the village. Faber opened the door, diluting the warm darkness with cold dawn light, stirring muffled noises from creatures not yet ready for the day.

They searched for eggs, but the hens had yet to lay. They went down to the other end of the barn where two cows waited, their udders heavy.

'So what do we do?' said Faber.

'It's easy,' said Weiss. 'Squeeze and the milk comes out.'

'Off you go then.'

Weiss knelt on the ground beside the cow's udder, wrapped his right hand around a teat and squeezed. Nothing happened. He tried again. Still nothing. Faber laughed.

'You try, Faber.'

The men switched places and Faber too wrapped his fingers around a teat, discomfited by the soft, flabby flesh. He squeezed but quickly released his hand and stepped back.

'Nobody will ever turn me into a fucking farmer,' he said.

Weiss laughed and tried again, squeezing so hard that the cow kicked at him and swivelled, turning her rump to him, damp faeces dribbling down her legs. The two men ran from the barn, roaring with laughter, and returned to the house. They had black coffee and army-issue crackers for breakfast.

By mid-morning, the other soldiers had collected eggs and milked both cows. Gunkel killed and plucked a few of the hens and, after lunch, brought one of the sheep to stand under the cherry tree. He put a pistol against its head and shot it, standing to one side as it twitched and jerked its way to stillness. He tied it by its hind legs to the tree, slit its throat and removed the pelt, blood draining from the animal as he worked. He sawed off the head and lowered the animal back to the ground, turning the carcass on its back, its shoulders tight between his calves. He sawed through the ribs, and, with a long, thin, tapering knife, cut from its neck to its groin, then dug his hands into the sheep, pulling out the stomach and intestines, jettisoning them so hard across the earth that they burst, half-digested hay spewing across mud and melted snow. He worked diligently, neatly, until the animal evolved into chops, roasts, racks and chunks for stew. Gunkel stood up straight, a neat stack of meat at his feet.

'Lamb and chicken for dinner tonight, my friends.'

The soldiers clapped, waited in line for their allocation and retreated to cook. They ate the meat with potatoes and boiled corn, and rested for two more days, stripping the barn of everything but the cows. They sang as they left, their bellies and packs filled with food. Faustmann shouted at the forest behind the village.

'What did you say?' said Faber.

'I told them they could go back now. That we'd finished.'

'We needed that rest.'

'We certainly did. It was well deserved.'

CHAPTER 9

Just before six in the morning, a surge of nausea woke her. She threw back the silk-covered eiderdown and ran to the bathroom, just in time to reach the cold porcelain of the toilet bowl. She pulled the chain, rinsed her mouth, splashed water on her face and went back to bed, rubbing herself against the linen to chase the cold from her feet.

CHAPTER 10

Russia, November 15th, 1941

My Dear Katharina,

The post truck has just stopped beside us. He is returning to Kiev and has told us that he will wait for ten minutes, allowing us time to write letters home.

I am well, Katharina, although missing you greatly. I want this whole thing to be over so that I can come home to you. In the meantime, could you do something for me? Could you send me a lock of your hair? As close to the full length as you can manage. I adore your hair. I wrap myself in it as I go to sleep. And a photograph; one of you smiling. I will keep them against my heart.

We have seen a little of the infamous Russian snow. It is already cold, Katharina. Colder than I have ever known it in November. How is the rest of winter in this godforsaken place?

We are marching again, obliterating all the enormous work that you put into my feet. It's such a huge place, Katharina. We march and march, but seem to get nowhere.

It helps me so much to know that you are waiting for me, although I do wish you hadn't moved apartment. I want you still in the bed we shared, in that room, as that is how I remember you, how I know you.

Wait for me nonetheless. I will be back soon.

Your loving husband,

Peter

CHAPTER 11

The driver sat on the step of his cab, passing round chocolate and cigarettes. Faber took both and handed in his letter.

'How do I get your job?' he said.

The driver sniggered.

'You're too skinny. Too fit. You have to be fat and wheeze a lot.'

'I can do that.'

'It takes years of practice.'

They watched as he hoisted himself back into the cab, revved the engine and headed back west, his wheels churning at the already churned earth.

'Lucky bastard,' said Faber.

'But no chance of a medal,' said Weiss. 'Of Iron Cross fame and glory. His picture in the newspaper, women fawning over the hero.'

'I'll take the chocolate, cigarettes and warm feet.'

Faber was wearing all his socks, but still the cold penetrated his feet, exacerbated by the steel across the toe of his boots. He walked a little faster to catch up with Kraus.

'How much further, Sergeant?'

'About sixty miles.'

'Three days?'

'Hopefully, Faber.'

'What did the driver have to say?'

'About what?'

'Our progress.'

'Struggling outside Moscow, but doing well around Kharkov.'

'So how does it look?'

'You know as much as I do, Faber. Judge it yourself.'

'But how long more will it take?'

'As I said, three days.'

'I meant the war.'

'I only know, Faber, about this march to Poltava. That's what I'm in charge of. Not the war.'

'Yes, Sir.'

'There's a place three miles from here where we can spend the night. Go and tell the others.'

The town square was quiet, and scattered with corpses. Some were German. Most were Russian. Faustmann bent down and rummaged through a Russian backpack. He pulled out a mink hat, the earflaps tied up.

'It's not that cold,' said Faber.

'It will be.'

'But we won't still be here.'

'So you say. No harm in being prepared though.'

'I don't know if I could do that,' said Faber. 'Wear dead men's clothes.'

'Up to you, Faber. But they're not using them.'

Faber squatted beside a corpse, its eyes already scavenged, peck marks on its cheeks and forehead. He took the felt boots from the man's feet, and put them on. They fitted perfectly. He kicked the corpse, hard, in the ribs, and moved on, his back bent over, picking at the dead. He found a mink hat of his own, as well as gloves, cigarettes, Belgian chocolate in an envelope, and two lengths of sausage. The houses, however, had already been stripped. He carried his booty to a small, wooden church. Weiss was there, at the front. They sat beside each other under gold-framed paintings and shared the sausage and chocolate.

'Do you think it's real?' said Faber.

'What?'

'The gold?'

'Probably.'

'We should take it with us.'

'I'm not carrying any of that shit.'

'We'll pick it up on the way back then. It must be worth a fortune.'

'It's kitsch, Faber.'

They slept in the church. It was cold, but drier than their tents. When they woke, a light layer of snow covered the ground. They buried the Germans and moved out, their boots breaking a crust of ice as they walked. Faber pulled his scarf over his mouth and nose, his breath condensing where the warmth of his body met the cold of the steppe. Weiss was beside him.

'How cold do you think it'll get?'

'This isn't cold, Faber. Winter hasn't begun yet. Not properly.'

'How do you know?'

'Faustmann told me.'

Faber looked at the sky, at the clouds heavy with snow. He kicked at the earth, at its muddied whiteness.

'I hate this fucking place.'

'It's not on my holiday list either.'

'We're wasting our time here. Let the tanks and planes do the job and we go home.'

'The perfect war. No infantry required.'

'Just bomb them all into submission. It worked in France, why not here?'

'Here they fight back, Faber.'

Weiss dug some chocolate out of his tunic and broke off enough for both of them.

In the afternoon, the snow came back, accompanied by wind, rain and hail that stripped it of its softness, hammering at the soldiers' faces, sharp pricks of pain on their eyelids. Faber wore his mink hat and blindly followed the men in front, glad of the blackness of their clothing, of the authorities' delay in sending winter camouflage. As darkness came, Fuchs halted and lifted the blanket off his head and face.

'What's wrong?'

'We're going the wrong way.'

'What do you mean?'

'We're lost, Faber.'

Fuchs bellowed at the sergeant, out in front.

'We've gone the wrong way,' he said.

Kraus trudged on.

'We're lost, Sergeant,' said Fuchs. 'You don't know where we are.'

Kraus stopped, turned slowly and lifted his head. His eyes were almost closed.

'You're right. I don't know where we are.'

'Shit,' said Weiss.

'We're walking north,' said Fuchs. 'Into the wind and rain. We have been for hours. Poltava is east, south-east.'

'I realize that.'

'When did you realize that?' said Fuchs.

'Just now, when you told me.'

'Damn it,' said Fuchs. 'You're supposed to be in charge.'

'I am,' he said, his eyes fully closing. 'I am in charge. We'll camp here for the night and get back on the right road tomorrow.'

'How will we know?' said Weiss.

'What?' said Kraus, his eyes still shut.

'That we're on the right road?'

'Set up camp, Weiss.'

They dropped their packs and pitched their tents on the sodden earth. Under wet fabric that stank of mildew, Faber and Weiss ate tinned sardines and crackers without talking, and lay down to sleep, burying their bodies under damp blankets and coats.

'Kraus is a fucking idiot,' said Weiss.

'He'll sort it out tomorrow.'

'We don't have a clue where we are, Faber. Or who the fuck is outside, lurking around.'

'I know.'

'Is your gun ready?'

'Yes, and my knife.'

'Mine too.'

'We should try to sleep, Weiss.'

'Good night, Faber.'

'Good night, Weiss.'

Faber closed his eyes and unpicked the pins from Katharina's hair, watching the locks unfurl, his gun across his chest, his finger on the trigger, ready for a dagger through the tent, or a pitchfork. He didn't know what he would do with a sniper bullet. Or a machine gun. A rocket launcher, grenade or tank. He moved closer to Weiss and buried his fear in his wife's hair.

He woke at dawn and heard Fuchs coughing.

'I never thought I would be glad to hear that bastard.'

'We're still alive then?' said Weiss, his head tucked under his blanket.

'Just about.'

Weiss sat up, plunged his arm into his pack and began to eat, voraciously.

'You'll run out of food if you keep eating like that,' said Faber.

'I'll die if I don't.'

Kraus gathered the men. He was rested. Awake.

'I regret what happened,' he said, 'but I will get us out of here.'

'How?' said Weiss. 'You're the one who got us lost in the first place.'

Kraus paused, waiting for the affront to pass. He spread out his map, turned his compass, and pointed at the flat featureless landscape.

'We need to head south again,' he said. 'It's about ten miles back to the main road to Poltava.'

'How can you be sure?' asked Fuchs. 'We have no bearings.'

'We came north, and now we have to go south.'

'Due south?'

'Yes.'

'Why not travel south-east, towards Poltava?'

'We should get back to the road first.'

'If we can find it,' said Weiss.

'That's enough from you, Weiss,' said Kraus.

'The whole place looks the same, Sir.'

'I realize that, Weiss.'

'Yes, Sir.'

'At least the wind will be behind us,' said Kraft.

'We should reach Poltava in three days,' said Kraus. 'Divide your rations accordingly.'

Faber had only enough food for two days.

'We'll manage,' said Kraft.

'How?' said Weiss.

'I don't know. We just will.'

They set off south, the wind against their backs, a pleasant relief until it grew too strong and pressed them to their knees, over and over again, their feet unable to keep pace with its strength. They slept again in their tents and Fuchs woke with a fever, his skin translucent, his eyes elsewhere. They draped him over their shoulders and trailed the sergeant and his compass, their minds and bodies numbed by the weather, rousing only when they heard Weiss shouting.

'Poltava.'

Faber and Faustmann surged forward, Fuchs between them, towards the light and the smoke rising from chimneys.

'We're there, Fuchs,' said Faber.

'We're not,' said Kraus. 'It's too small and too soon.'

'But it'll do,' said Weiss.

They knocked the ice from their weapons, loosened the bolts and moved towards the village, a tiny enclave of one barn and ten houses, all in darkness, wisps of smoke seeping from the chimneys.

'Move them out, Faustmann,' said Kraus.

The people slowly emerged.

'Tell them to give us their food,' said the sergeant.

'They say they don't have any. That other Germans have already raided the village. That the Jews and communists have already been taken away.'

'I don't give a fuck about the Jews and communists, Faustmann. Only food. That's all we want. Tell them to hand it over.'

Kraus was agitated, hungry for his men. The villagers were still. An old woman spoke.

'She says they have nothing left,' said Faustmann.

'Right then,' said Kraus, 'we'll just have to find it ourselves. Let's go.'

They crashed into the small houses, ripping up floorboards, emptying cupboards, cellars, vats and wardrobes, unearthing potatoes, sunflower seeds, bread and apples. But no meat. Kraus stormed back into the yard and the men followed, stuffing bread and apples into their mouths. He grabbed an old man by the collar of his tattered coat.

'Where are the animals? Where's the meat?'

Faustmann translated the sergeant's fury.

'We don't have any,' replied the old man.

Kraus pulled a warmed pistol from inside his tunic and placed it against the man's head.

'Where is it? My men need meat and I am going to find it.'

'We don't have any. It's all gone.'

Kraus squeezed his finger against the trigger and the old man fell to the ground, a puff of body heat and a scarlet flush across the muddied snow. The villagers covered their mouths, frozen, until a young woman with long dark hair hanging from beneath her brightly coloured cotton headscarf stepped forward.

'I will show you,' she said.

They followed her past the emptied barn to a small orchard at the end of the village, her plump, rounded buttocks shifting the material of her filthy, torn coat. Faber watched her. As she knelt down. As she scraped back frozen hail and lifted a sheet of wood, her bottom towards them. The chickens clucked, raucously, disturbed by the light. There were about twenty of them, on a shelf of earth scattered with seed.

'Clever,' said Faustmann.

'But not clever enough,' said Faber.

'How did they stop them suffocating?' said Gunkel.

'Who gives a fuck?' said Weiss.

Gunkel reached in and wrung the neck of each bird, passing them back to the waiting men. They ran to the houses, kicked the floorboards back into place and sat down, feverishly plucking the chickens with their coats and packs still on, resting only when the dampened fires had been restarted, when the roasts were on. Faber stuffed his mouth with sunflower seeds.

'Never thought I'd eat this bird food,' he said.

'Hunger is a great sauce,' said Kraft.

Faber laughed.

'Old mother Kraft is back. We have survived.'

'We're not there yet, Faber,' said Weiss.

'No. But at least we're here.'

He began peeling off his clothing, first examining his fingers, which had turned a dark red.

'Much longer out there and I might have been in trouble.'

'You're fine, Faber,' said Faustmann. 'It's not cold enough.'

'How are your feet?' said Weiss.

'They feel fine,' said Faber.

He removed his Russian felt boots. His feet were red, but safe. Kraft asked for help in taking off his boots. The leather was sodden, rotting near the heel and steel tips.

'You should have changed boots, Kraft.'

'I won't wear a dead man's shoes.'

Faber tugged at Kraft's left boot, laughing at the sucking sound as it loosened and came off. Newspaper and socks stuck like wet plaster to his friend's leg.

'You're disgusting, Kraft.'

'Just get it off, Faber.'

He unravelled the paper and fabric, but dropped the foot. It was riddled with lice. Kraft threw his hands over his face.

'Do the other one, Faber.'

'No way, Kraft. I'm not going near you.'

'You owe me. For not going to see my mother.'

'Bastard.'

Faber pulled off the second boot, tearing everything away as quickly as he could. He filled a bowl with water and placed it at Kraft's feet.

'There'll be eggs on your feet. You need to wash them off.'

'Thank you, Faber. You've been very kind.'

'I'm sorry I didn't go to see your mother, Kraft.'

'It's fine.'

'How is she?'

'I don't know. I'm hoping to hear when we reach Poltava. It's hard.'

'What is?'

'Being out here. Not knowing how she is. If she is even dead or alive.'

He looked at the ground, hiding his eyes from Faber.

'I hate this place, Faber. I want to go home. I want to see her.'

Faber patted his arm.

'We all want to go home, Kraft.'

They ate and slept. More snow fell and they stayed a second night. Fuchs slept most of the time, his lungs rattling with the effort of each breath, indifferent as the men tucked into bottle after bottle of home-made vodka.

'They're still here,' said Weiss.

'Who are?' said Faber.

'The villagers.'

'Where?'

'They crept into the barn this evening. They must have come in from the woods. Decided we were safe.'

'All of them?'

'Yep.'

'Including the woman?'

'Including her.'

They finished another bottle. Weiss stumbled to his feet.

'Let's go, Faber. Find out what they're up to.'

'Are you sure she's there?'

'She's there, Faber.'

Faber turned to the other men.

'Are you coming, Kraus? Kraft?'

'We'll have a look,' said Kraus. 'What harm?'

'I'll come too,' said Gunkel. 'Stretch my legs.'

'Come on Kraft,' said Weiss.

'I'm fine here,' he said.

They wore their boots, but left their coats and hats.

'Faustmann?' said Faber. 'Are you coming?'

'I'll stay here.'

'Why?'

'Not my thing, Faber.'

'Come on. We might need an interpreter.'

'I doubt it.'

'Suit yourself.'

They picked up their guns and stepped outside, into moonlight and sparkling snow. They walked across the village, crashing into each other as they went, loudly hushing each other's laughter. Weiss and Gunkel started to sing. Kraus told them to be quiet. They reached the barn and cocked their guns.

'All right, boys,' said Weiss. 'Who's first this time?'

'It must be you, Faber,' said Kraus. 'Your wedding present from us.'

They pushed open the door and swung torch beams until they located the huddle of staring eyes. Faber saw her, her headscarf still on. He walked towards her, but then he turned away and went back into the snow. He returned to the house to sleep between Kraft and Faustmann, his wife's hair and photograph pressed into his cheek.

CHAPTER 12

Katharina leaned back into the soft black leather chair, took a magazine from the walnut coffee table and angled her legs to the left, her feet crossed at the ankles like those of the other women in the room, although their fur coats closed neatly across their chests. She flicked through the pages, scanning pictures of ball gowns, gas cookers and tips for the perfect family Christmas, listening to the near silence of the other women, the polite coughs, the low whispers to already quiet children.

The nurse opened the door across thick cream carpet.

'Mrs Faber.'

Katharina did not lift her head. It was rude to stare. She turned onto a new page.

'Mrs Faber, please.'

The other women's coats had obviously been bought for them. She could tell. No straining at the buttons. She felt herself in shadow. It was the nurse. Standing over her.

'Mrs Faber. Please. Dr Weinart is waiting for you.'

'Oh. That's me.'

'I know it's you.'

Katharina stood up, fumbling with her bag, coat and magazine, her face flushed. The women were staring at her. She hurried after the nurse, across a hall and into a room overlooking the city.

Dr Weinart rose as she entered.

'Ah, Mrs Faber. The daughter of Mr Spinell and wife of Peter Faber.'

'That is correct.'

'Your father is a fine man. A very loyal supporter. I can assume the same of you?'

'Of course, Doctor.'

'Good. And your husband seems to be so, too. How is his campaign?'

'I have not heard from him for several weeks, I'm afraid.'

'He is a busy man, fighting for his country. It's often hard to find time to write.'

'That's what my father tells me.'

'Listen to your father.'

'It is very kind of you to take me on, Dr Weinart.'

'We can't have our loyal supporters attending the son of a Jew.'

'We didn't know, Dr Weinart.'

'He hid it well, Mrs Faber.'

'Which of his parents was it?'

'His mother. He fooled a lot of people, as they do. Now, how can I help you?'

They sat down on leather chairs on either side of a large mahogany table.

'I am pregnant. At least, I think I am.'

'That is very fine news. But it will take a couple of days to find out for certain.'

'I see.'

'I need a sample of your urine.'

'Yes, Doctor.'

'You understand why?'

'I have read about it in the newspaper. It sounds very interesting, although a little hard to understand, I must admit.'

'Great German science, Mrs Faber, is never simple.'

'Could you explain it to me?'

'I will inject your urine into a rabbit's ear and the reaction of its ovaries will tell me whether you are pregnant.'

'I see.'

'The response of a female African clawed toad is much faster, Mrs Faber, but they are hard to come by at the moment.'

'I'm sure.'

'Give the nurse your sample and come back to me on Friday. We will know the truth then.'

'Yes, Doctor.'

She handed in her sample, and went back downstairs, onto the street, where the wind cut at her chest. She would have to find a new coat. And a stole. Preferably matching. She turned right along the boulevard, glancing at coffee shops, looking for the one with the most customers and therefore the most supplies. She found one a couple of streets down from Dr Weinart. It was warm and quiet; the patrons were well-dressed, their heads buried in newspapers or books. They didn't look up as she walked in. The waiter was polite but brisk, unwilling to linger.

She sat at a window and ordered hot chocolate. It was sweet, sugary rather than chocolatey, and the milk was thin, but it was hot and frothy. She wrapped her hands around the thick white porcelain. Pregnant, she would receive extra rations. Full fat, creamy milk.

She dropped her right hand to her belly. She knew he had taken hold. She didn't need the rabbit. She could feel the growth, the frantic multiplication of cells, the sense of something other feeding on her. She rubbed her womb, her hand over the space where their baby was growing, wanting it, but afraid of it.

What if her husband was already dead? Or worse, injured. Those shadows of men she remembered from the end of the last war, hanging around street corners, maimed and scarred, dependent on their wives, without jobs, without pensions. She stirred her drink, dredging up the chocolate stuck to the bottom to blend it with the milk. How would she feed the baby then? How would she become anything other than her mother? She didn't want to be her mother. Anything but that.

She finished her drink, paid the waiter and started the walk home, dawdling at the shop windows displaying fur coats, stoles and evening dresses, walking quickly past the boarded-up windows, past the Jewish draper defiantly open for business, with nothing to sell and no customers. She stopped at a stall and bought some flowers for her room. White roses, short stemmed. Would she tell her mother now or on Friday? She should wait. Enjoy the privacy, the quietness. When would she write to Peter? Would he want a boy or a girl? What did she want?

She took a quick, sharp breath. Nothing deformed. She didn't want anything maimed. And shocking. The field trip to that house south of Berlin had been shocking. When she and the other girls were taken by bus, led up a marble staircase by a nurse in crisp white and brought into a room with tall windows, ornate ceilings. The noise. The screeches. The stench. The faeces on the wall. The puddles of urine. The nurse shoved her further into the room of metal cots and screaming children in stained lilac cotton gowns.

'You are here to learn, young lady.'

Katharina stared at the twisted limbs shunting across the green linoleum floor towards her, closing her eyes as they pawed at her feet and legs, as they pulled themselves up with her skirt, smearing her with snot and saliva drooling from faces contorted by birth or faulty genes.

'They are happy to see you,' said the nurse.

Katharina ran through the door when it reopened, down the stairs to the reception room, towards coffee and cakes with thick fresh cream. Later the nurse addressed the youth movement girls in neat uniform and tidy hair on the importance of choosing the right husband.

'It's vital to ensure there are no impurities – of blood, flesh or brain – that might pass from one generation to the next.'

'What will happen to them?' said Katharina.

'That is to be decided. It costs a lot to keep them here, money that could be better spent on healthy children.'

Katharina walked faster, her feet pounding the pavement. She knew nothing about her husband, or his family. Nothing about the child growing inside her. She chose him for the strength in his sinewy hands. For the light smile on his face. The kindness of his eyes. She knew nothing about his parents. His grandparents. About what lay inside him. It was inside her now.

She turned the key in the lock. She would say nothing to her mother now. Not yet. Nor to Peter. She would wait until she knew more.

CHAPTER 13

He read her letter six, eight, ten times, folded it, slipped it back into its envelope and, still in his socks, walked down the stairs of the house in Poltava. Faustmann, Kraft and Weiss were by the stove, at cards.

'I'm going to be a father.'

'Bloody hell, you're a fast mover,' said Faustmann.

'Congratulations,' said Kraft. 'When is the baby due?'

'July.'

'We'll be done here by then,' said Weiss.

They toasted him with vodka and dealt a new hand.

CHAPTER 14

Katharina tied her scarf more tightly and moved up the line, closer to the ducks and geese hanging from steel hooks in the butcher's window. Mrs Sachs came towards her, a brown parcel under her arm, white string in a neat knot.

'I got a duck,' she said.

'It looks big,' said Katharina.

'I'd have preferred a goose. More traditional.'

'I'd be happy with either.'

'You should have been here earlier.'

'I didn't know.'

'Word went around last night.'

'We didn't hear.'

'You would have heard if you hadn't moved,' said Mrs Sachs. 'The new people in your old place got a goose. A big one.'

'They'll have a good Christmas then. And how are you, Mrs Sachs?'

'Well enough under the circumstances. My son is outside Moscow. The cold is killing him.'

'The cold is killing us all, Mrs Sachs. Have you any coal?'

'We haven't the luxury of a fireplace, Katharina. As you will no doubt remember.'

'It's a curse rather than a luxury, Mrs Sachs, when there is no coal and the wind blows into the apartment.'

'How is your husband?'

'Fine. Safe. We're expecting a baby in the summer.'

'Congratulations.'

'Thank you. I'm very excited.'

'How is your mother? I never see her now.'

'She's well, Mrs Sachs. Enjoying the new apartment.'

Katharina moved up the queue, close enough to see the spikes of the S-shaped hooks digging into the birds, their flaccid necks shifting in the breeze from the open door. She craned her neck. There were eight birds in the window, all of them ducks. In front of her were ten women. The butcher was still drawing on stocks from inside the shop. She turned to the woman behind her.

'It's nerve-racking, isn't it?'

'Awful.'

A car stopped outside the shop and a woman got out, her hair and make-up perfect, her body sculpted by a woollen jacket and skirt. Her driver, in black uniform, shifted the queue to one side. The woman walked into the shop.

'Who is she?' said Katharina.

'I think it's more "what" than "who",' said the woman behind her.

Katharina watched the suited woman point at the ducks in the window. The butcher removed three from the display. A woman ahead of Katharina started to cry, but fell silent as the suited woman left the shop, her driver carrying the ducks to the boot of the car. He drove off and the queue moved back to its previous position. The butcher served eight more women, then shut his door and pulled down his blinds. Katharina knocked at the door. He didn't answer. The remaining women shuffled away, hiding their tears from their children.

She climbed into bed when she got home as it was too cold in the apartment of high ceilings and large rooms without coal. She missed the cloying cosiness of their old kitchen. Her mother did too, although neither woman would admit it.

She woke in the darkness of a winter afternoon. She got up, wrapped a cashmere blanket over her shoulders and went to the living room, braced for the cold, and surprised by the warmth. There was a fire in the grate. Her parents sat on the sofa in front of it, giggling.

'There is more,' said her father.

She looked at the mound of coal still on the slate, waiting to be burned.

'So I see,' she said. 'It's fantastic.'

'Go and look in the kitchen, Katharina.'

On the counter, lying between the cooker and the sink, were a goose, a leg of lamb, sausages, a bag of potatoes, carrots, two turnips and a bottle of wine.

She shrieked and embraced her father.

'And there's more,' he said. 'Let me show you.'

He dipped his hands into the pockets of his jacket.

'Stand in front of the fire please, ladies.'

He draped gold and emerald around his wife's neck, silver and sapphire over his daughter's wrist. They each kissed him and looked at themselves in the hall mirror, above their new bust of Wagner. Mrs Spinell was crying.

'You're a marvellous man, Günther Spinell,' she said. 'You have served this family well.'

Katharina fingered her bracelet.

'It's just a pity we have nowhere to wear them,' she said.

'Oh, but you do,' he said. 'We're going to Dr Weinart's house tomorrow. To hear the Führer's Christmas message.'

Their backs straight, the two women walked either side of Günther Spinell up to the first floor of the doctor's house. A coal fire blazed there too, but the other guests, the women in silk, were indifferent to it as they drained their champagne and picked canapés from the train of passing plates. Mrs Spinell whispered to her daughter.

'Don't guzzle, Katharina. Remember that we have plenty to eat at home.'

Katharina moved about the room, introducing herself, admiring dresses and jewellery, accepting admiration of her bracelet, revelling in the conversation. Mrs Weinart was especially charming.

'I have heard about your family, Mrs Faber. You should come for morning coffee with your lovely mother.'

Dr Weinart demanded their silence and called the company to gather around the radio, Katharina towards the front. The voice entered the room, and people bowed their heads. She listened to the rise and rise of his pitch, but drifted off to replay her success at the party, to run her hand across her expanding womb, to relish the growth of her new life.

CHAPTER 15

Kraft pushed into the house, panting.
'Close the damn door,' said Weiss.
'Give me a chance to come in first.'
He swept snow from his eyes.
'The lieutenant wants us.'
'Bloody hell,' said Faber. 'What for?'
'To award you the Iron Cross, Faber,' said Weiss.
'For services to fatherhood.'
They laughed.
'It'll be the only one I get,' said Faber. 'Stuck in this pit.'
'Why does he want us?' said Faustmann.
'I don't know,' said Kraft, 'but he's wound up.'
They swore as they pulled on their outdoor clothes. Kraft stoked the stove.
'I'll make coffee when we're back,' he said.
They stood outside the lieutenant's house, snow and wind cutting into their faces, darkness on its way. Faber stamped his feet. He should have put on a second pair of socks.
Reinisch came out of his house, his shoulders straight, but his face pale.

'We're moving out tomorrow,' he said. 'At first light.'

A shock of cold rushed up Faber's legs.

'It's January, Sir.'

'I'm aware of that, Private.'

Reinisch stepped back from the men, towards his house.

'Where are we going?' said Weiss.

'Kharkov. The Russians are on the move there. Our boys need support.'

'But that's a hundred miles away.'

'A little less, I think, Private.'

'What, ninety?'

'About that.'

Faber started shivering, his teeth chattering.

'I could die, Sir, if I go out there again,' said Fuchs.

'Have the doctors told you that?'

'No, Sir.'

'Well then, you've nothing to worry about.'

The lieutenant turned his back on the men and went back into his house, shutting the wooden door against them, shoving it tight into its buckled frame. The wood shuddered. Together the men moved towards it, two, three steps. And then they stopped, turned away towards Kraus. He threw his hands into the air.

'Those are our orders. They want us to shore up Kharkov.'

'It's impossible,' said Weiss.

'We are expected to walk thirty miles a day and will be given enough food for ten. There are villages along the way where we can rest.'

'It's madness,' said Fuchs. 'We can't walk thirty miles a day in snow. Russian snow.'

'I have been told that most of the road has been cleared.'

'It's madness, Sir.'

'That's enough, Fuchs. Back to your houses, everyone, to rest and prepare.'

They were still.

'Who will lead us?' said Weiss.

'The lieutenant will,' said Kraus. 'It's a straightforward route.'

Faber suddenly wanted to sleep. To forget what he was hearing.

'What'll we eat?' said Gunkel. 'What'll we do for meat? We need meat in the snow.'

'I'll talk to Stockhoff,' said Kraus. 'See what extra rations he can give us.'

They drifted back to their houses. Kraft began to make the coffee sent by his mother, to bang pots and hum.

'Shut up, Kraft,' said Faber.

'Leave him alone, Faber,' said Weiss. 'He's making coffee.'

'That piss! You call it coffee?'

'Forget it.'

'No, I won't. I hate his humming. He's like an old woman.'

'Leave it. Write a letter to your wife.'

Weiss picked up a newspaper. Faber paced the room and settled beside Fuchs, crumpled by the stove.

'So what do you think, Fuchs? Will you survive out there this time? All that snow?'

'I doubt it.'

'What are you going to do about it?'

'There's nothing I can do.'

'You could go back to Reinisch,' said Faustmann. 'Refuse to go.'

'And be lined up and shot? In front of you all?'

'But you're not fit, Fuchs,' said Faustmann.

'The doctors say I am. So that's that.'

'You shouldn't be going,' said Faustmann. 'None of us should be. We should refuse the order. Collectively.'

'Don't be a fucking idiot, Faustmann,' said Faber.

'So what do we do, Faber? We go out there, march Fuchs to his death?'

'It's an order. From a proper army. Not your Soviet rabble.'

'Right then, Fuchs,' said Faustmann. 'Off you go, out into the snow. Pack up.'

'Leave it, Faustmann,' said Weiss.

'But write to your wife and children first, Fuchs. Tell them you won't be coming back.'

'Shut up,' said Weiss.

'Tell them that you are about to die because you're following some stupid fucking order to walk ninety miles through January snow. Tell them all that.'

Fuchs' cheeks flushed. He shoved his knuckles into the floor and vaulted onto Faustmann, pummelling his chest and face. The other men wrenched him off.

'Shut the fuck up, Faustmann,' said Fuchs.

Faustmann dragged a sleeve across his bloodied nose and lit a cigarette. He handed the rest of the pack to Fuchs.

'Thanks. How's your nose?'

'Fine.'

'You're right anyway. I'll never last another week out there.'

'Of course you will,' said Faustmann. 'I was talking rubbish.'

'I'm beaten. I don't have it in me.'

'You'll be fine,' said Weiss. 'The road has been cleared and we'll have plenty of food.'

The coffee spluttered on the stove.

'It's ready,' said Kraft.

They drank in silence and played cards, without money.

Faber was unable to sleep. He took his blanket to sit by the stove. Faustmann was already there, smoking and staring at the flames.

'How's your face?' asked Faber.

'Sore.'

'He whacked you.'

'I deserved it.'

Faber threw three more logs on the already blazing fire.

'We may as well use them up.'

Faustmann lit a cigarette.

'They don't give a damn if we live or die.'

'Who?' said Faber.

'Those idiots in Berlin.'

'What do you mean?'

'They don't give a damn about us.'

'Of course they do.'

'We're cannon fodder, Faber. Just like in the last war. Nothing has changed.'

'Don't be ridiculous. We are crucial to the inevitable victory.'

'Cannon fodder. That's all. For Russian guns and German ambition.'

'Have you been drinking, Faustmann?'

'Reinisch will be promoted because we've walked through ninety miles of Russian snow.'

'I'm not listening to this, Faustmann. You're just looking for another fight.'

'I'm not, Faber. I'm just sick of being used.'

'You're a soldier, Faustmann, and there's a war on.'

'But what's the war about?'

'A greater Germany.'

'At whose expense? Not theirs in Berlin, with their stuffed gullets. At our expense, Faber. With our lives.'

'You sound like a communist, Faustmann.'

He laughed.

'I'm not a communist.'

'But you speak Russian, your grandmother's Russian and your politics sound Russian.'

'I'm German, and you know it. But these

105

Russians have done nothing to us, so what the hell are we doing here?'

'We need a bigger Germany.'

'For what?'

'For food, space, oil, coal.'

'Can't we just buy it all?'

'You'd better shut up.'

'Why?'

'You might be reported.'

Faustmann placed a log on his thighs and picked at the splinters.

'By whom, Faber?'

'It could be dangerous for you. That's all.'

'I'm not a communist.'

'You speak Russian.'

'So what? Weiss speaks French. What does that make him?'

'I'm only concerned with you.'

'Why? Why the sudden concern with me? You were never concerned before.'

'I have a family and a future to think about. I can't have our campaign in Russia jeopardized by communists spreading disaffection.'

'Is that what you think I'm doing? Spreading disaffection?'

'You just need to be careful. That's all.'

Faustmann went to the end of the room where Weiss, Kraft and Fuchs were sleeping. Faber stayed, relishing his easy victory, and fell asleep by the stove, his feet against the shrunken woodpile.

★   ★   ★

They moved out just after dawn, towards the sun rising into a cold, cloudless sky. The road was clear, as promised, and the sixty men made steady progress, about twenty miles that day, before finding an abandoned village at dusk where they built fires and sheltered for the night. The second day, too, began well, but in the middle of the morning the road suddenly disappeared under a drift of snow that reached up to their thighs.

'We must have gone off course,' said Fuchs.

Reinisch, who checked his map and compass every half-hour, was adamant.

'This is the right way,' he said. 'No doubt about it.'

'That's old, compacted snow,' said Faustmann. 'They haven't cleared it. They stopped here.'

'They wouldn't do that,' said Kraft. 'We must be lost.'

'We're not lost, Kraft,' said Kraus.

Faber looked at the tyre tracks in the snow, at the traces of turning circles.

'We should go back,' said Weiss.

'I can't allow that,' said Reinisch. 'There's a village two miles from here.'

Faber followed the lieutenant. The snow melted into his trousers and coat, chilling his sweat, confusing his senses so that he did not know whether he felt cold or hot. He took off his gloves and hat, but put them back on again. He removed his scarf. He was comfortable for a short time, but then too cold again, his body drained by the changes. After four hours, they reached the edge of the village. He checked his gun. It was frozen. Fuchs was coughing.

'Why can't I see any roofs?' said Faber.

Weiss peered through the fading light.

'Damn it,' he said. 'It's been burned out.'

'Right men,' said Reinisch. 'Find a bed for the night.'

Fuchs coughed, bending at the waist.

'We'll find shelter,' said Kraft. 'You'll be all right, Fuchs.'

'And there'll be something to slaughter, Fuchs,' said Gunkel. 'There always is.'

They walked towards the centre, marked, as usual, by a wooden bench and a cherry tree, both blackened. They stubbed at the charred remains of the village with their boots.

'Who did it?' said Faber.

'It's a thorough job, lots of petrol,' said Weiss. 'Must have been our boys.'

'Thanks lads,' said Fuchs.

'We'd better move,' said Weiss, 'or all the best places will be gone.'

'There aren't any best places,' said Faber. 'It's a hellhole.'

'Let's look,' said Kraft.

They moved from house to house, but stoves, beds and cupboards were lost under blankets of snow. The only roof they could see was on the south-facing gable end of the barn, but it was already packed with other soldiers, their backs set firmly against the gusting northerly wind.

'Let's keep looking,' said Kraft. 'Fuchs needs proper shelter.'

'There isn't any,' said Faber.

'We'll go around again,' said Weiss. 'One more time.'

They headed towards an orchard at the other end of the village, its branches reaching into the darkness. Weiss stopped and hunkered down to peer through the trees.

'I think there's something over there,' he said. 'On the other side.'

Suddenly they could all see it. Walls with a roof, unblackened, intact.

'Saved for another day,' said Fuchs. 'Hallelujah.'

They charged at it, guns to the front, packs bouncing against their backs, hurrying in case somebody else got there first. Weiss yanked open the small, wooden door and the five piled into a darkness sweetened by ripened fruit. Kraft switched on his torch, and they cheered, ecstatic at their good fortune.

'What's there to eat?' said Faber.

Kraft swung his torch, across apples, pears, plums and two women wrapped into each other, one old, one young.

'It's all right,' said Kraft. 'We won't hurt you.'

He held his hand towards them and the younger woman stepped forward, apples rolling at her feet. Faber was shocked by the beauty of her pale, unblemished skin, by the brightness of her green eyes and the strength of her strong, straight shoulders.

'She looks German,' he said. 'Talk to her, Faustmann.'

'In Russian, Faber?'

He put his gun barrel on her left breast, over her heart.

'Speak,' he said.

She did, so softly that Faber heard the melody of the language for the first time.

'Russian,' laughed Faustmann. 'Go on. Out.'

He dragged the older woman, the grandmother, by the arm and threw them outside, into the snow.

'What are you doing?' said Faber.

'They're Russian,' said Faustmann.

He planted them in front of an apple tree and aimed first at the old woman, who held her hands in front of her face, then at the young woman, who held his gaze. He fired into the middle of her face.

'What the hell did you do that for?' said Fuchs.

Faustmann shot the old woman too.

'They're Russian,' said Faustmann. 'I can't share a shed with Russian peasants.'

'Jesus, Faustmann,' said Fuchs, 'your grandmother's Russian. It's like you just shot your own grandmother.'

Faustmann went back into the shed, bit into an apple and dug in his pack for food. Kraus and Gunkel followed them inside.

'You bastards,' said Kraus. 'How did you find this place? Make room for us.'

'Just you two,' said Weiss.

'We'll fetch our packs. Right, the rest of you men, back to the barn. Incident over.'

Faber sat down to eat, to settle the churn of his stomach. Faustmann leaned into him, and whispered.

'Now, Faber. Accuse me again. See who'll believe you.'

'Fuck you. You shouldn't have shot her.'

'She was Russian.'

'Maybe you shot her because she looked German.'

'You're a bastard.'

He moved away, leaving Faber next to Fuchs, a rattling wheeze in his chest.

'How are you feeling?' said Faber.

'I'm glad to be inside. What's going on between you two?'

'What do you mean?'

'You and Faustmann. You're hissing at each other like an old married couple.'

'I don't like his politics.'

'I told you before. There's no room for politics here.'

'He's talking like a communist.'

'Faber, before you went to Berlin, you barely knew what a communist was.'

'But it's important.'

'It's rubbish. What's important is to stick together and get out of this hellhole in one piece.'

'It's important to me.'

'Why is it so fucking important to you?'

'We're here for a reason, aren't we?'

'Yes, because we're soldiers.'

'No, Fuchs, we're here to clear the communists and Jews from Russia. So that my wife and child have a better future.'

'We're here because we're soldiers, Faber. That's it.'

'It's not that simple.'

'Make it that fucking simple.'

CHAPTER 16

Katharina read the letter a second time, her mother curled into her.

'It doesn't say there's anything wrong with him, Mother. You should be happy. He's coming home.'

'They'd never send him back, Katharina, unless there was something wrong.'

'So he injured his arm, his leg? He'll recover. The main thing is that he's coming.'

She kissed her mother on the cheek.

'We should prepare for him, Mother. Decorate his room. We still haven't hung up those badges and certificates. Come on. We'll do it now.'

She helped her mother to her feet and they went to his room.

'He'll be fine, Mother.'

CHAPTER 17

There was no shelter the following evening and they stood stranded on the steppe, only thirty-five of the ninety miles behind them.

'We should walk through the night,' said Kraft. 'Keep moving and stay warm.'

'It's too cold and we'd lose each other,' said Reinisch. 'We'll camp here.'

Faber stuck his rifle down through the snow, but found no earth for pegs, only thick sheets of ice.

'What do we do now?' he said.

'Dig into the snow,' said Weiss. 'We'll make a cave for the tent.'

'I'm exhausted,' said Kraft.

'Let's just pitch them on the surface,' said Faber.

'We need shelter from the wind,' said Weiss.

'There is none,' said Kraft.

'There might be. Start digging,' said Weiss.

'Nobody else is bothering, Weiss,' said Faber.

'That's up to them.'

They burrowed for twenty minutes, until they had created a cavity deep enough for the tent ropes and pegs.

'We're like bloody Eskimos,' said Faber.

'I can't believe this is happening to us. That they are doing this to us,' said Kraft.

'Who?'

'Those bastards in Berlin. The ones who sent us out here.'

'Have you been listening to Faustmann?' said Faber.

'No.'

'You sound like him.'

'Like Faustmann?'

'Yes, he talks like that. Like a communist.'

Weiss's laughter exploded in the tent.

'Kraft's too rich to be a communist.'

'So why is he talking like one?'

'I'm not,' said Kraft. 'I'm just wondering what the hell we are doing out here. What purpose does it serve?'

'See, that's communist cant.'

'No, Faber. It's me wondering what the fuck I am doing in Russian snow when I should be at home in front of the fire, looking after my mother.'

They slept, until brutally cold air filled the tent. It was Fuchs, Faustmann and Gunkel, forcing their way inside.

'Ours is fucked,' shouted Faustmann. 'Ripped apart. Everybody's out there, scrambling for shelter.'

'But there's no room in here,' said Faber.

'There has to be,' said Fuchs.

Faber, Weiss and Kraft squeezed their knees against their chests and the other three pushed their way in, dragging packs and guns after them.

'It was the wind,' said Fuchs. 'Cut through us like a knife.'

They hunkered, backs against the tent, knees pressing up against each other, six men compressed into a space created for two. Fuchs coughed for most of the night, spitting up phlegm in a tent already full of sweat and stale breath. Faber woke at dawn, gasping for fresh air. It was bitterly cold outside, but still. He lit a cigarette and watched the sun climb into the sky, its strengthening light rinsing the snow pink, illuminating three men wrapped in their collapsed tents. Faber walked towards them. They were dead.

'Poor bastards,' he said.

He finished his cigarette, threw the butt to the snow, and went back to the sleeping men, nudging them to open up the space that had been his. He slept again, woke with the others, and ate.

They tugged at the dead men's clothing. Everything was frozen. Their hats glued by ice to their heads, their packs sealed shut.

'The snow will bury them for us,' said Kraus.

Fuchs coughed and spat green phlegm onto the snow.

'I hope you'll bury me, Sergeant,' he said.

'You'll be fine, Private.'

Fuchs wiped the sweat dribbling from his forehead and the bridge of his nose.

'Let's hope you're right, Sergeant.'

They gathered around the dead, said some prayers and moved out, heading north-east, following the map and compass, supporting Fuchs when he stumbled, then taking turns to carry him through the snow. When evening came, there was again no village, no shelter, only the never-ending whiteness. Kraus leaned his head against Fuchs', the eyelashes of both men shrouded in ice.

'I'm sorry Fuchs.'

Fuchs opened his eyes, then closed them again.

'It's not your fault, Sergeant.'

'We should have disobeyed him.'

'Then you'd be dead too, Kraus.'

'I may be, anyway.'

Weiss put a hand on the shoulder of each man.

'We'll rest for the night,' he said.

'I can't dig,' said Faber.

'We've got to,' said Weiss.

'I can't. I'm worn out.'

'Nor can I,' said Kraft. 'Let's just pitch on the surface.'

'What if there's wind, like last night?' said Weiss.

'It can't happen two nights in a row,' said Faber.

'I suppose not.'

They fell into deep, consuming sleep, oblivious to the high-pitched whistle of wind across the steppe. It kicked their tent as though it were a football, sending it into the air, dropping it again and rolling it over and over, their hips, knees, heads and guns crashing into each other. They tumbled over and under one another, screaming, howling, Kraft sobbing that they would fall off the edge of the earth. And then it stopped. Suddenly. The men untangled their limbs and tried to still their rasping breath.

'A ride at a fucking Russian funfair,' said Weiss.

They laughed, grateful for the release. They were bruised and grazed, but no one was cut. Nothing seemed broken. They shoved their way out of the tent, through the ropes and fabric. Kraus, Gunkel and Faustmann were beside them, their tent pushed the same direction by the same wind.

'Some fucking country,' said Gunkel.

They gathered their belongings and walked the quarter-mile back to camp where the others still slept undisturbed under the early morning moon. They tried to pitch the tent again, but the fabric was torn, and ropes and pegs were missing.

'It's almost dawn, anyway,' said Weiss.

'We should just huddle together,' said Kraft.

Faustmann laid his tent across the snow.

'Stand on this,' he said, 'and we'll drape the other one over us.'

'And put Fuchs in the middle,' said Gunkel. 'Breathe on him to keep him warm.'

Fuchs looked lost. He was no longer coughing.

'Are you all right, Fuchs?' asked Faber.

'Yes. You're all very kind.'

They fell silent in the thin, brittle air, listening to Fuchs' breath, the plaintive wheeze of a man drowning in his own lungs. Faber rubbed his gloves over Fuchs' face, knocking off the icicles, breaking the ice spreading across his nose and lips. He was determined to stay awake, to be with his father's old pupil, but at dawn a wave of sleep dragged him under, holding him down until he felt something fall against him. It was Fuchs, already freezing. He held him briefly, but then let him fall further, face first, into the snow.

'He's dead,' he said.

They all woke and looked down. Weiss bent over the body.

'I'll take his paybook and tag,' said Weiss. 'For his wife.'

They bent as Weiss did, taking things no longer of use to a dead man – a knife, a torch, a hat, scarf and gloves, moving quickly before the corpse froze any further. They covered him with snow and left.

'So, what do you think now, Faber?'

'About what, Faustmann?'

'Are we cannon fodder?'

'Shut up.'

'No, he's right,' said Weiss. 'What the hell are we doing out here, anyway?'

'I am doing as I am ordered to do by my leaders.'

'Where are they?' said Weiss. 'Why aren't they here?'

'Because we are,' said Faustmann. 'On their behalf.'

'We'll end up dead or mad,' said Weiss.

'Or both,' said Kraft.

'I can't think about it,' said Faber.

'You have to think about it,' said Faustmann.

'No I don't, Faustmann. What I have to do is stay alive.'

'You're ignoring the facts, Faber.'

'The facts? The facts are that I am starving and freezing to death thousands of miles from home. For what? For a bigger, stronger Germany free of communist Jews. Those are the facts. That's why I'm here. Why are you here, Faustmann?'

'I have no fucking idea.'

The snow began to fall again, the flakes landing on already frozen snow. Faber covered himself in everything he had, glad of his mink and felt, so that only his eyes were visible. But it was hard to see. The snow was thick and the sky was dark. He moved towards the front of the group, exposing himself to more of the wind, but getting closer to Reinisch and the compass.

In the early afternoon, they came upon a village, intact but empty of people and food. Gunkel found nothing to slaughter. They lit fires and drank boiled snow. Kraft began to remove his leather boots, the steel tops cleaned by the snow, glistening in the firelight.

'I'm not sure you should do that, Kraft,' said Weiss. 'It's probably best to wait until we're there.'

'I want to wash my feet. Warm them up a bit.'

Faber helped him with his boots and watched as Kraft removed the left sock. The skin underneath was darker than the rest of his leg, with a scattering of white dust across it.

'What's that?' said Faber.

Kraft brushed at it. It didn't move. He took off the rest of the sock, lifting it over the ball of his foot and over his toes.

120

'Shit! That hurts.'

Kraft's toenails were gone. All five of them. Faber lifted the sock, turned it inside out and found them, stuck to the material, black and rotten. The flesh of Kraft's right foot was even darker. Those toenails came away too, and the small toe was blacker, squashed and elongated. Nobody spoke. Everybody stared. Kraft stood up and hobbled to the stove. He filled a pan with luke-warm water, sat back down and put his feet in the water.

'They'll go back to normal in a minute,' he said.

The feet lightened a little in colour, but the little toe remained black and spongy. He dried his feet and applied the frostbite cream from their first aid kits. Faber found a pair of thick, dry socks in a pair of Russian slippers by the door.

'Looks like I should have worn dead men's shoes,' said Kraft.

'I'll see if I can find some for you here,' said Weiss.

'Don't even bother,' said Faustmann. 'Russians only have one pair of boots. They're wearing them.'

In the morning, Faber, Weiss, Gunkel and Faustmann walked with Kraft, moving slowly at the back, ushering him through snow that reached up to their thighs, along a vague path left by the men who had gone before them.

Cold snow seeped in through Faber's clothes and hot, damp sweat seeped out, his body exhausted and confused, uncertain of its own temperature, of its own strength. He wanted Stockhoff's beef stew. Katharina's long hair. He wanted it all to be over. For the stupidity to end.

CHAPTER 18

They waited, with cake and coffee ready, listening to the clock tick each irretrievable second of the afternoon.

Katharina went down to the street every half-hour to check that he was not wandering up and down, lost, uncertain of the new address, but found no sign of him.

'Maybe his train was delayed,' said Mrs Spinell. 'Nothing can be relied on any more.'

'I'll go and check,' said Mr Spinell.

'I'll come with you, Father.'

'It's raining, Katharina. Stay with your mother.'

Katharina sat back down in front of the fire, opposite her mother, and resumed her sewing. The clock ticked on.

'That damn thing,' said Mrs Spinell. 'I don't know why they ever bought it. It's so loud.'

She stood up, took a cloth from the kitchen and dusted the ornaments she had already cleaned.

'I'm sure he's fine,' said Katharina. 'There's probably some simple explanation.'

'But he was always so punctual. Do you remember how he raced to school every morning to be at the top of the line under the teacher's nose so that she could praise his timekeeping?'

'I remember.'

'He was never, ever late. You always dawdled and dreamed your way to school.'

'I know, Mother.'

Mr Spinell returned after two hours, his coat and suit sodden.

'There was no trace of him. All the trains from the east have come and gone.'

Mrs Spinell picked up the cake, wrapped it in a clean towel, placed it in a tin, and went to her room. Her husband changed his clothes and took the place she had warmed on the sofa.

'Do you think he's all right?'

'I'm sure he is, Katharina. We haven't been told otherwise.'

'But who would tell us?'

'In war, you always hear bad news. I'm sure the explanation is simple. You should go to bed, Katharina. You look tired.'

Early the next morning, at around six, the doorbell startled her out of sleep. She threw back the covers and hurtled to the front door, tying the belt of her dressing gown as she ran. Her parents were already there, talking to a soldier, a young man who was not Johannes. He passed them a letter, saluted and left. Mrs Spinell squeezed her husband's arm, her upturned face shut tight against bad news.

'Please, Günther. What does it say?'

His reading was silent.

'It's all right, Esther. He's fine.'

She opened her eyes.

'Oh, thank God.'

'He's in an army hospital in Poland. He was taken off the train for treatment and will be home next week.'

'We can wait a week,' said Mrs Spinell.

'I wonder what happened,' said Katharina.

'He was always a strong boy, Günther.'

She brought the cake to the living room table, removed the cloth and began to slice it.

'It's a bit early, Mother.'

'No point in wasting those precious eggs,' said Mrs Spinell.

They sat at the table and ate the cake.

'Maybe he has influenza,' said Mr Spinell.

'Or a stomach bug,' said Katharina. 'On a packed train.'

They laughed.

'It can't be anything too serious,' said Mr Spinell, 'or we would have been informed.'

A second army letter arrived, telling them to collect Johannes from the station at three on the following Thursday. Katharina went with her father this time, running her hand across her belly until the train arrived and the doors opened, spewing hundreds of dirty uniforms onto the platform.

'We'll never find him,' she said, 'they all look the same.'

'Look carefully. He'll see us.'

She did look, at the blanched cheeks and hollowed eyes, at the lines of hunger, cold and exhaustion ploughed into the men's faces.

'My God, Father.'

'The fighting in Moscow is hard, Katharina. But we shall prevail.'

A fleck of white distracted her, bobbing along the platform amid the swarms of staggering grey. It was a nurse in a sparkling-white cap, holding the arm of a frail man and steering him through the crowd. He was oblivious to the nurse, to the crowd, to the sliver of drool sliding from the side of his mouth. Katharina put her arm on her father's sleeve.

'I found him, Father.'

'Where?'

'In front of you.'

'Where, Katharina? I can't see him.'

'In front of you. With the nurse.'

'Oh no, Katharina. No.'

The young man's uniform hung in folds. The thin, papery skin of an old man had been stretched across his face.

'My poor son.'

The nurse walked past them, Johannes with her.

'Come on, Father. Let's go to him.'

'I don't know if I can.'

'It's definitely him.'

She tapped the nurse's arm and introduced herself.

'Hello, Johannes. Welcome home.'

He turned towards the voice, but looked through her, his blue eyes seeing nothing. Mr Spinell stepped towards Johannes and took his arm.

'Come on, son. Let's take you home. Your mother is waiting.'

Johannes started off again, down the platform, shuffling his feet, unwilling, or unable, to lift them. Katharina stayed with the nurse.

'He's in shock,' said the nurse. 'It happens a lot. The doctors have given him three weeks' leave, so take him home and put him to bed for a few days. He'll be fine then. His gun and pack are back in Poland, but his documents are here. They tell you everything you need to know.'

She handed over an envelope.

'The sedation should wear off in a couple of hours. Have him asleep in bed before that happens.'

'Why?'

'He'll be easier to manage.'

'Oh.'

'He'll be fine. It's really very common.'

'How long does it last?'

'It varies. But he should be better within the three weeks. Contact your own doctor if you need to.'

'Thank you.'

Katharina followed her father and brother, and caught up quickly, easily. She took Johannes' left arm, lifted his hand to her lips and kissed it.

'Hello, Johannes. It's me, Katharina.'

They led him down the steps to the underground and onto a train, all three silent until they stood in front of the door to their apartment.

'I need to talk to your mother first. To prepare her a little.'

He tried to put the key in the lock quietly, but his wife heard him, opened the door abruptly and pushed past him to greet her son.

'Johannes,' she said, reaching out her arms.

She stopped, her body stilled, her arms outstretched.

'Johannes. My darling, handsome son.'

She stepped towards him, took his face between her hands and kissed him on both cheeks.

'Welcome home, my sweetheart. Mama will look after you. You're safe now.'

She took his hand and led him into the living room, plumped up the cushions, sat him down and took off his boots.

'Katharina, fetch a blanket for him. Günther, bring the coffee from the kitchen. It's on the stove.'

They did as she bid, each relieved to have a task that distracted from the mangled shape on the sofa. Katharina tucked the blanket around Johannes' legs and Mr Spinell handed his son the coffee, but Johannes' hands remained inert and the cup tipped to one side, spilling coffee onto the blanket.

'Günther, what are you doing?'

'I didn't realize.'

'Pour another cup. Give it to me this time.'

She lifted the cup to Johannes' mouth and tipped

a little of the coffee between his lips. Some went in, but most dribbled out of the right side of his mouth, mottling the white linen napkin draped across his chest. Cake followed, crumbs that she fingered through his lips, gently, refusing to accept his failure to chew and swallow.

'I made it this morning, my love. Especially for you.'

'The nurse said the sedation would wear off soon,' said Katharina. 'That we should have him in bed before it does.'

'What nurse?'

'At the station.'

'I'm giving him a bath first. The water's hot.'

'I'll get it ready,' said Katharina.

She turned on the taps and looked at her reflection, tracing her fingers over her weariness.

Mr and Mrs Spinell raised Johannes to his feet and steered him to the bath.

'Now, ladies, out please. I will take it from here.'

'No, Günther. I will bathe him.'

'Esther, he is a twenty-year-old man, far too old to be bathed by his mother.'

'I need to check his skin, for lice, for infection. I want to see him, Günther. He's my son.'

'We'll do it together, then. But not Katharina. That's too much.'

She left them and sat back on the sofa to alter a maternity summer dress, in blue silk. The man in the pawnshop had kept it aside for her.

Her mother left the bathroom, hurried to the

kitchen, opened a cupboard, closed it and headed back to her son.

'He has lice. Though only in his hair. And no infections or frostbite, thank God.'

She closed the bathroom door, then snapped it open again.

'Oh, Katharina, could you get his pyjamas?'

She rose slowly, her lower spine and pelvis feeling the strain of the day as she moved to his room. She ran her fingers over his awards, lingering over the brass horse on its wooden plaque, the city boy's triumph over the country riders. She left his clothes on the floor outside the bathroom and knocked.

'Pyjamas.'

He emerged, washed and shaved, blue cotton sagging from his shoulders, a parent holding each arm as he was led to the sofa.

'I'll make him something to eat,' said Mrs Spinell.

'Mother, we really need to put him in bed before the sedation wears off.'

'Katharina, that boy has not eaten properly for weeks. I won't let him go to bed without food.'

'Fine, then.'

Katharina lifted his legs onto the sofa and covered him, overriding his silence with her chatter about her new husband and baby, about the new apartment and the things to be found in the pawn-shops. He said nothing. Noticed nothing. The less he responded, the more she talked, relieved when her mother returned with a bowl of soft, milky, infantile potato. Mrs Spinell spooned it into his mouth, mopping away his spews and dribbles.

'You like that, don't you, sweetheart?'

Mrs Spinell scraped the bowl and spooned what was left into her own mouth, reassuring herself that he had eaten well.

'Good boy.'

Katharina took both his hands.

'It's time to get him to bed, Mother.'

'Katharina, I haven't seen him for months. Leave us be.'

'But the sedation will wear off.'

'And what will happen then?'

'I don't know. I never asked.'

'Just five minutes more.'

Mrs Spinell sang to him and, with her husband's help, took him to the lavatory and then to bed. Katharina went to bed too, grateful for the rain clouds hanging over the city. The English would not be coming.

In the morning, in a warm, thick cardigan, she went to see her brother. He was motionless, but for his lips, which moved frenetically, feverishly. His eyes were open.

'Johannes? Are you awake?'

She put a hand to his forehead, but found no fever. She sat on a chair at the side of the bed and folded his papery hand into hers, until her mother came in, a house smock already on.

'How is he, Katharina?'

'He's awake and calm, but muttering to himself.'

'He's been doing that all night.'

'Have you been up?'

'Your father and I took turns to sit with him.'

'Why didn't you tell me? I would have helped.'

'You have little enough rest as it is.'

'Did he sleep?'

'Not much. A little at the beginning of the night. For the rest of the time, he just lay like this.'

'It's so awful.'

Mrs Spinell sat next to her son's feet.

'What do we do, Mother?'

'We'll have to wait and see what happens. Your father saw this in the last war. Men tended to come out of it.'

'Unscathed?'

'Sometimes. Sometimes not.'

'How long did it take?'

'Days, weeks, sometimes months.'

'The nurse said three weeks.'

'Let's hope so.'

'I forgot about her letter.'

Katharina retrieved the nurse's envelope from the hall. Inside were Johannes' paybook, leave pass and a letter addressed to their parents. She opened the paybook and looked at his photograph, taken at the start of the war. He was smiling at the camera. She turned the pages, tracking his clothing allowances, equipment, payments and route across Europe into Russia, the scrawled signatures, entry and exit dates, the institutional stamps. The names of three hospitals.

'Johannes has been in hospital before, Mother.'

'What? How do you know?'

She passed over the book and the letter from an army doctor who wrote that Johannes had been treated three times for trauma, without any success. It was decided that he would be better off at home and would, without doubt, recover quickly after a short break from the front.

'How are we supposed to make him better if the doctors can't?'

'We can only do our best, Katharina. You should get ready for work.'

The bank was busy. Many of her colleagues had left the city to live with relatives in the country so she had been moved from the back room to the front desk, answering questions from customers wondering whether their money was safe, whether it could be hit by British bombs. She reassured them, often the same person several times a month.

When she got home, she went to Johannes. He was the same, but there was a sour smell in the room. She pulled back the sheets. He had wet himself, plastering the pyjamas to his skin.

'My God, Johannes, what has happened to you?'

She took off her coat, opened the window, drew a couple of deep breaths and lifted him upright, stripping him down, exposing what had been hidden from her for over a decade.

In dry pyjamas, she led him to the living room and sat him on the sofa, in front of the fire.

'What are you doing?' said Mrs Spinell. 'He's supposed to be in bed.'

'He wet himself.'

'And you changed him?'

'I'll sort his bed out now.'

'But, Katharina, you shouldn't have done that. He's your brother.'

'Mother, I'm married and pregnant. I can manage.'

She stripped the sheets, washed them in the bath, and mopped the mattress with a towel before propping it against the open window to catch the end of the cold spring day. She sat beside him, picked up her sewing, and caught the smell again.

'No, Johannes.'

She repeated the procedure, this time with her mother's help.

'He needs a nappy.'

'He's a grown man, Katharina. We can't put him nappies.'

'We need something, Mother.'

'We'll use towels.'

They ate chicken, beetroot and potatoes as Johannes lay on the sofa, his muttering running in parallel to their table conversation.

'Dr Weinart has promised to visit over the next couple of days,' said Mr Spinell. 'He says that he has seen plenty of cases like this.'

'That's kind of him,' said Mrs Spinell.

'What's going to happen to Johannes, Father?'

'Let's wait and see, Katharina. In the meantime, we must keep him calm and rested.'

She fell into a deep sleep early that night, unaware of the blustering wind that cut through the clouds and cleared the skies. The sirens blared and she groaned, resenting their harrying wail, their interruption of her sleep. She began to dress, methodically adopting a rhythm that would allow her to reach the shelter on time. Only when she was buckling her shoes did she remember her brother.

Her parents were in his room, already dressed, trying to slip a sweater, the one with swastikas, over his head.

'I'm sorry. I was fast asleep.'

'Fetch his shoes and socks, Katharina,' said her mother.

They bundled him into his coat and into the hall. At the door, he wet himself.

'Oh my God, Johannes,' said Katharina. 'Not again.'

'I'll get fresh clothes.'

'No, Esther. We have no time.'

'We can't take him like this, Günther. The shelter will stink, and we'll never be forgiven. Or forgotten.'

Katharina stripped him and her parents dressed him, all three struggling to keep him upright. They steered him down the stairs and onto the street, relieved, as their eyes adjusted to the dark, to find others still there, women with young children and old parents. But Johannes sat down on the pavement, under a siren. The others were quickly gone.

'Hurry, Johannes,' said Mr Spinell. 'They'll shut the doors very soon.'

Katharina could see the huge concrete shelter towering over the street, but it seemed miles away. They lifted Johannes to his feet and hurried him forward, his laces undone, his feet stumbling. Mr Spinell shouted at two men shutting the doors at the top of the concrete staircase. They didn't hear him, and the bombs started to fall on the outskirts of the city, far to the west, but falling nonetheless. Mr Spinell shouted louder. At his son. At the men. He waved the arm that was not holding Johannes and the two men caught sight of him. They grabbed Johannes under his arms and dragged him up the steps. Katharina and her parents followed and the doors slammed shut, heavy bolts and bars thrown across their width.

'Thank God,' said Mr Spinell. 'And thank you, gentlemen.'

'Don't do that again,' said one of the men.

'No. No, we won't. We're hoping he'll improve soon.'

Katharina and her parents normally sat on the ground floor during the raids, with a little bag of books, cushions, puzzles and sewing. This time all the lower floors were full and they had nothing with them.

'You'll have to go towards the top,' said the man at the door.

They followed the trail of fluorescent paint that led to the staircase and began to climb. Johannes moved easily, as though more compliant when sheltered from the outside, from the cold, the wind. The first, second and third floors were full. They found space on the fourth, close to the flak towers on the roof.

'I don't like being so high,' said Katharina. 'We're nearer to them.'

'These towers are indestructible, Katharina. The Führer designed them himself.'

'I know that, Father, but I still prefer to be lower down.'

They walked through rooms full of people already settled into their routines as they waited for it all to be over. Mothers and grandmothers sitting on wooden benches were reading to young children while old men scraped out pipes and talked quietly to one another. The older children knew to behave, knew to resume sleep or unfinished schoolwork. They looked at Johannes, but then looked away. It was rude to stare.

In the last room on the fourth floor, they found a space next to a group of families with young children. Mrs Spinell guided Johannes to the bench and sat him down, tilting his back towards the dusty concrete wall. She smoothed his hair.

'Now, my love, we're here, and you're safe.'

Katharina's parents sat either side of her brother. She flopped down beside her mother, sighed and laughed.

'What is it?' said her mother.

'Look, he's wearing odd shoes.'

'We'll get it right next time,' said Mrs Spinell.

One of the anti-aircraft guns on the roof kicked off, closer than Katharina was used to, and noisier. She decided to ignore it, to drift off towards sleep, but her mother's movements were agitated.

'What's wrong?'

'I don't know. He's trembling.'

'Maybe he'll settle in a minute.'

A second, then a third gun started firing. Katharina put her hands to her ears, then to her belly, which was becoming round and firm. Her mother sat forward. Johannes was shaking, his arms and legs rattling in time to the weapons. Mrs Spinell tried to rock him, to sway him as though he were back in her arms, her troubled infant, whispering into his ear. He settled a little. Katharina sat back against the wall, but a blast pushed her forward. A single bomb. People screamed, but only briefly, regaining their composure when they realized that the walls and ceiling were intact.

But Johannes' breathing did not settle, and the emptiness of his eyes was gone, displaced by a vivid, frantic blue. Katharina slid to the floor and rubbed his legs. Her mother pulled at her.

'Get up, child. People are looking at you.'

'Mother, we need to keep him calm.'

'Get up. You're pregnant. You look ridiculous.'

She got up, and sat beside her father, nestling

into her brother, the tremor of his limbs passing into hers.

'Sssh. It'll soon be over.'

Another bomb fell. Then another. Four of them, six, battering at the people's calm and confidence. The children wailed. The adults ordered them to be quiet, told them it would soon be over. They obeyed, but Johannes was on the floor, rolled in a ball, his hands over his ears, his eyes shut tight, his mouth wide open in a scream that made no sound. Katharina tried to lift him up.

'Come on, Johannes. It's not that bad.'

Johannes remained on the floor, still curled up.

'Come on, son,' said Mr Spinell, 'you don't want to worry people.'

'Maybe you should leave him there, Father. Let him recover. He's not doing any harm.'

'It's shameful, Katharina. Help your father.'

She bent down, but lost her balance and toppled onto her brother's chest and head, throwing him into darkness. He shrieked, so piercingly that the children began to cry. In time they responded to their mothers' soothing. But Johannes fought off all attempts to soothe him, and continued screaming. The mothers carried their children to another part of the shelter, away from Johannes, the man made mad by war.

CHAPTER 19

Dr Weinart came, carrying a cake box.

'For you, Mrs Spinell.'

She received it awkwardly, almost with a curtsey.

'That's very kind of you, Dr Weinart. Thank you.'

'It's nothing.'

She shifted the box from one hand to the other.

'Let me help, Mother.'

'I'm fine, Katharina. People don't really give cakes any more, do they, Dr Weinart?'

'Don't they, Mrs Spinell? I hadn't noticed.'

'We must be very lucky.'

She passed the cake to her daughter.

'Günther, take the doctor's coat.'

Katharina balanced the cake evenly on her palms and walked towards the kitchen, salivating. She lifted the lid. It was a chocolate roulade filled with fresh cream and decorated with sifted icing sugar and mint, the sprig set perfectly in the centre of the cake. Mrs Spinell came in behind her.

'Let me see it.'

'It's gorgeous, Mother.'

Katharina transferred the cake onto a white rectangular gilt-edged plate and stood over it, inhaling the chocolate and mint.

'I have to do this.'

She dipped her finger into the cream and licked it, scraping her skin with her teeth to ensure none had been left behind. She rolled the cream over and under her tongue, and swallowed.

'Heavenly.'

'Let me.'

Mrs Spinell took more than her daughter, a large blob that covered a third of her finger.

'That's not fair.'

Katharina laughed and dug in a second time, using a teaspoon to smooth over the holes.

'Why is Dr Weinart so kind to us, Mother?'

'He and your father go back a long way. He was a lieutenant in the last war, very young but very gifted, and your father recognized that, accepting his youth when others wouldn't.'

'And they stayed in touch all this time?'

'This war brought them back together.'

Mrs Spinell carried the plate and coffee to the table. Katharina followed with a knife and cut into the cake, first serving the doctor, then her father, her mother and herself, sneaking the mint sprig onto her own plate, hidden from her mother's view. They set their plates on the table and waited for Dr Weinart to stop talking, to start eating so that they could follow his lead. But he carried on, talking about the war, the eastern front, their triumphs,

141

oblivious to the poured coffee and unfolded napkins, indifferent to their torment. Mr Spinell coughed; Mrs Spinell spoke.

'Please, Dr Weinart, do start.'

'Thank you, Mrs Spinell.'

He raised his plate, allowing them to raise theirs, but his fork remained on the table.

'It'll all be ours by the summer. Once this spring campaign is under way, they are finished.'

'That's certain,' said Mr Spinell.

'We must concede that we were somewhat thwarted by their winter weather, but that is behind us now. We will again prove our strength.'

'Indeed,' said Mr Spinell.

'Please, Dr Weinart,' said Mrs Spinell. 'Your coffee will go cold.'

He picked up his fork and poked at the edge of his cake. He didn't eat, but the movement was sufficient for the others to start on the rich, dark and obviously expensive chocolate sponge.

'This cake is marvellous,' said Katharina, 'where did you find it?'

'I am glad you are enjoying it, Mrs Faber.'

'Where can I find one? Is there a special bakery that you go to? I would use a week's salary to buy one.'

Dr Weinart cleared his throat. Mr Spinell echoed the polite cough.

The doctor returned his plate to the table, half of the cake uneaten, and wiped his mouth with their best linen.

'Mrs Faber, this is a cake made by one of the Führer's bakers. It is not available to you.'

'Oh, I see. Then I am honoured to eat it.'

'Indeed.'

The doctor finished his coffee and declined to take any more.

'Now, Mrs Spinell, how is your son? Johannes.'

'The same, Dr Weinart,' said Mrs Spinell. 'He lies all day staring at the ceiling. He moves his mouth less, though, and makes the occasional sound. An improvement of sorts, I suppose.'

'That's good.'

'His food intake is small but steady. Beyond that, there is little I can tell you.'

'May I see him now?'

'Of course.'

They followed the doctor into the bedroom where Johannes lay awake but motionless on the mattress.

'Johannes,' said Mr Spinell. 'This is Dr Weinart. He has come to examine you.'

Dr Weinart sat on the edge of the bed. He picked up Johannes' hand and shook it.

'Hello, Johannes.'

Johannes' limp fingers slipped from the doctor's and fell back onto the sheet. Dr Weinart checked his temperature and pulse. He clicked his fingers and clapped his hands beside each ear.

'We shall just have to wait. I will come back in a week unless something changes and you need me sooner.'

'Thank you, Doctor,' said Mrs Spinell.

'And he hasn't made any sounds at all, Mrs Spinell?'

They trailed behind him as he walked to the hall door.

'Only at the bomb shelter. He became a little upset there.'

'Ah yes, I heard about that.'

Dr Weinart wrapped his scarf around his neck and began to fasten his coat, which was made of fine dark wool. He stopped at the third button.

'I think it is better not to take Johannes to the shelter in future.'

'I don't understand,' said Mrs Spinell.

'In the interests of German science, I want to see if Johannes can sleep through a bombing raid, to find out if his subconscious will allow him to rest.'

'We can't do that to him, Dr Weinart,' said Mrs Spinell.

'Keep him in bed, Mr Spinell. Without sedation.'

'He shouldn't be left like that,' said Katharina.

'One of you, unfortunately, will have to sit with him.'

'Oh,' said Mr Spinell.

'I think it is for the best. For him. And, indeed, for your neighbours.'

'Our neighbours?' said Katharina.

'We don't want them seeing a soldier frightened of bombs. It's bad for morale.'

'Why would it be bad for morale?' she said. 'It's just the truth.'

'I'm sure your parents understand, Mrs Faber.'

'Indeed,' said Mr Spinell.

Mrs Spinell wrapped her arms tightly across her chest as the doctor resumed buttoning his coat.

Her husband spoke again.

'I will arrange it, Doctor.'

'Thank you, Günther. And thank you for your hospitality.'

'Thank you for the cake,' said Mr Spinell.

Mrs Spinell closed the door, listened until she could no longer hear the doctor's shoes on the stairs, and turned on her husband.

'How could you, Günther?'

'What?'

'Pander to him like that?'

'Esther, that man has been very kind to us.'

'So kind that we have to stay here during a bombing raid.'

'That's enough. It might help Johannes.'

'Or kill him. Kill us all.'

'Stop it, Esther. We have to do what he says.'

'"We have to do what he says."'

'Stop it.'

'Good old Günther Spinell. Always does what the big boys say.'

'That's enough. It's done now.'

She slumped into the sofa.

'What if the house is hit?'

'That's very unlikely, Esther.'

'You can't be sure. You don't know.'

Katharina sat down beside her mother.

'I'll stay with him,' she said.

'You?' said Mrs Spinell. 'You're pregnant. You can't.'

'I'll be fine, Mother.'

'What would people think of us, Katharina?'

'Who will know?'

'It's out of the question. Your father and I will do it. Günther will do the first night.'

'Fine,' he said.

'Let me do it,' said Katharina.

'If you're sure,' said Mr Spinell. 'I should really be with your mother.'

'Günther, that's your pregnant daughter. You can't let her do it.'

'I'll be fine, Mother. You'll frighten Johannes if you stay with him. You'll be too nervous.'

'And you won't?'

'I'll be fine.'

'Let her do it, Esther. She can rest on our return.'

'How can you do this? You're a coward, Günther Spinell.'

Katharina returned the cups and plates to the kitchen, cut a piece of cake for Johannes and sat on his bed to tuck the chocolate into his mouth.

'Taste it, Johannes. It's by the Führer's baker. And it's far better than Mother's.'

She stroked his hair, kissed his forehead and ran her hand over his cheeks, still hollow despite a week of mashed potatoes and vegetables, the weight of his head and body making barely a dent on the bed linen.

'Come back to us, Johannes.'

She sat down in a chair, covered her knees with a blanket, and stared at him, the stillness enhanced by the quiet rhythm of his breathing and the occasional flutter in her belly. She ate what remained of the cake and read for a short while from an American detective novel that was being passed around the women at work. Her father disapproved, so she read it out of his sight.

Her parents were by the living room fire, reading newspapers. She showed them the empty plate.

'He liked the cake.'

'How is he?' said Mrs Spinell.

'Asleep.'

'We left some cake for you.'

'Thanks,' said Katharina.

She extended her legs along the sofa.

'Dr Weinart is obviously more used to cake than we are.'

'What do you mean?' said Mr Spinell.

'He left half of his on his plate.'

'He's a very important man, Katharina, and that brings its privileges.'

Mr Spinell ate dinner and left the apartment, leaving the women to bathe Johannes.

'We should get him to bed early,' said Mrs Spinell. 'It's a perfect night for the English.'

When the siren sounded, Katharina snapped awake. Her parents were already in the doorway, her mother clutching a pack of cards as she would an evening bag.

'Will you be all right, Katharina?'

'Just go, Mother.'

She pushed the door tightly behind them, shutting out any bombs that might land in the hall, and twice checked that the windows were shuttered and the curtains fully drawn. Johannnes was asleep. She heard planes, to the west of the city.

'Please God, let them stay there.'

She tried to read her American book, but it was boring. She was bored. And safer than she had expected. She stood up.

'I know I shouldn't do this, Johannes.'

She switched off the light, drew open the curtains, opened the shutters, raised the window and looked out. The air was cold, exhilarating, the street dark and still, emptied of everything but feral cats evicted from homes that no longer had food for them.

The sky was a chalky orange, a mixture of fire and dust. She could see the planes, little black dots waltzing over houses and shops, over people; swirling and twisting around each other in a dance of incongruous beauty. She closed the window, shutters and curtains, sat down on the chair beside Johannes' bed and pulled the blanket over her shoulders and chest, her feet against her brother's hand, her hands over her womb.

She didn't hear the plane until it was overhead, a single one, straying from the pack, its engine quiet and light. She begged it to move on. It didn't.

It released a bomb, a sharp, single whistle, an exhilarated child rushing down a slide. She dived under her brother's bed, pleading for his protection. He slept on. The house shook and the windows rattled. She remained under the bed, listening to the lightness of her brother's breath until her mother returned.

'He slept through it all,' said Katharina.

'Thank God for that,' said Mrs Spinell. 'Are you all right?'

'I'm fine.'

'You look exhausted. Go to bed. I'll warm some milk for you.'

'Where's Father?'

'He has gone to help. A house three streets away was hit by a bomb.'

'It sounded so much closer. I thought they were going to kill us.'

'Go on, Katharina. Go to bed.'

Under the covers, still in her clothes, she cupped her belly, mumbling apologies over and over to the baby. Mrs Spinell sat on the edge of the bed, rubbing her back through the blankets.

'Drink your milk while it's still warm.'

'I'll get it in a minute. Leave it on the table.'

Mrs Spinell remained where she was until Katharina emerged.

'I can't believe that Johannes slept through it, Mother.'

'Maybe Dr Weinart is right and it will do him some good.'

'It was the machine guns that upset him the last time, wasn't it? I wonder if something happened with machine guns when he was in Russia.'

'I can't bear to think about it, Katharina.'

'I have to think about it because what if Peter comes back like that? His brain turned to mush? Or without arms or legs? What happens then? What type of life do I have then?'

'You should sleep. I'm sure Peter's fine.'

'You don't know that. You can't know that. The whole damned thing goes on and on, with no end.'

'There is an end. The summer.'

'They said Christmas. Now it's summer. How long are we supposed to wait? I am sick of it all.'

'It will all be over soon. You heard Dr Weinart.'

'And you believe him?'

'I have to, Katharina.'

CHAPTER 20

Russia, March 4th, 1942

My darling Katharina,

I am jealous. There. I have admitted it. Johannes is home with you. I am not. He is in clean clothes, sitting down each evening to have dinner with you. I am still in this fleapit, no closer to being home than I was when we set off down these godforsaken roads.

I hate this place. I am worn out, Katharina. By the war, by being without you, by these stupid, ugly Russians who come at us with whatever weapons they can find, in whatever clothing. They are relentless.

I am trying to focus on cheerful things, on the fact that spring is coming, that the wind is abating and that tiny little flowers are pushing their way up through the melting snow. But it is hard. I miss you so much and I miss my friend, Fuchs. He seems to have died so needlessly, Katharina. If we had been allowed to wait at our previous camp until the snows had melted, Fuchs would be alive now. As it is, we have made little difference to Kharkov. It still belongs to us. The Russians are too weak. It was all so bloody pointless. Except for Reinisch. He is to be promoted. For his good work in marching us through the snow.

I don't know if this letter will evade the censor, but if it does, forgive my grumpiness. It is only that I am fed up, worn out by the Russians and their scrawny, lice-ridden women who possess none of your beauty. They even send their women to fight, Katharina.

I'm sorry, my love, to burden you in this way. I am, on the whole, quite well and safe, if a little tired. But I do miss you, terribly, and I fret in the darkness of night that this war will go on so long that you will forget me. By tomorrow morning, when the sun has warmed me a little, I will feel more positive, certain that it will all be over soon and that I will be back to you and our baby.

I am looking forward to it very much, Katharina. To being with you and our child. I can't decide if I want a boy or a girl. Have you a preference? Whatever it is, I know we will make it a happy and healthy child.

I do miss and love you.

Yours in love,

Peter

CHAPTER 21

Katharina stretched as she walked into the living room, chasing sleep from her limbs. Johannes was already there, upright on the sofa, awake. Mrs Spinell was beside him.

'He got up by himself,' she said.

'Has he said anything?'

'Not yet.'

Katharina lifted his hand and kissed skin that was still pale but softer. No longer paper dry.

'Good morning, Johannes. It's nice to see you up and about.'

In the afternoon, he began to pick at things. His pyjamas. His dressing gown. Plucking threads, twisting and tugging, working them over and over until they were tiny balls of dense cotton.

'Is he getting better, Mother?'

'So far as we can tell.'

The following day, he switched to newspaper, tearing long strips first, then shredding the war reports into tiny pieces, scattering black and grey confetti on the sofa and floor. Mrs Spinell reprimanded him, tidied up, washed the ink from his hands but then gave him a second newspaper.

'I suppose it's doing you some good,' she said.

But he wasn't interested. He stood up, walked to the table and sat down, extending his large, elegant hands across the mahogany.

'Are you hungry, Johannes?' said Mrs Spinell. 'Dinner will be in about an hour.'

He remained there, still, even as Katharina worked around him, placing mats, cutlery and glasses on the table, chattering as she went. She put down his napkin and he lifted it up, unfolded it and placed it across his knees.

Mr Spinell came home, hesitated, and kissed the crown of his head.

'Hello, son. Have these women not got your dinner ready yet?'

They sat down and started with soup. Mrs Spinell ladled from a ceramic tureen, serving Johannes first.

'You can start, Johannes,' she said. 'It's vegetable.'

He lifted his fork, dipped it into the bowl and brought it to his mouth. He sucked, but the orange soup dribbled to his chin, little bits of vegetable tumbling to his chest. He tried again, his mother's ladle suspended over the blue and white tureen, his father and sister staring into bowls that had nothing in them. Mrs Spinell reached across the table.

'Here, Johannes,' she said, 'let me help you.'

154

She wiped his chin and chest, and gently prised the fork from his hand, replacing it with a spoon.

'You might find this easier.'

He became more dextrous with each movement of the spoon. He ate most of his soup, lifted the napkin, rubbed his chin and pushed back his chair.

'Thank you,' he said, tipping his head into a small bow. 'That was delicious.'

He walked towards the sofa, his slippers slapping against the wooden floor. They stared after him, their own soup uneaten.

'He spoke,' said Mrs Spinell.

'And ate,' said Katharina. 'By himself.'

'Let's not make a fuss of it,' said Mr Spinell.

Dr Weinart returned a couple of days later. Johannes was sitting on the sofa, staring at the pages of a newspaper, neither ripping nor reading.

'It's a miracle, Doctor,' said Mrs Spinell.

'Has he said much?'

'Not a lot, no, but they were words.'

'And used appropriately?'

'Oh yes, Doctor.'

Dr Weinart checked his pulse and temperature.

'What is your name?' he asked.

'Johannes Spinell.'

'Do you know the names of the people in this room?'

Johannes said nothing, but stared again at the newspaper.

'I have no wish to force him. Things are obviously improving. When is his leave due to end?'

'In ten days,' said Mr Spinell.

'I will have them give him an extra week. There is no point in rushing him.'

'Thank you, Doctor,' said Mrs Spinell. 'We are very grateful.'

'We have to look after our soldiers.'

Johannes followed the doctor to the hall. He stopped in front of the mirror, ran his fingers over his hair, straightened the collar of his pyjamas and leaned into his reflection. He smiled at himself. A little laugh.

'Don't worry,' said Dr Weinart, 'he's improving, although it is a strange journey for you all.'

The doctor left.

'Who was that?' said Johannes.

'It was Dr Weinart,' said Katharina. 'He has been looking after you.'

'A doctor. Have I been unwell?'

'Just a little,' said Mrs Spinell. 'But I think you are getting better.'

'I feel fine. Although hungry.'

Over an early lunch of meat and potato pie, he talked. Feverishly.

'When did we move here? It's very grand.'

'Before Christmas,' said Katharina. 'We brought all your things with us.'

'That's very kind. You look like you've been eating well, Katharina.'

'I'm pregnant, Johannes.'

156

'Oh. A baby?'

'I got married in August. To a soldier.'

'A soldier.'

'He's in Russia.'

'Why? Why does he want to be in Russia?'

She looked at her parents. Her mother put her hand on her father's arm.

'He's fighting in the war, Johannes,' said Mrs Spinell.

'The war?'

'On the eastern front,' said Mr Spinell. 'You were there too, Johannes.'

'I've never been to Russia, Father. It holds no interest for me.'

They went for a walk and sat on a park bench, Johannes squeezed between his parents, Katharina against her father's arm.

'This is a good day, Father.'

'It is, Katharina.'

When the doorbell rang the following week, Johannes opened the door.

'Hello, Dr Weinart,' he said. 'Come in.'

'Oh, hello, Johannes. It's a pleasure to meet you properly. How are you enjoying being home?'

'Very much. It is a fine apartment.'

'Can you tell me the names of the people in this room?'

'The names? Of course I can. Over there, by the fireplace is my father, Günther Spinell. On the sofa, to the right, is my mother Esther Spinell and beside

157

her is my sister, Katharina Faber. And you, should you need reassurance, are Dr Weinart.'

'Thank you, Johannes. That's excellent.'

He held up his hand.

'How many fingers can you see?'

'Three.'

'Good. And now?'

'Two.'

'Excellent. And what is the date?'

'March the thirtieth, nineteen forty-two.'

'Excellent.'

Dr Weinart laughed, picked up Johannes' hand and shook it.

'Congratulations, young man. You have made an excellent recovery. Enjoy the rest of your leave.'

'Thank you, Doctor. Leave from what?'

'What do you mean, Dr Weinart?' asked Mrs Spinell.

'I see no reason why he should not return to his unit.'

'But he has been so ill.'

'He is well now, Mrs Spinell. You can see it yourself.'

'He needs more time,' she said. 'He talks to himself in the mirror every day, preening himself, fixing his collar, telling himself that he is off out. He's not better yet.'

'I have already given him an extra week. He must return.'

'Even another week, Doctor?'

'I'm sorry, Mrs Spinell.'

'He has improved so much over the last few days. One week more will not make any difference to the army.'

'Esther.'

Mr Spinell took his wife's hand.

'This is always hard for a mother, Dr Weinart,' he said.

'I understand.'

Mrs Spinell took her hand from her husband.

'He can't go back, Doctor,' she said. 'I won't let it happen.'

'Mrs Spinell, he is a soldier. We need him for our decisive spring campaign. The sooner he goes, the sooner we bring this war to an end.'

'Doctor, he might be a soldier, but he is also my son. I tell you that he is still too weak to go anywhere.'

Mr Spinell took his wife's arm.

'Esther, please.'

'Günther, please, talk to Dr Weinart.'

Her husband walked away, towards the tall windows coated with rich, glossy, white paint. He placed his hands on the oval brass handle and looked down at the street.

'What about a second opinion?' said his wife. 'An army doctor?'

'Mrs Spinell, my judgement is final. Your son will return next week.'

'Günther, please, say something.'

Mr Spinell continued to stare into the street.

'Mrs Spinell, your husband understands the army's position.'

'Günther.'

He turned back to his wife.

'There is nothing to be done, Esther.'

'The matter is settled then,' said Dr Weinart. 'Good man, Günther. Keep well, Johannes, and good luck.'

'Goodbye, Doctor,' said Johannes.

Dr Weinart left. Mr Spinell went with him. The two women sank into the sofa.

'His own son.'

'There must be something we can do,' said Katharina.

'How could he?'

Johannes sat between them.

'What's wrong with Mother, Katharina? She looks a bit pale. Is she ill?'

'Johannes, did you understand what Dr Weinart said?'

'I'm afraid I stopped listening, Katharina. I hate it when Mother is emotional.'

'They want to send you back.'

'Who does? Back where?'

'The army. To the front.'

'Oh. I had quite a good time there, considering.'

'Where?'

'France. When I was in France.'

'No, they want to send you back to Russia.'

'Katharina, as I have never been there, it is surely hard to send me back.'

'You were there, Johannes. Outside Moscow.'

'Must be a different brother, Katharina. I was in France.'

'But after France?'

'I came here. To Berlin.'

She rubbed his thigh and dropped her head onto his shoulder.

Mrs Spinell started to shiver, her teeth to chatter.

'You need to rest, Mother.'

She covered her mother with two woollen blankets and went to the kitchen, to bake, to create something warm, something soft and sugary. But there were no eggs. She began to peel and chop vegetables. She would make soup. Johannes came from the living room.

'Let me help.'

She handed him a carrot, already peeled.

'The knives are in that top drawer,' she said.

He picked his way through every piece of equipment, testing each one before settling on a small, wooden-handled knife.

'This will do.'

He placed the carrot on a round chopping board and set to work, moving the knife slowly but meticulously along its length. He measured one piece against the next, matching their widths.

'Is this all right?'

'Perfect, Johannes. You're doing a fine job.'

She diced two onions, a turnip and two parsnips in the time it took him to cut one carrot.

'Johannes?'

'Yes?'

'Do you remember using a gun?'

'Of course. I used one in France. Why?'

161

'But what about in Russia? Did you use your gun in Russia?'

'You must miss your husband very much, Katharina.'

'What do you mean?'

'Because he's there, you assume every other soldier has been there too.'

'That must be it.'

'I've done the carrot. Anything else?'

'No, thanks, Johannes. Go back and sit beside Mother. She'd like that.'

Katharina was finishing the soup, removing the frothy brown scum from the surface, when her father returned. He stood in the archway to the kitchen.

'How's your mother? Has she been asleep long?'

'About an hour. She was very upset.'

'There is nothing we can do, Katharina. Believe me. I would stop it if I could. But I can't.'

'You have to. He can barely use a kitchen knife, never mind a gun. He can't go back. It's as simple as that.'

'Dr Weinart is a very powerful man, Katharina. We can't go against him.'

'But it's your son. My brother.'

'I know that. But we will all be in trouble if he doesn't go back.'

'What do you mean?'

'What's for dinner?'

'Just soup. We have nothing else.'

'Take this.'

He handed her two large brown paper bags. She

162

opened both and found a large leg of mutton, sausages, chocolate, coffee and bread.

'This is from Dr Weinart?'

He nodded.

'I'll prepare the sausages now. We can have the lamb tomorrow.'

Her mother woke as the sausages turned a golden brown.

'What's that smell?'

'Sausages. Father brought them.'

'I see. Where's Johannes?'

'In his room.'

'How is he?'

'Fine. Oblivious.'

'Probably as well.'

Mr Spinell stood again by the window.

'Did you talk to him, Günther?'

'No.'

'You just took the food.'

'Esther, there is no point. He is not a man to change his mind.'

'How do you know if you don't ask?'

'Please, let's stop this.'

'Stop? Your son is being sent back to war and you want to talk about something else?'

'Esther, please.'

'I can't talk about anything else. I can't think about anything else. You won't defend your own son.'

'I can't defend him. Every son in Germany is being called to fight. Ours too.'

'He's not going. I won't let them take him. He's too ill.'

'Have you any idea what you are saying? What they will do to him? To us, if we keep him here?'

'I don't care. He's not going back.'

'Esther, he has to go. Dr Weinart said so.'

'"Dr Weinart said so."'

'Stop mocking me.'

'He's your only son. Our only son.'

'There is nothing I can do. He has to go.'

'Lamb to the slaughter. And you know it. Talk to him, Günther, please.'

'I can't, Esther. The decision is made. I can't start annoying him with our problems.'

'Our problems? You are talking about your son's life.'

'Please, Esther.'

'Good old Günther Spinell, always in with the boys, no matter which bloody war it is.'

'You didn't mind until now, Esther.'

'What do you mean?'

'This apartment. The extra food. The fur coat that you wore all winter. All from the boys, Esther.'

'And this is the price?'

'Every eligible son in Germany is being called up.'

'Ours is not eligible.'

Mr Spinell slammed his hand against the wall, marched into the hall and took his wife's fur coat from the cupboard.

'Off you go, then, and tell them that. See if they will listen to you. Here's your coat. Your bloody

164

fur coat. You go tell Dr Weinart and the army. Go! Go on!'

She got up, took the sausages from the hob and set the table, tears running down her face.

'I don't want him to go back. He's my baby boy.'

'I know, Esther. I don't want him to go either. But there's a war.'

She wiped her face with a napkin.

'All right, Günther. But it's on your head.'

He sat down.

'It's on yours too, Esther.'

They took him to the train station, the concourse crowded with new recruits.

'They seem younger,' said Katharina.

'Who?' said Mrs Spinell.

'The soldiers. Younger than when I was here with Peter.'

They steered Johannes through the crowds, Mr Spinell carrying his papers, Katharina his food bag filled with bread, salami, chocolate and dried fruit. The train was already at the platform.

'We should get him on, Esther. Find him a seat.'

'It's over an hour before departure.'

'It'll fill up fast, Mother.'

They found a carriage in the middle of the train.

'It's safer here,' said Mr Spinell. 'If the bastards attack it, they'll probably target the front or the back.'

They put Johannes in a seat by the window, with a table to lean on, and packed his things around him.

'You'll be able to sleep here, darling,' said Mrs Spinell.

She sat beside him, Katharina and Mr Spinell opposite them, on the other side of the table.

'Nice train,' said Mr Spinell. 'Good and clean.'

They were silent until the other soldiers arrived. A sudden rush of men. Hundreds and hundreds clamouring for seats and space for kitbags and guns.

'We'll have to go now, Johannes,' said Mr Spinell.

They kissed and hugged him, the women's tears on his dry face. They squeezed their way through the soldiers and stood again on the platform, waving as the train pulled away, Johannes smiling and waving back, the seats around him still vacant.

CHAPTER 22

Faber was already awake when the shelling started. He had known it would come. Just not when. But there it was. At first light in the middle of May, the earth shaking under the force of the Russian attack.

'That's our wake-up call, boys,' he said.

In the dimness of the Kharkov house, they pulled on their clothes, their battle kit, and picked up their guns.

'They're heavy weapons,' said Faber. 'Long range.'

'And a lot of them,' said Faustmann.

'Nothing we can't handle,' said Weiss.

'But listen to it, Weiss,' said Faber. 'It's organized. Orchestrated.'

'They're finally learning how to fight a war,' said Weiss. 'That's all it is.'

'That's bad news for us then,' said Kraft.

'We'll piss on them, Kraft,' said Gunkel. 'Come on, lads. Let's get to it.'

Kraus was already on the street, tucked behind the gable end of a house.

'Let them play with their guns. Then we'll move forward and teach them some manners.'

'Yes, Sir,' said Weiss.

He pointed to the area on the edge of the city where he wanted them to wait until they were ordered to advance.

'Off you go, boys. And keep down.'

They moved out, the shells arching and falling, felling trees, gouging holes in the earth, into other men's bodies. They turned their backs on the barrage, leaned against a wall and lit cigarettes.

'I wish we had coffee,' said Faber. 'Wake us up a bit.'

'How awake do you want to be?' said Weiss.

'Good point.'

'How far away do you think they are?' said Kraft.

'About ten, twelve miles,' said Weiss.

'Poor bastards underneath it,' said Faustmann.

'At least it's not us,' said Gunkel.

'Not yet,' said Kraft.

Kraft took a pipe from his pocket.

'What are you doing with that?' said Faber.

'My mother sent it to me. It belonged to my father.'

'Are you going to use it?'

Kraft opened his knife, scraped at the bowl and filled it with tobacco. He lit the pipe and sucked on it, then passed it to Faber who drew on the smoke and coughed.

'I think I'll stick to the cigarettes.'

'It uses less tobacco,' said Kraft.

'Too much effort,' said Weiss. 'All that cleaning.'

'It keeps you calm,' said Kraft. 'The routine of it.'

'Your father was never calm,' said Faber.

'True.'

'How is your mother, anyway?' said Faber.

'Much better, thank you.'

'Did you tell her about your feet?'

'No. There's no need to worry her.'

They fell silent, listened to the Russians and lit more cigarettes.

'Any news on Reinisch?' said Faustmann.

'He got what he wanted,' said Gunkel.

'Which is?' said Faustmann.

'First lieutenant,' said Gunkel. 'With the reconnaissance battalion.'

'Bastard,' said Faustmann.

'Will Kraus do the same?' said Kraft. 'Use us to get promoted?'

'Kraus is loyal,' said Weiss. 'We're not a tool for his career.'

'So he won't care if we sit out this battle?' said Faber.

'He has no interest in being shot either,' said Weiss.

Kraft cursed at the pipe and threw it to the ground.

'Has anyone got a cigarette?'

They laughed, momentarily masking the sound of the planes. Faber looked around the wall. He saw a mass of aircraft coming from the east, flying low, bombs already falling. They were Russian.

'I thought they had no fucking planes, the bastards.'

They ran, scrambling back towards the city,

towards the already blasted houses. Kraft was in front, but stopped suddenly.

'Move,' shouted Weiss.

'I don't want to be in the lead.'

The bombing and strafing was almost above them, the bullets cutting into the soldiers behind them, scattering bodies across the earth, a fresh crop of death. Weiss bellowed at Faustmann.

'Where do we go?'

'Over there,' said Faustmann. 'We need a roof.'

They lunged at the remnants of a house. But there was no roof, only an overhang barely big enough to cover them. They huddled tightly into each other. Kraft was whimpering.

'Don't move, anybody,' said Faustmann. 'Don't attract attention.'

Faber looked up at the sky, tracking the planes as they flew overhead, as they travelled west towards Germany, willing them onwards, horrified when they banked and turned back towards them, flying even lower than before, even closer. Kraft started screaming

'We're going to die. We're going to die.'

Faber pulled his knees to his head, making himself as small as he could. Kraft was babbling. Pleading for his mother. Weiss shouted at him.

'Shut the fuck up. I want to listen.'

'Why do you want to listen to that?' said Faustmann.

'Because I can't fucking listen to him crying for his mother.'

Faber closed his eyes. He didn't want to see the pilots, or find out whether they had seen him. He covered his ears with his hands but the thunderous roar drilled into his head anyway. Prayers flowed from his lips, one after the other, prayers from his childhood, when he stood in church beside his father, his big hand enveloping his own small hand. He wanted to go home; to retreat behind the laurel hedge, into the garden where the earth did not shake. He opened his eyes, briefly, and saw the planes mowing the earth, cutting down men, over and back, over and back, the movement as methodical and thorough as his father mowing the grass on a Saturday afternoon.

After twenty minutes, the planes left, flying back east, their bellies emptied. The men stumbled to their feet, unable to speak, their trousers wet. Kraus yelled at them to move forward. They started to run, over the bodies of the dead and the not yet dead; charging and scurrying across open ground towards the Russians, their backs bent, shoulders rounded, as though that might protect them from the storm of bullets and bombs.

Faustmann dived into a freshly formed crater.

'We'll set up here. Use it as our trench.'

'Their weapons reached here,' shouted Faber.

'Their weapons reached fucking everywhere, Faber.'

Faustmann slid the machine gun off his shoulder, opened it up, locked it in place and began firing, Faber feeding in belts of ammunition, Weiss pointing out targets, Kraft preparing the next round. They threw grenades, fired their rifles and moved on to the next crater, staying longer in each newly held position, fighting even harder, battling until night fell, when they took turns to go back for food, cigarettes and ammunition. They dug into the ground, and crawled into their holes, Faber and Weiss together.

'Any idea how many we got?' said Faber.

'I lost track.'

'It's pretty stupid, isn't it?'

'What?'

'Running like that,' said Faber. 'At a machine gun. It seems so pointless. And terrifying.'

'They seem intent on using up all the men in Russia.'

'And women, Weiss. We shot them too.'

They slept, woke and began again, covering the ground with another layer of bodies.

'Death to Bolshevik Jews,' shouted Faber.

He had slept well.

'We really are invincible,' said Faber.

'We'll have to be,' said Faustmann.

Word came that the Russians had surrounded a village occupied by German soldiers, cutting them off.

'They're not capable of that,' said Faber.

'They obviously are,' said Weiss.

'They're copying us. What we did at Kiev.'

'We should be flattered. They won't be there long.'

German planes flew over from the west and dropped

172

food, fuel and ammunition to the stranded soldiers, loud cheers erupting from the battlefield. The tanks and heavy artillery followed, breaking through to free the men.

Stockhoff cooked beef stew.

'You see, Faustmann. They do care about us.'

Faustmann lit a cigarette.

'We're crucial, Faber. Absolutely crucial.'

CHAPTER 23

Kharkov, May 23rd, 1942

My dearest Katharina,

You would be so proud of us. We fought so hard and have pushed the Russians back again, further east, beating their attempts to take back control of land that is no longer theirs. They seem to struggle to accept this basic fact.

As you may have already heard, they surrounded some of our troops, but Berlin sent in wave after wave of rescue missions until every man was freed. It was marvellous to watch, Katharina. The planning and precision of the operation, the elegance of it all. It is marvellous to know that we have so much support from other regiments and from Berlin. It warms me to know how much you care about us all out here, because I have to admit that sometimes it is hard to know whether anybody back home is concerned about what we are doing.

Ours is a great country, Katharina. We are indeed lucky to have been born German. I would certainly feel despair today if I had been born a Russian. I would see myself as being without hope. Without any future.

But we have a great future, Katharina. You, me and our child. We will raise him or her to be proud of our country, not embarrassed as our parents were. As my parents still are. I wish my father could be more like yours and understand what the Germans are capable of. You understand it. I am not sure that I understood it before, but I understand it now. And I have witnessed the Fatherland's commitment to its people, each planeload dropped onto those men stranded in that village expressing that commitment.

I am so happy today to be German, to be part of all this. To be part of this great living history.

I will be home very soon.

Your loving husband,

Peter

CHAPTER 24

The letter came late one midweek afternoon as Mrs Spinell was preparing a cut of lean beef. Katharina walked into the kitchen, her gait awkward, her body tired from eight months of pregnancy.

'Mother.'

Mrs Spinell turned to her daughter. Then back to the sink. She vomited. She rinsed the sink, brushed back her hair and went to the sofa, to the place where her son had sat. They opened the letter and huddled into each other as the words assaulted them: death, regret, service, Fatherland. They remained silent, Katharina stretched along the sofa, Mrs Spinell, upright, staring at the ceiling, until Mr Spinell came home. The tears came then, and angry accusations. He read the letter and left.

CHAPTER 25

Mrs Spinell went to bed and remained there under the blankets in her dressing gown.

'Should we fetch Dr Weinart?' asked Katharina.

'She'll come out of it,' said Mr Spinell. 'Just give her time. It is a terrible thing for a mother.'

'And for a father?'

'Of course.'

'Do you feel guilty, Father?'

'No, Katharina. Should I?'

'I don't know. I do.'

'Why?'

'That he went back.'

'There was nothing to be done.'

'How can you be so sure?'

'We have to play our part, Katharina. To follow orders.'

'No matter what the consequences?'

'Otherwise it's chaos.'

'It's chaos, anyway.'

'It will be worth it.'

'Worth Johannes?'

'He would have understood.'

CHAPTER 26

'It's happened, boys,' said Faber.

'What has?' said Gunkel.

'The birth. I'm a father.'

'Congratulations,' said Weiss. 'Boy or girl?'

'Boy.'

'Fresh fodder for the empire.'

'His name is Johannes. After her brother.'

They toasted him and his son with their water bottles and resumed lunch in the sunflower field, jaws chewing on stale bread and tinned meat, eyes fixed on the soil burned black by retreating Russians. Faber opened the letter again. His hands smudged the white paper.

'Apparently he looks like me. Long and skinny, with dark hair and blue eyes.'

'Poor bastard,' said Weiss.

'It was a hard labour. Nineteen hours.'

'That's tough,' said Kraft.

They fell silent then. Faustmann touched the right side of his mouth.

'That tooth is getting worse.'

'You'll have to see the dentist,' said Weiss.

Faber leapt to his feet and kicked at the earth, showering them in black soil that reeked of petrol.

'Bloody hell, Faber,' said Weiss. 'We're trying to eat.'

'Well, excuse me for disturbing your fine repast in this splendid dining hall.'

'Piss off.'

He bowed, obsequiously.

'And what will Mr Weiss have for his main course today? Fetid meat from a tin? Or would sir prefer a can?'

'Shut up, Faber.'

'No, you shut up. All of you shut up.'

'Calm down,' said Weiss.

'No, I won't. And stop telling me what to do, Weiss. You're always telling me what to do.'

'Act like a child, and I have to tell you what to do.'

'You fucking don't.'

'Sit down,' said Faustmann. 'You're wearing yourself out.'

'I'll do what the fuck I like, Faustmann. And I certainly won't take orders from some half-Russian bastard.'

'Right, Faber,' said Weiss. 'What's the matter?'

'Nothing.'

'Out with it.'

'I've just become a father. You could all have been a little more enthusiastic.'

'Jesus, Faber,' said Faustmann. 'We said congratulations. What do you want? Baby booties?'

'That would be a start.'

'Fine. I'll find some at the baby boutique in the next village.'

'Leave it, Faustmann,' said Weiss. 'Look, Faber, everybody is tired. You've had a baby, congratulations. Can we go back to our food, please?'

'You do that.'

'Jesus, Faber.'

Faber slumped back into his place.

'I'm fed up of this hellhole.'

'We all are.'

'I thought I'd be home by now. Instead I'm still here, chasing tanks across the fucking steppe. I want to see my child.'

'It'll be over soon,' said Weiss.

'How many times have you said that? You're wrong every time.'

'Not this time, my friend. I'm certain of it.'

'He's right, Faber,' said Gunkel. 'There can't be much left to do.'

Kraus shouted at them to move out. They stood up, crumbs and burned sunflower petals falling from their uniforms. Faber ran after Kraus.

'My wife has just had a baby boy.'

'Congratulations.'

'Thank you. I need home leave. To see him.'

'Not a chance.'

'Please, Sergeant. Even a week.'

'Forget it. No more leave until this is all over.'

He held back and waited for the others to catch up.

'What did he say?' said Weiss.

'Not a chance.'

'You should write to your parents. Tell them the news. A first grandchild.'

'Maybe Katharina will send me a picture. So I can see him.'

'I'm sure she will. It won't be long, Faber.'

'I hope you're right.'

The rhythm of moving feet calmed his nerves.

'I thought I'd be home by now. There for the birth. I'll never see him now as a newborn. Never know what that was like.'

'You'll have other children. Other newborns.'

'But never a first one again.'

In the evening they arrived at a village. The locals carried on with the tasks they had to complete before nightfall, moving between their whitewashed houses and the brick well, ignoring the soldiers as though their arrival was normal, or expected. Faustmann went to them.

'They say the partisans beat us to it. The food is all gone.'

Kraus shot an old man. Nobody moved. Then he shot another. Still no response. He brought a young woman forward, a mother, and shot her, her young boy screaming beside her. The food appeared. They sat in the village square and ate.

'It's idyllic here,' said Kraft. 'Such a simple life. Mother would love it.'

'It's a tip,' said Weiss.

181

'But imagine,' said Kraft, 'a big house, a farm with pigs, apples, geese, room to stretch our cramped urban limbs.'

'You have a big house,' said Faber. 'And room to farm if you want to.'

'But the air here is so clear. You can really breathe.'

'And winter?' said Weiss.

'Tolerable in a house with proper heating,' said Kraft.

'I doubt it.'

'Think of spring and summer – Faber's little boy running through that orchard over there, reaching up his hands to catch falling blossoms. It could be heaven.'

'Or hell,' said Weiss. 'No matter how many houses we burn, there'll always be lice.'

'I'd forgotten about them,' said Kraft.

'And partisans,' said Gunkel.

'We'd get on well with them in the end, when all this is forgotten. When they can practise their religion and own their farms again.'

'This will never be forgotten, Kraft,' said Faustmann.

They rummaged through the houses, looking for things that might be of use. Weiss held up a baby's bonnet with ear flaps and strings. It was covered in dried mud.

'Do you want to send this to your wife, Faber? For the baby?'

'My child's not wearing that, Weiss.'
Weiss slapped Faber on the back.
'Don't say I didn't try, my friend.'
They moved out.

CHAPTER 27

She read his letter at the breakfast table, over and over, each time struggling to contain her disappointment.

'He's not coming.'

'Of course he's not,' said her mother.

'He's been refused leave.'

'So he says.'

'He's very upset about it. And apologetic.'

'They always are. In the beginning, anyway.'

Mr Spinell spread butter on his bread.

'Don't worry, Katharina,' he said. 'Your husband will be home soon.'

'Unlike your brother,' said Mrs Spinell.

He hurried his chewing.

'I'll be back tonight.'

'Off with the boys again, are you?'

He slammed the door as he left. Katharina stood up to gather the dishes.

'Leave them,' said Mrs Spinell. 'I'll do them.'

'Are you sure?'

'I feel better today. I'll manage them.'

'That's good, Mother. I'll get the baby ready.'

Johannes was awake in his cot by her bed, the

trace of a first smile on his face. She scooped him up, rubbing her lips across the downy softness of his head. She sat on the chair that had been in her brother's room and laid the infant across her thighs, humming and smiling at the squareness of his small chin, at the curl of hair hanging over his forehead. He yawned, then cried and snuffled. She pushed aside her nightdress, and lifted him to her nipple, her back taut, waiting for the shot of pain as he sucked. She slapped her feet against the floor and sang until the pain passed, until the nerves coursing up and down her spine settled into the rhythm of his feeding.

'I got a letter from your daddy, sweetheart. You're going to have to wait a little longer before you meet him.'

She returned to the living room, the baby on her shoulder, the dishes still on the table, her mother motionless, staring at nothing.

'I told you that you should have married the doctor's son,' she said. 'He liked the comforts of home. You could see that in him.'

'Stop it, Mother.'

'He'd be here now. With you and your child. Not off with the boys.'

'There's a war on, Mother.'

'You'll end up like me, Katharina. You chose a husband as useless as your father.'

Katharina paced the room, rubbing small circles into her son's back to release the tension in his tightly curled legs.

'That's just what Johannes used to do,' said Mrs Spinell. 'He looks so like him.'

'He looks nothing like him, Mother. Johannes was round and chubby.'

'But he has his eyes.'

'They're Peter's eyes. Please, Mother, not again.'

The baby burped and his legs relaxed. Katharina slid him off her shoulder to cradle him in the crook of her left arm.

'Will you hold him while I tidy up?'

'No.'

She laid Johannes on a blanket, a towel beneath his bottom, and took off his nappy. She gathered the dishes and filled the sink with hot, soapy water, deliberately using more than her mother would have permitted, and scrubbed furiously at the light stains on the crockery, at her mother's words, at her husband's letter, harder and harder, certain that nothing would ever be clean again, never back to the way it had been. To the way it should be.

'Damn you, Peter Faber. Damn you.'

She dried and put away the dishes, washed and dressed the child and went downstairs to the pram Dr Weinart had given her. It was large, elegant and modern, made of navy fabric and shining chrome. She liked the way the other women looked at her as she pushed it.

She set the child into it, tucked blankets around him and pulled his white cotton cap over his ears. She rolled back her shoulders, raised her head and wheeled him onto the street, where the air was fresh but warm, the day's heat still to come. She turned towards the park, to sit and watch the waltz of sunlight and leaves.

She chose the bench she had shared with Peter, turned the pram against the sun and inhaled the newness of the day. She closed her eyes and rested, and then took a magazine from the bottom of the pram. The doctor had given her several back issues from his clinic. Before, leafing through a magazine, she would pause at the pictures of coats, dresses and hats, but now she found herself poring over kitchens, bedrooms and living rooms. She wanted a home for her child. To be away from her parents. From her mother.

A shadow fell over the magazine. Katharina looked up. It was a woman, in a summer dress that had once been elegant, a baby at her hip and a young child hanging from her skirt. Both were boys.

'It works well, doesn't it?' she said.

The dark circles under her eyes covered much of her face.

'Sorry?' said Katharina.

'The pram. It's very good. I used to have one just like it.'

'Yes, I like it a lot.'

'The suspension is excellent. Better than the model I had for my first child. My daughter.'

Katharina shielded her eyes from the sun to look up at the woman, at the yellow star dirtied and torn.

'Yes. Yes. It is.'

Silence fell between them.

'How old is your child?' said the woman.

'Six weeks.'

'Your first?'

'Yes.'

'Congratulations.'

'Thank you.'

She wanted to return to her magazine, but all three were staring at her, snot dribbling from the older boy's nose.

'How old are yours?'

'Almost one. And the boy is three.'

'And your daughter?'

'Eight. Only she's gone. Taken with her father.'

The woman's legs buckled, and she pressed her hand onto the back of the bench for support. Katharina looked at her, at her hand on the bench, at the doctor's pram, at the people who passed by. They could see everything. They could see Katharina talking to a Jew.

'You can't sit down here,' said Katharina.

'I know that. I'm just tired.'

The woman straightened her back and moved the baby to the other hip. She walked away, the boy still hanging onto her skirt. Katharina checked her child, shifted him out of the light and returned to her magazine.

CHAPTER 28

Berlin, August 20th, 1942

My dear Peter,

The Führer has just announced that we are to take Stalingrad. To hear it from our leader's lips is thrilling. Imagine it, Peter, a German Empire stretching from the Atlantic to the Volga. It is beyond anything I could have hoped for. The man is truly a genius.

And you are to be part of it, Peter. I am very proud of you and promise to stop badgering you about home leave. You have an important task to achieve. Your son and I will support you as best we can. I have enclosed three bars of chocolate to help you along a little of the way.

Everything here is fine. You have nothing to worry about. Johannes is thriving. My father and I took him on a little trip to the lake the other day, when the weather was hot, and dipped his feet into the water, although not for too long, as the water remains quite cold. He is a good child, Peter. You will be entranced, my darling. I am sure that I am

189

hearing his first attempts at a giggle, especially when I tickle his belly.

My parents are well, and very much enjoying their first grandson.

My father tells me that Stalingrad will be ours within a few weeks, that the war will end quickly after that and that you, my darling husband, will be home by Christmas. For ever.

Good luck on your road to Stalingrad, my love. Go speedily so that you come home faster.

All my love,

Katharina

PS I will have a second photograph taken of Johannes very shortly and will send it to you. You will see how much he has grown, in such a short space of time. All my love, again.

K.

CHAPTER 29

She sealed the letter and put it on the hall table, ready for posting. But then picked it up again. The table was dusty. So was the mirror. The bust. And the floor was grubby. She wiped the end of her apron across the table surface and set the letter down again.

She was exhausted by it all – by the night feeds and day feeds, by the queuing for food, cooking food and the laundering, increasingly with cold water. She went back to the living room. Her mother, her skin pasty and flaccid, lay on the sofa, reaching for another cigarette.

'Mother, I've asked you not to. I want Johannes to have fresh air to breathe.'

Mrs Spinell lit her cigarette and inhaled, throwing her head back to look at the ceiling.

'How long is this going to last, Mother? I can't do everything.'

There was no reply. Katharina went to the kitchen and made coffee, aware that she had only a short time before her son would wake, wet and hungry. She sat on the floor at the end of the room, and wrapped her hands around the cup. It was a sunny afternoon, but she was cold. The apartment was cold.

Her father came home, sweating.

'I'm going to Russia,' he said.

'God, we must be in trouble,' said Mrs Spinell.

'Are you not too old, Father?'

'I'm not fighting, Katharina. I'm going to look after the harvest.'

'You know nothing about farming, Günther.'

'I'm security, Esther. Making sure we reach it before those bastard partisans.'

'It's their wheat, Günther.'

'It's our wheat, Esther. It's on German soil and German families need it for the coming winter.'

'I expect Russian families do too.'

'That's enough from you, woman. I'm going in an aeroplane, Katharina. With Dr Weinart.'

'That's so exciting, Father.'

'We'll be gone for about a month, and Mrs Weinart has asked that you visit her, to keep her company.'

'We'd love to, Father. Wouldn't we, Mother?'

Mrs Spinell said nothing.

'And I have some other news,' he said.

He went back to the hall door, opened it and brought in a young woman, his hand tugging at her arm.

'Cleaning is no longer a job for a German woman. She will do it for you so that you ladies can go off and enjoy yourselves with Mrs Weinart.'

Katharina hugged her father.

'That's marvellous news. Will she be able to mind Johannes sometimes?'

'Of course. Whatever you want. She doesn't speak German, so you will have to show her things.'

'Is she Russian?' said Mrs Spinell.

'Call her Natasha,' said Mr Spinell. 'They're all called Natasha.'

Mrs Spinell sat up.

'I'm not having a Russian in my house.'

'She's here to help you, Esther. And she'll sleep in the basement.'

'I don't want her.'

'I do,' said Katharina.

Mrs Spinell went to her room and closed the door. Katharina took Natasha to the kitchen.

CHAPTER 30

His feet were sore and his face was sunburned. He flopped onto the ground.

'How much longer?'

Weiss hunkered down beside him and lit two cigarettes.

'Kraus says one more day. The bombing is already under way.'

'They shouldn't have started without us.'

'Well, they have.'

Kraus shouted at them and pushed them on until the city spread out in front of them, a mass of white-painted concrete shrouded in black cloud.

'That place is finished,' said Weiss.

'Let's go home now, then. Leave them to it.'

'And miss the big show?'

Stockhoff gave them pea soup and bread. They stared as they ate, at the planes weaving in and out of the clouds, at the explosions of fire and trails of smoke across the sky.

'We have them,' said Weiss. 'Their backs against the river.'

'I can feel the vibrations,' said Faber. 'How far away are we, Kraus?'

'About ten miles.'

'It's the longest river in Europe,' said Faustmann.

'The longest in the German Empire,' said Weiss. 'What's it called again?'

'The Volga.'

'Oh yeah. I remember,' said Weiss. 'I'll swim in it. To mark our new frontier.'

'And freeze your balls off,' said Faustmann.

They laughed.

They sang and marched all day. That night Stockhoff fed them beef and carrot stew, the meat so tender that even Gunkel was pleased.

'It's almost as good as what you'd get in my shop,' he said.

Kraus told them to rest, to prepare for the next day when they would move towards the north of the city. Kraft drank, more than he should have.

'You're lucky, Faber, to have a wife and son,' he said.

'Why's that, Kraft?'

'It's something to fight for, Faber.'

'You have your mother.'

'She never wants me to leave her. To go out on my own.'

'She'll have got used to being without you now. You've been away so long.'

'I have no life. Nothing of my own.'

'Kraft, you're not even twenty-five. Something will turn up.'

'Maybe. She's ill, you know.'

'I know, Kraft.'

'No, really ill. I got a letter from a neighbour.'
'She'll be fine. She always is.'
'Kraus won't let me go home. To see her.'
'This won't take long.'
'I hate it.'
'What?'
'Killing. Watching people die. I hate it.'
'You'll be fine.'
'I've always hated it. Killing. Hunting. My father called me a coward.'
'I have a photograph of my son.'
'He was always mocking me. Maybe he was right. That's what I am.'
'Do you want to see it?'
'What?'
'The photograph of my son?'
'I should sleep, Faber.'
Faber reached into the inside of his tunic for the picture that had been taken not long after the birth, his son asleep, a loose fist resting against his right cheek. He kissed the child, and his wife's hair.

At dawn, they began their march towards the city, hundreds of thousands of them.
'This is it, Faber,' said Weiss.
'Home by Christmas, Weiss?'
They both laughed.
'We'll be heroes, Faber. Feted for generations to come.'
They stamped their feet into the ground, claiming it as their own. The planes rolled and dived over

their heads, owning the sky, thrilling the soldiers underneath, schoolboys on the winning team. They fell quieter on the outskirts of the city, silent but for their steps and breath as they moved along streets of mud and wooden houses, past neatly curtained windows. Inside, the tables were set for breakfast, but everyone was gone. Shoes and bags littered the roads.

They turned left onto a boulevard, its tar blasted and cratered, concrete strewn across the middle of the road, fires smouldering, apartments razed, shops blackened and burned, a thick veil of smoke and dust hanging over it all. He could now identify the smells of death – the initial stench of copper and shit, followed by the suffocating sweetness of rotting blood that lingered for days. He pressed on, past the infant boy, his body charred, only his fingernails still white. He found Kraus, crouched behind a chimneystack that no longer had its house. Weiss, Kraft, Gunkel and Faustmann were with him.

'We've walked into hell, Sergeant,' said Faber.

'There's a school close by that will serve as our company base. We'll move across the city from there.'

'How long will it take, Sergeant?'

'Not long, Faber.'

'You always say that.'

'So stop fucking asking.'

The school still had most of its roof and all of its desks, though no longer in neat rows. The men went down into the basement, and found an extensive network of passages and rooms. Stockhoff was already there, preparing his kitchen. Queues had formed for the barber, tailor and cobbler, and small amounts of hot water were being dispensed for washing. The doctor was busy with blistered feet. Faber went there first.

'I prefer the way my wife does it,' said Faber. 'Letting them soak in hot water first.'

'I presume she only has one husband. Go on, out of here.'

Washed, shaved, his hair and nails cut, he settled down to clean his gun, stripping it back to dust and oil each part, his fingers practised in the routine. He slept well, despite the barrage of tank and artillery fire that continued through the night. It was not his problem. He was safe.

CHAPTER 31

Katharina went to her mother and opened the curtains.

'Up you get, Mother. We're going to Mrs Weinart's today.'

Mrs Spinell groaned.

'Go without me, Katharina.'

'She's expecting all of us.'

'There is no all of us.'

'Stop it, Mother.'

'I don't want to go.'

'I'll help you choose something to wear.'

She held up dresses, one in each hand.

'Either of these?'

'No.'

'Mother, you can't stay in bed for ever. You'll rot.'

'I already have rotted.'

'Oh, get up. Natasha is making breakfast. Eggs and toast.'

'Don't let her have any.'

'No, Mother.'

The Russian had a heavier hand in the kitchen than either Katharina or her mother, so that her cooking was not always successful. But she was good with clothes; cleaning too, and Johannes liked her.

Katharina took the baby from the Russian and fed him, running her fingers over his fontanelles, willing the gaps to close. They had to be at the doctor's house at ten, and her mother would require all her attention.

Mrs Weinart had a selection of cakes ready for them in her living room. She took Johannes immediately, fussing over his tiny hands and nose.

'He must bring you so much pleasure, Mrs Spinell. Your own grandchild.'

'Oh, I enjoy him thoroughly, Mrs Weinart.'

Katharina wanted to sit down.

'Do, Mrs Faber, do. First-time motherhood is exhausting. But you have help, I hear.'

'Indeed, Mrs Weinart,' said her mother. 'She is settling in well. We are lucky to have her.'

The doctor's wife passed Johannes to Mrs Spinell, and poured coffee.

'We'll let your daughter rest, Mrs Spinell.'

'Indeed.'

Katharina looked at her mother, who smiled down at her grandson and held out a finger for him to hold. He took it.

'Have you heard from your husband, Mrs Weinart?'

'I was talking to him on the telephone last night, Mrs Faber. He is well. They both are, but the work is hard as the partisans keep setting fire to the crop. Can you believe it? Such wanton destruction.'

'It seems to be a very hard place, Mrs Weinart. They are a hard people.'

'True, Mrs Faber. But we'll sort them out soon enough. How is your husband?'

'He is at Stalingrad. I am very proud of him.'

'You should be.'

They ate and drank, and Mrs Weinart took charge of Johannes again, playing with him, singing to him, and calling on her own children to come and see the baby. They played gently with the infant and sang when their mother asked them to. The girls danced too. Katharina laughed.

'They're gorgeous children, Mrs Weinart.'

'I'm sure your son will grow up to be just like them, Mrs Faber.'

CHAPTER 32

Kraus woke them at five and Stockhoff fed them hot coffee and warm bread with jam. At six they left, moving north-east towards the factory district, the sky lightening and clearing, promising heat, a last surge of summer sun. Tanks, machine guns and heavy artillery announced the start of the assault and Faber ran down a boulevard, scurrying from one fragment of wall to the next, barely able to hear the weapons over the sound of his own breath and pounding heart.

'I don't like this,' said Faber.

'Nor do I,' said Faustmann. 'It's not what we're used to.'

Snipers fired towards them from the right. Faber saw three men go down, each shot through the head.

'Training wasn't like this,' said Weiss.

A captain circled his arm through the air, pressing them forward.

'Keep going,' he shouted. 'They can't get all of us.'

'Fuck that,' said Kraus. 'This way, boys.'

He pushed through a door and Faber followed,

turning to let Weiss know, but he was already behind him, followed by Kraft, Faustmann and Gunkel. Faber focused on Kraus' boots, on the leather fraying over the heels, as they clambered over rubble, across tables, beds, dressers, along bullet-punctured walls sieving dust and smoke; his trousers were wet with urine, and sweat poured from his cold, clammy skin. Sniper fire dissected the air, slicing through gaps between walls and doors, between one building and another, one street and the next. Faber grabbed Kraus' boot and pinned him to the rubble. He shouted at his sergeant.

'I want to go back.'

'You can't.'

'I can't do this, Kraus.'

'You have to. You're a fucking soldier, Faber.'

'I'm not. I'm a schoolteacher. A fucking provincial schoolteacher.'

'Act like a soldier, Faber, or you'll never be a schoolteacher again.'

Faber followed him, crawling on his belly when Kraus did, tracking the heels and soles of his boots to places snipers could not reach. But mortars could. And grenades. They scrambled behind a piece of corrugated iron, their backs against a west-facing wall, sweating and panting, separated from the rest of the group.

'It's harder than I expected,' said Kraus.

'They're bastards.'

They waited until it was dark and crawled back

to the school. The others were already there. They all shook hands.

'We didn't see any point in staying out there, Sergeant,' said Weiss.

'We'll try again tomorrow when we're a bit more familiar with the territory,' said Kraus.

Stockhoff soothed them with bacon and potato.

'It might take a bit longer than Kharkov, lads,' said Kraus.

'How many dead, Sergeant?' said Kraft.

'Six. All sniper fire. No wounded.'

'We're not used to this, Sir.'

'I know, Faustmann.'

'We know trenches and open spaces. Not this.'

'I know. But we're going to have to find a way.'

The following morning, when it was still dark, they raced through the streets, moving before the sun rose, before the snipers could see them. They reached so far forward that they could no longer go back. They settled behind a wall that hid them from the east, and Faustmann set up his gun. They waited, still and silent, until the sun began to move towards the west, revealing a sniper they had not been able to see in the morning. Faustmann took him out. They moved on again, found a cellar, moved in, and waited for Stockhoff to find them. The cook brought soup, rations for the next day and a letter for Faber from his wife.

'She sent me two bars of chocolate, lads.'

He passed them round. The third he slipped back into his pocket with the envelope.

CHAPTER 33

Katharina went to the pawnbroker. He always managed to find things that interested her. She bought a winter suit for Johannes and a bead necklace for her mother. Under a bundle of watches, she saw a pen, black with gold trimmings, the name 'Samuel' etched into the clip.

'I can remove the name,' he said.

'Then it would be perfect.'

'Would you like another name instead?'

'Peter.'

She would give it to him at Christmas.

CHAPTER 34

Faber was awake at five. He had an hour. He drank coffee, ate bread, and sat down to write to Katharina. His hand was still. What would he say? That he loved her? Loved their child? That he missed her? He tore the paper. It was all pathetic and pointless.

Why did they want a tractor factory anyway? It was a wreck. The roof and walls were already gone, the complex decimated. The planes and tanks should carry on until there was nothing left, nowhere to hide, just a mound of rubble running down to the river. He hated going in after them, picking through the remains. The more often he did it, the harder it became. And Kraft kept crying. For no reason.

At six the order came as usual. They moved out of their cellars, rats emerging from the sewers, and scrambled forward into the darkness, the carcass of the factory looming in front of them.

'We're heading for the southern end,' said Kraus. 'Stick together and we'll be fine.'

'Are you sure?' said Faber.

'As sure as I always am.'

He fell in behind the sergeant, again focusing on the heels of Kraus' boots. The fraying had been neatly stitched – the gaps closed, the leather gathered, all of it reinforced and repaired. He liked that expertise. His army's attention to detail. He let out a deep sigh. It would be all right. They knew what they were doing.

The planes came, the tanks rolled in and the explosions shook every fragment of his body. Kraus ordered them to catch up with the tanks, walking behind them, close enough for protection, but not too close to be a target. And in they went, into an enormous cavern of collapsed roofs and tumbled pillars, the floor buried under tank and tractor parts, conveyor belts, screws, spanners, twisted fenders, and bodies, dozens of them, bloated and black, riddled with maggots.

'I don't know why we want it,' said Faber. 'Any of it.'

'For your great German Empire,' said Faustmann.

'Fuck off, Faustmann.'

They set up their gun behind a wall, its barrel peering through a gap. They began firing, taking turns loading, reloading, throwing grenades, defending, attacking; but they ended the day as they had started, cowering behind the same wall. They ate and slept there, starting again in the morning with new rations and more ammunition, the same pattern day after day, but none of it ever enough to thwart the waves of men that came at them, the colour of their skin and hair shifting from pale to dark, from west Russia to further and further east. An endless stream of men. Kraft began to scream. He was shaking. They laid him down and covered him with Weiss' large coat. Kraus pointed at a doorway.

'There must be an opening on the other side of that door. We need to seal it off.'

Faustmann went out in front, his gun spraying from left to right, the others behind him. They reached the door and hurtled through, into a building that scarcely had walls. They could see the river. And then the Russians. Dozens of them rising from the rubble and charging at the four men. Faustmann unfolded the tripod and set up the gun. Kraus fed him. Faber and Faustmann threw grenades but still they came. Faber used his gun, but it was too slow. Loading. Reloading. They were too close. And there were too many of them. He used his bayonet, their warm blood running over his hands and thighs, splashing his face. He preferred his gun. He stuck his knife in a man's neck, left it there, and ran back out the door after Faustmann, back to the wall where Kraft lay quietly, his eyes open.

'There's no end to these bastards,' said Faber.

'It's a big country, Faber.'

Kraus shoved Kraft.

'We're out of here. I'll go back and organize support to block that opening.'

They went to the cellar, but Kraus kept on going, back to the school. Faber, Weiss and Faustmann lay on the floor to sleep. Kraft began to tidy, to arrange the shelving, table and chairs.

'Why are you bothering?' said Faber.

'I may as well make it comfortable.'

'We're not staying. We'll be out of here soon.'

It was night when he woke, the dark sky lit intermittently by bursts of Russian phosphorescence.

Stockhoff sent soup, carried by two fresh recruits, their faces pale.

'How is it looking, boys?' said Weiss. 'How are the other sectors faring?'

'We are not really sure, Sir,' said the older of the two. 'But there are a lot of bodies.'

'Russian or German?'

'Both, Sir.'

'They're easy to trip over,' said the younger one. 'And we spill the soup. Burn our hands.'

'Stop spilling the soup,' said Faustmann. 'We're hungry.'

'Yes, Sir.'

They slept until morning. Kraus woke them.

'Right. You're rested. We need to take over that building. We're kicking off in half an hour.'

They gathered behind their wall and waited with Kraus and twenty other men.

'We need more than this, Kraus,' said Weiss.

'It's coming.'

Just before the half-hour was up, four men emerged from the west, pushing a six-barrelled rocket launcher. Faber cheered. They all cheered.

'That should sort them out,' said Faustmann.

The launcher blasted through the walls and its operators forced it on towards the river, its rubber wheels bouncing over the rubble. The men followed, firing guns, hurling grenades, forcing the Russians from the southern end of the factory. They were winning. It was easy. Thrilling. Faber was chuckling at the simplicity of victory, so triumphant that he didn't hear the hiss of the mortar gun, only the landing of each shell on top of their rocket launcher, on top of their men, scattering body parts. He ran from the building, back behind the wall.

'Nothing's working, Kraus,' said Faber. 'Our guns are too big and heavy. Nothing's agile enough. Fast enough.'

'I can see that, Faber.'

After an hour, they went back into the building. Just infantry. Some went upstairs. Faber and Weiss stayed down, moving along what was left of the walls to the end of the building overlooking the river. Down below them, in the distance, they could see hundreds and hundreds of men leaving boats and running up the riverbank into the city.

'We'll never beat them like this, Weiss.'

'Of course we will. We just have to be clever about it.'

'I need to eat.'

They crawled under the staircase and pulled a sheet of corrugated iron over them. They ate crackers and tinned meat, and drank water. Weiss looked out, saw nobody and lit a cigarette. He inhaled and passed it to Faber.

'Thanks.'

Faber held the cigarette against his own until the flame took hold. He handed it back.

'So what do we do?'

'I don't know. I'm sure they'll come up with something.'

Faber finished his cigarette and tumbled into a sleep that teetered on wakefulness. He felt something beside him. Feet. Russian. Silent in felt boots. He pushed back the iron sheeting, fired a shot, checked for more, found none and went back to sleep, deep this time, waking in the near darkness. Uncertain. Weiss was still beside him. Still asleep. He woke him.

'We should get out of here.'

Weiss shook his head.

'How long have we been asleep?'

'I don't know. Hours. Kraus will lynch us.'

'Who's going to tell him?'

Weiss yawned and scratched his face.

'Where's everybody else, Faber? We're on our own.'

Faber shoved back the corrugated iron, looked at the dead Russian and pulled it back over them.

'What are we going to do, Weiss?'

'I don't know. That guy stinks.'

'This whole place stinks.'

Faber ran his hands through his hair. The lice were back.

'Any sign of the others?' said Weiss.

'Not that I can see.'

'So what'll we do?'

'I don't know.'

They lit cigarettes, waving at the smoke to break it up, diluting its trail.

'It's so quiet,' said Weiss.

'We should go back. Find them.'

Weiss slipped out from under the corrugated iron and back through the door, towards the west. Faber followed.

'We're in hell, Weiss.'

'It's too fucking cold to be hell.'

'I think I see men.'

He peered harder into the fading light.

'They're ours.'

'You sure, Faber?'

'Certain. Come on.'

On their bellies, they crawled out of the factory to the remains of a junction.

'You cross first,' said Weiss.

'I always follow you.'

'Now I want to follow you.'

'I don't want you to. I want to follow you.'

'Just go, Faber.'

'No. You're older than I am. You've always gone first.'

Weiss cursed at him and moved forward. Faber followed, staring at Weiss' boots, at the gaps in the stitching, surprised when the boots suddenly flipped in a rush of wind, noise and exploding earth, and he found himself staring instead at their steel-tipped toes.

'Jesus, Weiss. What are you doing?'

Everything was muffled; his own voice, the thump of cement and soil falling on his back and head. But he could see that Weiss was screaming, that his mouth was wide open, that his eyes were startled, that his hands were shaking over the place where his stomach had been, his intestines spilling onto the ground beside him. Faber scrambled to Weiss, deaf still to everything, even to his own crying and screaming. He scooped up the intestines, shoving the ragged and bloodied flesh back into the hole, all the time shouting at Weiss to get off the road, to get back behind a wall, to hide. Weiss stopped screaming. He cried instead, and called for his mother.

Faber heard the hiss of a new attack.

'Get up, Weiss. Get up.'

Faber ran to a wall, and listened to the crash of each mortar shell onto the earth. He counted twenty-four of them. And then silence.

'Weiss?'

Nothing.

'Weiss?'

He stayed there, behind the wall, as night came, his helmet off, his knees against his chest, his fingers picking at pieces of his dead friend's flesh.

213

CHAPTER 35

Berlin, October 30th, 1942

My darling Peter,

It is hell here, Peter. Absolute hell. My mother shouts at my father all the time. Any little thing turns into the most enormous row. Yesterday, she accused him of having an affair with another woman. Somebody called Maria. He laughed at her and walked out the door. Again.

I'm always on my own, Peter. It's just me and Johannes, and it feels so lonely. My mother is about, of course, but she only moves from her bedroom to the living room, just as my brother did, wearing her dressing gown all day, staring at nothing, scavenging all the time through the kitchen cupboards so that she is becoming bloated, fat at a time when everybody else is losing weight. I no longer bother talking to her as she just shouts at me, even when I am holding the baby.

I spend all day at the park, though it's freezing. But I've nowhere else to go to find peace. Come home please soon, my love. I need you to take me away from all this. I do hope that your mother will be a better grandmother to our child than my own.

With love,

Katharina

PS I hear from the radio and read in the newspapers that the fight for Stalingrad is going well. Keep up the good work, my darling. I am very proud of you, of your bravery. Johannes is too. PPS I hope that you are not having an affair with some Russian woman. Natasha here is a little dull to look at, but I am sure there are others who are prettier. You wouldn't, would you?

CHAPTER 36

Faber flopped onto the cellar floor, waking Faustmann.

'Where's Weiss?'

'Dead.'

Faustmann rolled into a tight ball.

'What happened?'

'Shrapnel. His stomach. Mortar shell.'

'The poor bastard. Are you all right, Faber?'

'No.'

Kraft handed Faber coffee in a tin cup.

'Drink, Faber. And then sleep.'

He slept, tucked between the two men, the warmth of their bodies soothing him. He woke at five again and sat with his hands over his mouth, watching morning creep into the room and light up the shelf Kraft had decorated. A porcelain ballerina, one arm missing, a sepia picture of his mother, a candle, a flower of blue tattered silk and a black carriage clock that no longer told the right time, stuck on half past six. The other two woke and Kraft made more coffee.

'What about his parents?' said Faustmann.

'What about them?'

'Will you write to them?'

'The army will do that.'

'But you should too, Faber. You were the last person with him.'

'What? And tell them their son died with his gut spewing out all over the ground? I can't do that, Faustmann.'

'Somebody should.'

'You do it. You didn't see him. It's easier then.'

'Maybe Kraus should. Does he know yet?'

'No. Not yet.'

Kraft poured coffee into cups and gave them each a chunk of chocolate.

'How do you find this stuff?' said Faber.

'I pay lots of money for it. More than others are prepared to.'

'Or able to,' said Faustmann.

'That may be so,' he said, handing them each another piece of chocolate. He stood up and began to tidy their packs, to hang coats and hats from makeshift pegs he had hammered into the wall.

'Aren't you having any?'

'I'm not hungry, Faber.'

'You didn't fight at all, Kraft?' said Faustmann.

'Did they miss me? Your coats stink.'

'They'll execute you if they find out,' said Faustmann.

'What? That I'm buying chocolate.'

'That you're here. Hiding. Not fighting.'

'I don't like it. The noise. The blood. It's not for me.'

'None of us likes it,' said Faber. 'But we're supposed to do it.'

'And I've decided not to.'

'They'll be looking for you,' said Faustmann.

'It's chaos out there. They won't notice.'

'Kraus will,' said Faber.

'Is he looking for you? Does he know you two have quit the battlefield to sit here with me drinking coffee and eating chocolate?'

Faustmann drained his cup.

'We should leave. Thank you for the hospitality.'

Faber followed Faustmann up the rattling staircase and through the hatch.

'Are you all right, Faber? Are you up for this?'

'I'll have to be.'

CHAPTER 37

The wind and rain were laced with ice. Faber, Faustmann and Kraus curled into a hole in the ground that faced east, blankets over their heads and shoulders.

'We're going to have to accept it, lads,' said Kraus.

'What?' said Faber.

'That we're here for the winter. That this will not be over soon.'

'You can't say that, Sergeant.'

'Do you want me to say it again, Faber?'

'All we need is more men,' said Faber. 'They've been promised.'

'There aren't any.'

'I've seen them, Kraus.'

'Convalescents and seventeen-year-olds. They're no use to us.'

'And officers back from leave,' said Faustmann. 'Looking fat and rested.'

'But they're on their way,' said Faber. 'They must be.'

'So it's said. Either way, we need shelter.'

In the early morning darkness, they prised sleepers from the railway line that ran through the city and carried them back to their end of the tractor factory. They dug into the ground and built a wooden cave big enough for them to sleep and squat in, the entrance hidden by a bank of earth, the dampness attenuated by a wood fire in a small metal barrel.

'How much longer do you think we'll have to put up with this, Kraus?'

'I don't know, Faber.'

The routine was firmly in place. As structured as his father's teaching. He got up at dawn, urinated, ate and crawled through the rubble with Faustmann and Kraus to find a place for their gun, a nest safe from snipers. A different place each day.

At nine, sometimes earlier, sometimes later, the Russians began firing; rockets and shells hissed and screeched across the river, blasting the already blasted dead, blowing holes in the already mangled earth. He shut out that noise, focusing instead on the sound of a footstep, a breath, a whisper in a language he did not understand. And shot it. Dead. Always dead. Only the dead counted in their end-of-day tally.

'I'm beating you, Faustmann.'

'I've given up keeping tabs, Faber.'

'Bullshit.'

'I couldn't be bothered, Faber. Too many dead.'

When it was dark, they went to the trench behind them and waited for Stockhoff. He gave them coffee, cabbage soup, chocolate, a day's rations, razor blades, cigarettes and lice powder.

'It's always good to see you, Stockhoff,' said Kraus. 'But where's the meat?'

'You get what I get.'

'It's cold. We need it.'

'I do tell them that.'

'And what do they say?'

'Nothing, so Gunkel is helping me. We are trying.'

'Any news on replacements?'

'First-timers again.'

'They won't last long then. And winter clothes?'

'Nothing yet, Sergeant.'

'And post?'

'Not a lot. It's slow too. Only one for Faber and one for Kraft.'

Kraus took both letters, passed one to Faber and looked at the one addressed to Kraft.

'Has anybody seen him, Stockhoff? Any news?'

'Nothing, Kraft.'

He threw it to the ground, Faber picked it up and slipped it into the inside pocket of his tunic, next to the photographs of his wife and son. He opened the letter from Katharina. He laughed.

'She wonders whether I'm having an affair.'

'Take your pick of those fine Russian women soldiers,' said Faustmann. 'Just be careful what she does with her knife.'

'You're sick.'

'Sick and getting sicker.'

Stockhoff left, but his orderlies remained to heat water and clean out the latrines, the darkness lit by a single oil lamp and Russian phosphorescence.

'There are advantages to being a frontline soldier,' said Faustmann.

They lit cigarettes and waited until the orderlies left. The latrines still stank and the water was only warm. Faber dipped his spare vest into the water, squeezed it, rubbed soap into the fabric and cleaned his face, ears, neck, underarms, groin and bottom. He scrubbed his teeth, ignoring the blood, and shaved without a mirror. He dunked his head into the dirty water, shook off the heavy droplets and threw on lice powder, digging it into his scalp with his nails. It would have to do. Everything would have to do.

When it was dark, he went back with Faustmann to the cellar. Kraft was lit by candlelight, dusting, using a sock to wipe away the concrete and rock chippings that fell with each bombardment onto his furniture and decorations. Faber handed him the letter. He didn't take it.

'I know.'

'How can you know?' said Faber. 'You haven't opened the letter.'

'I already know. Open it if you like.'

Faber read the words written by a neighbour.

'How did you know?'

'I just did.'

They sat as he made coffee, their coats still on. It was freezing, colder than in their bunker, but Kraft didn't seem to notice.

'Are you eating?' said Faber.

'I'm not hungry.'

'You need to eat, Kraft.'

'I pick up my rations most nights. What I don't eat is in my pack. You take it.'

Faber found crackers and six tins of meat.

'And nobody notices?' said Faustmann.

'I put on my helmet. My kit. Take the rations. Come back. Nobody cares.'

They finished their coffee.

'We should get back,' said Faustmann.

'Stay. Please. Just one night. I don't want to be on my own.'

'We might be caught,' said Faber.

'I haven't been,' said Kraft.

They lay down either side of him, each with an arm over him as he wept.

CHAPTER 38

Stalingrad, November 19th, 1942
My darling Katharina,

I laughed at your suggesting I might be having an affair. If only you could see how I live. I am so riddled with lice again that no woman would come near me. I promise I will clean up before I come home!!

I am still waiting to hear about my application for Christmas leave. Faustmann has applied too, and may receive it before me as he has not been home once since we were in France. Kraus has said that he will remain to hold the tractor factory. I imagine that he will be by himself, as everybody else is madly keen to get home.

I hope things have settled a little between your parents. And don't worry, I'll whisk you and Johannes out of there as soon as this war is over. Which must be very soon. We are so close to the Volga that I could dip my toe in it from here, although they still come at us, hurling whatever weaponry they have. And they are still fighting furiously in the northern and southern sectors. But don't worry, I am perfectly safe, if filthy, bitterly cold and hungry. I am quite a good soldier now, Katharina. A winter suit would be nice, but I don't intend on being around here long enough to need it.

Please find some chocolate for me. And meat. Beef. They are the only two things I want. Apart from you. But no more crackers. Never do I want to see a cracker again. Or snow. It is beginning to fall again. I have had enough snow to last me a lifetime.

I love you and our son very deeply.

Wait for me. It will not be long.

Your loving husband,

Peter

CHAPTER 39

Faustmann turned his head towards the west.

'What's wrong?' said Kraus.

'I don't know. Something's happened. Back there. At the trench.'

They packed up their gun and moved back, even though it was long before nightfall. The trench was full of men, ashen-faced and staring at Stockhoff.

'We're surrounded, lads,' he said.

'Bullshit,' said Faber. 'They're not capable.'

'Well, they've done it, Faber. They took out the Romanians to the north, then the lads in the south. Zip. We're locked in.'

'Those fucking Romanians,' said Kraus.

'They were on their own up there, Kraus,' said Stockhoff. 'It's not their fault.'

'Well, it's not my bloody fault,' said Kraus.

He slumped to the trench floor. Faber hunkered down beside him.

'Are you all right?'

'I'm just tired, Faber. I'll be fine.'

'It won't last,' said Faber. 'They did it at Kharkov and it only lasted a few days.'

'That was only a few hundred of us,' said Stockhoff.

'Why?' said Faustmann. 'How many are you talking about here?'

'All of us.'

'What do you mean?'

'The entire Sixth Army. Almost three hundred thousand of us.'

The trench fell silent, but the Russian artillery continued firing, its tone gloating, mocking.

'They can't hold us all,' said Faber. 'We'll break out.'

'I'm sure they'll come up with a plan,' said Kraus. 'Like they did at Kharkov. That worked well.'

'You can't supply three hundred thousand soldiers from the air,' said Stockhoff.

'Those airmen can do anything they put their minds to,' said Faber.

'When did you last have a proper meal, lads?' said Stockhoff. 'They can't even supply us from the ground.'

'They'll come up with something,' said Kraus.

Stockhoff stood up. 'I'm going back to the kitchen. See what I can make for you lot.'

'Let us know when it's rat,' said Faustmann.

Faber wanted to laugh, but didn't. He went back to the bunker and fiddled with the fire, throwing on some still-damp wood, then sloshing petrol over it. A flame took hold.

'What do you think, Kraus?' said Faber. 'A break-out?'

'It's hard because all the tanks have gone north.

227

The horses too. It would be hard on our own. It's easier if they come for us.'

They drew heavily on their cigarettes.

'And what?'

'Clear a passage out for us. Hold back the Russians until we're through.'

Kraus fell asleep.

'He looks awful,' said Faustmann.

'We should go and tell Kraft,' said Faber.

They found Kraft humming and still dusting.

'Gentlemen, I shall make coffee.'

His lips and skin were dry. Flaking.

'Are you eating, Kraft?' said Faber. 'Drinking?'

'I'll do it now. Sometimes I forget.'

They drank his coffee. There was no chocolate.

'We're surrounded, Kraft,' said Faustmann.

'We are?'

'You can't really be here on your own any more.'

'Why not? What's the difference?'

'We need you with us,' said Faustmann. 'For when the break-out comes. We won't have time to come and get you.'

'Where are you sleeping? You both stink.'

'In a bunker,' said Faber. 'Near the tractor factory.'

'I'm not going back there.'

'But it's dangerous for you to be here,' said Faustmann. 'On your own.'

'I'll take my chances.'

Faber ran his hands through his hair.

'Will you at least bloody look after yourself, Kraft? Eat and drink properly.'

228

'You don't exactly look a picture of health, Faber. Or you, Faustmann.'

They shook his hand. Faber pressed him to his chest.

'Mind yourself.'

'You too. Both of you.'

They climbed again through the hatch, their exit hidden by a mound of soil and concrete. They scuttled east, back towards their bunker. Kraus woke as they barrelled in.

'You look like shit, Kraus,' said Faustmann.

'I feel like shit.'

After soup and coffee in the trench, Kraus went to the rear with Stockhoff, to the medics. Faber and Faustmann went back to the bunker. To wait.

CHAPTER 40

Katharina dressed for the food queue. The Russian usually went but Katharina had heard the rumours. Her father was silent. Her mother knew nothing. She walked onto the street. There was snow on the ground, but her feet were warm in fur-lined boots with a slight heel. And she finally had a mink coat that fastened across her chest. Her own.

She joined the queue outside the baker's, behind a woman whose thin-soled shoes slapped against the icy ground each time she stepped forward. It was an irritating noise.

The women in front and behind her were deep in conversation. Hushed and fevered. She tried to join in, repeating their words, asking questions, but she was shut out, the women's eyes on each other, away from her with her fur coat and well-fed hips. She stared ahead. They were skinny women anyway, in ragged clothing. She would find out some other way.

She headed further into the city, towards the east where she knew Mrs Sachs shopped. She waited outside a butcher. Mrs Sachs came out of the shop, a light weight at the bottom of her bag. She looked gaunt. Strained.

'You look well, Katharina. How is your mother?'

'Fine.'

'I never see her out.'

'She enjoys being at home.'

'I was sorry to hear about your brother.'

'Thank you, Mrs Sachs.'

'You've heard the news? Your husband's there, isn't he?'

'It can't be true, though, Mrs Sachs. The Russians don't have the capacity.'

'So we were told.'

'Do you believe it? There's nothing about it in the newspaper.'

Mrs Sachs snorted.

'It must be nice up there in your new apartment, Katharina.'

'Yes, it is,' she said, but Mrs Sachs had already gone along the road to join the queue for vegetables. Katharina waited, stamping her feet like the other women, although she was not cold. Then she gave up. She didn't even need meat.

She went home and fed Johannes, scooping the food prepared by the Russian into his mouth. She put him to bed and sat on the sofa, waiting for her father to wake. A door opened, but it was her mother, still in her nightgown. She nodded at Katharina, and disappeared into the bathroom. Katharina picked up a magazine and turned its pages, crumpling them, irritated by the relentlessness of her mother's grief, by the possibility that she was already a widow without ever having been a wife.

Her mother shut her bedroom door and her father emerged from his. Her brother's old room.

'Good morning, Katharina. How is my beautiful daughter today?'

'It's nearly afternoon, Father.'

'Then I slept well.'

'Was it a late night?'

'More of an early morning.'

He sat beside her on the sofa, yawning and scratching his chest.

'How is young Johannes?'

'Fine. No air raid, so he slept through.'

'I think they're running out of bombs.'

'What's happening in Stalingrad, Father?'

'Nothing our men can't handle.'

'Have they been surrounded?'

'There's talk of it, but it's nothing serious. A few days more and they'll have broken out of it.'

'How can you be so sure?'

'They're German soldiers, Katharina.'

'Am I going to be a widow?'

'Your husband will be fine.'

'That's what you said about Johannes. About Mother. And look at them.'

He peered at her.

'You're beginning to sound more like your mother, Katharina. Trust me. Peter will be fine. They're working on plans right at this moment.'

She put her head on his shoulder.

'I'm just so worried about him. About Mother.'

'She could stop if she wanted to, Katharina.'

'What do you mean?'

'The hiding. The not eating.'

'You think so?'

'She's trying to make me feel guilty, that's what it's about.'

'And do you?'

'What?'

'Feel guilty, Father?'

'He had to go back, Katharina. We had no choice.'

'I feel guilty. All the time. I see him sometimes, alone on that train, no idea where he was going. Was it really necessary, Father?'

'Wars cannot be won without sacrifices, Katharina.'

'She has no interest in Johannes. She doesn't even look at him, never holds him. Her own grandson.'

'Grief is the morose indulgence of the idle.'

'That sounds very pompous, Father.'

'Dr Weinart said it. Now, let me see what Natasha can do for me. I'm hungry. Peter will be all right. They'll all be all right.'

CHAPTER 41

Faber and Faustmann sat in the early morning against a west-facing wall to stare at the sky, its clear, bright blueness and wisps of light cloud undisturbed by wind.

'They'll come today,' said Faber.

'They'd better,' said Faustmann.

Faber lit a cigarette and inhaled, deeply to blur his hunger, to warm his lungs.

'The weather is perfect,' he said.

'It was perfect yesterday.'

He inhaled a second time, still deeper, and held his breath, waiting for the nicotine rush. It didn't come. Nothing but the swirl of acid in his stomach.

'I wonder why they didn't come yesterday,' said Faber.

'They'd better come today.'

Wrapped in coats, blankets and scarves, the two men pressed against each other. Not for warmth. There was none.

'This will test your theory, Faustmann.'

'Which one? I have many.'

'That we're cannon fodder.'

'Are we, Faber?'

'There's been almost nothing. No supplies, no men, no food. It's as though they're not interested. They don't care.'

'They're telling us to wait, Faber. That's all. To hold on.'

'And you believe them?'

'Do I have any choice?'

CHAPTER 42

She squealed when she saw them. The white envelopes with gold trimming. One for her parents. One for her. She opened it, still in the hall. An invitation to the dinner. The Weinarts' dinner. She hugged herself and ran upstairs to tell her mother.

CHAPTER 43

Gunkel led a chestnut horse into the shell of an apartment block and shot it. He sharpened his knives and set to work, his wrists moving habitually. Stockhoff stood at his side.

'Find something else to do, gentlemen,' said Stockhoff. 'This will be served later.'

They drifted off, back to the bunker. Kraus was asleep.

'We should see how Kraft is,' said Faustmann.

They moved through the snow, a shroud over the dead, over the flies and their maggots. Faber was glad of it.

The cellar stank of shit; there were large mounds in the corner under the stairs, amid scatterings of torn newspaper. Kraft sat on a chair, combing his hair and humming, the table set for food.

'Jesus, Kraft. It's disgusting in here.'

'Is it?'

'You shit under the stairs.'

'There's no bathroom, Faber.'

'Go outside, you bastard.'

'No.'

'What do you mean, no?'

'I'm not going out there. It's too noisy. I don't like it.'

Faber looked at him, at his cracked, bleeding lips and papery skin.

'Are you all right, Kraft?'

'I'm fine.'

'Have you eaten? Drunk anything?'

'I had a little water. My stomach hurts, though. It keeps cramping.'

'I'll clean up.'

Faber opened up his shovel, wrapped his scarf over his mouth and scooped up the excrement, his face turned away, his eyes half closed, his stomach curdling. He climbed the stairs, opened the hatch and hurled it as far as he could, then scraped his shovel across the snow. He went back down the stairs, but left the hatch open.

'The bombs will come in,' said Kraft. 'They'll find us.'

'We'll be dead anyway if we have to inhale that smell. Next time, shit outside.'

'It's terrifying out there, Faber.'

'It's terrifying in here.'

Faustmann took the dusting sock, rinsed it in water from his can and began to clean Kraft's face and hands.

'You stink, Kraft. You need to eat, drink and build a fire. It's freezing in here.'

'Is it? Let me make some coffee.'

He pushed the chair away from the table and stood up. Shit stains ran the length of his trousers, both legs. Faber retched. There was nothing in his stomach to vomit.

'I'm sorry. How forgetful of me. I have no coffee.'

He picked up the photograph of his mother and stared at it.

'You're so lucky to have your wife and child waiting for you, Faber. So fortunate.'

'You should sleep,' said Faber.

'I'm not tired.'

'You are. You're exhausted.'

'Stop telling me what I am, Faber. I'm not exhausted.'

'What are you then?'

'I'm nothing. A nothing with nobody.'

'You've got us.'

'You'll all move on once this is over. Back to your homes. Your families. I'll go back to an empty house, a big empty house to be on my own.'

'You'll find someone. The women will be queuing up to live with you, to be lady of the manor.'

'That was my mother, Faber. Nobody else can be my mother.'

'Just get some sleep, Kraft. You'll feel better.'

'I'll never feel better. It'll always be like this.'

'Wars end, Kraft.'

'Its ending won't bring back my mother, Faber.'

'But at least you'll be able to go home.'

'I have no home. Not any more.'

'You should sleep.'

'So you keep saying.'

Kraft bent over.

'Are you all right?' said Faber.

'I need to shit.'

'Not in here. Go outside.'

Kraft climbed the staircase, shit seeping down his leg, his arm across his stomach. He went through the open hatch. They heard him sigh as he released his bowel at the top of the staircase.

'I need paper,' he said.

Faber passed up a Russian newspaper.

'What are they saying about us, anyway?' said Faber.

'Who?' said Faustmann.

'The Russians. In the paper.'

'Oh, that we're fucked. That they'll blow us to oblivion.'

'They probably will,' said Faber.

'Probably.'

They listened as Kraft tore and crumpled the newspaper.

'Clean yourself properly,' shouted Faber.

They heard him buckle his belt, but not his footstep on the staircase.

'What's he doing now?' said Faber.

He climbed a few steps, enough to see Kraft's shit, but not Kraft himself. He climbed further and saw the man scrambling up the snowbank.

'What are you doing, Kraft?'

The bullet hit him in the neck, his larynx, so that he was silent as he fell backwards, blood bubbling and spurting from the freshly made hole. Faber fell back down the stairs, away from Kraft, tumbling into Faustmann.

'The bastard, the mad bloody bastard,' said Faber.

'What happened?'

'They shot him. He let them shoot him.'

Faustmann pulled the hatch shut. Artillery fire followed, tracking the sniper's victory over Kraft.

'The bloody idiot has given us away. We're stuck here till nightfall.'

'We'll miss the horsemeat,' said Faber.

They waited until dusk and crawled out on their stomachs, through Kraft's faeces and over his body. They reached the trench in time, their smell no different to anybody else's.

'Where were you?' said Kraus.

'Looking for food,' said Faustmann.

'Find any?'

'No.'

Stockhoff had distributed the horsemeat through vats of turnip soup. He gave them each two portions and four pieces of bread.

'Rations are being cut tomorrow, lads.'

'It's too cold, Stockhoff,' said Kraus. 'The men need more food, not less.'

'Nothing to be done. Nothing's coming through.'

'The planes?' said Faustmann.

'We've seen canisters fall,' said Faber.

'Almost none of it is food,' said Stockhoff. 'Or it has fallen behind Russian lines.'

'By how much?' said Kraus.

'What?' said Stockhoff.

'Cut by how much?'

'By more than half.'

'How much more than half?'

'By almost two thirds.'

Faber buried his head in his hands.

'But I'll do what I can for you, lads. Gunkel and I will find a way.'

They shook the hands of the cook and butcher, thanking them for their effort, their commitment to them. Faber, Faustmann and Kraus went back to their bunker and stoked the fire.

'How are you feeling, Kraus?' said Faber.

'Better.'

Kraus lit a cigarette.

'We'll go back out again tomorrow, lads.'

'Is there any point, Sergeant?' said Faber.

'It'll give us something to do,' said Kraus. 'I can't look at the sky any longer.'

'Shouldn't we keep back our ammunition for the break-out?' said Faber.

'If there is one,' said Faustmann.

'What do you think, Kraus?' said Faber.

Kraus drew on his cigarette.

'Do you think they're coming, Kraus?'

'I don't know, Faber.'

They fell asleep, but Faber woke in the middle of the night. He was hungry. He put his hand under his tunic and touched his ribs. He could feel each one. And his stomach was hollow. He found some crackers in Kraus' pack, ate them and went back to sleep.

In the morning, Faustmann and Kraus prepared to return to the tractor factory.

'Come with us, Faber,' said Kraus.

'There's no point, Sergeant. Another dead Russian will do nothing for us.'

'I could report you.'

'Will you?'

'Not today.'

They left and he stoked the fire, throwing on scraps of wood from an old table and staring at the flames. He was glad not to have to look at the two men, at their hunger.

He took out his pictures of Katharina and Johannes and attached them to rusty nails sticking out of the bunker wall, next to where he slept. He ran his fingers over the pictures and kissed his wife on the lips. She smiled at him. At his flaking skin and thinning legs. Three and a half weeks.

He tried not to think about it. Three and a half weeks and nobody had come. The planes that flew in always left with a heavier load, captains, first lieutenants, majors, their faces coloured yellow as though they had jaundice. But he saw that their eyes were white, and healthy.

He stabbed at the fire, stirring sparks. He wasn't going to fight any more, to risk his life for officers too cowardly to stay, expose his belly to the Russian rockets now bouncing off the icy ground, fragmenting and gouging ever bigger holes in German bodies. No. He would keep himself safe, so that he could be a father to his son.

He lay down by the fire, curled up in a ball and closed his eyes. He liked the snow. It muffled the sound of battle so that he could no longer hear the men to the north of the city fighting to hold back the Russians. He appreciated their effort, but didn't want to listen to it. He fell asleep, woke and read until the others returned. Kraus had a small cut on his hand.

'Probably from a knife,' he said. 'Maybe even my own.'

They went to the trench and ate horse sausage. Stockhoff told them to prepare for the break-out.

'They're coming for us from the south,' he said.

'Anything official?' said Kraus.

'Not yet,' said Stockhoff. 'We just have to wait. And be ready.'

'He hasn't abandoned us,' said Kraus.

'I knew he wouldn't,' said Faber.

They waited in the bunker, their guns, bullets and grenades ready. Faber tucked his photographs back into his pocket, beside his wife's hair. They waited a second day. And a third. A bitter thin wind cut across the steppe, delving into clothing and skin. It was impossible to be outside.

'We'll miss it,' said Faber. 'They'll leave without us.'

'They won't,' said Kraus. 'Nobody can move in that.'

Thunder echoed across the city.

'That's it,' said Kraus. 'We're on.'

They rushed outside, into the darkness, ready to head south, but found the noise was coming from the east, from the river. It was freezing over, huge ice floes crashing into each other, fusing under a fall of fresh snow. They were surrounded from every direction, north, south, west, and now east. They returned to their bunker.

'We're done for,' said Faustmann. 'They'll be able to bring over everything they need to finish us off.'

'We can bomb holes in the ice,' said Faber.

'We can't,' said Kraus. 'No artillery left.'

Faber fiddled with his gun.

'They have to get us out of here,' he said.

They went back to Stockhoff and drank donkey soup.

'They're not coming,' he said. 'It's been called off.'

'Why?' said Kraus.

'Don't know. No reason given.'

CHAPTER 44

Katharina raised the skirt of her crushed velvet gown and walked up the marble staircase of the Weinart house, her path lit by candles and shimmering light from the enormous Christmas tree decorated with bows of silver silk.

Her parents went in front of her, her father in a crisp, black suit with a hand-tied bowtie, her mother in green chiffon, a fox fur draped across her shoulders, its head and feet still attached.

They turned right at the top of the stairs to join the queue waiting to greet the doctor and his wife, Mrs Weinart in a silver lamé dress that shimmered in the candlelight. She kissed Katharina's mother on both cheeks.

'Mrs Spinell, I am so, so glad that you came.'

'Thank you, Mrs Weinart. It's lovely to be here.'

'It is a difficult time for you. The first Christmas. I know that one day you will understand the significance of your son's sacrifice. And here is Katharina. How beautiful you look!'

Katharina stepped forward, her royal purple dress curving around her hips and breasts and cascading to the floor.

'Thank you.'

'I can only agree with my wife, Mrs Faber.'

'Thank you, Dr Weinart.'

'Go in, Katharina. Have some champagne. We'll dine after we have heard from our soldiers.'

Katharina took champagne from the waiter's tray and handed a glass to her mother who took it without a word and walked towards a woman in a floral dress. Her father hesitated momentarily, but left her for a man in party uniform staring into the coal fire, his face reddened by the heat, their conversation immediately intense. Katharina sipped from her glass. Embarrassed at her sudden isolation, she turned her back on the guests and stepped towards a tree, smaller than the one in the hall but also covered in silver bows. Beneath the branches was a hill of presents, each beautifully wrapped. Theirs was with the butler downstairs.

She took a deep breath, turned back into the room and walked towards a gathering of women, most of them her age, a circle of silk, lace, velvet, bodices and bows. They made space for her, as they exchanged tales of their Russian housemaids, suitable schools and holiday homes. One woman, a blonde in a ruby silk dress with matching jewels, wore a blue and gold enamel cross on the strap of her dress. Katharina nodded towards it.

'Congratulations. That's quite an honour.'

'Thank you. I am very proud of it.'

'Did the Führer present it to you himself?'

'He did. Only six weeks ago, so it's still exciting for me.'

'How many children do you have?'

'Eight.'

'That's very impressive. You're so young.'

'I've been married for seven years. And you?'

'I married last year. I have only the one child.'

'You have plenty of time, then. I'm Elizabeth Bäker, by the way.'

'Katharina Faber. A pleasure to meet you.'

Dr Weinart turned up the radio.

'It's from Stalingrad,' he said.

The room fell silent. They heard men singing carols and hymns, in strong, confident voices. They sounded warm and well fed. Katharina bowed her head and tried to catch a tear with her finger before it stained her make-up. The woman in the ruby dress passed her a handkerchief.

'I wonder if it's my husband,' said Katharina. 'He has a very good voice. He was in his school choir.'

When it was over, Katharina composed herself, and promised to return the handkerchief.

'Keep it.'

'No, no. My Russian girl will wash and iron it, and return it to your home.'

'Bring it yourself, Katharina, for lunch on New Year's Eve. And bring your son.'

'I'd be delighted, Elizabeth.'

Katharina tucked the address and handkerchief into her black clutch bag. The gong sounded for dinner. Elizabeth remained on the first floor, Katharina went to the second, again trailing her parents. They were sent to a front room overlooking the street, she to a rear room that looked out onto a courtyard lit by candles. Others were still climbing the stairs, towards rooms on the third floor.

Her room was duller than the one downstairs, with only two windows instead of four and a plainer ceiling. But it was still handsome and large enough for five tables of ten people, a plate at each place holding four oysters on a bed of ice, still in their shells. Panic rushed through her. She smiled nervously at the other people in the room. She had never eaten oysters before. She wanted to go home. But she also wanted to stay. She would copy someone else. Do as they did.

The men gathered at the table and waited for the women to sit. An old man helped her with her chair, waiting until she was settled in front of her name perfectly written in rich, black ink, the thick cream card matching the napkins, the tablecloth and the three tall roses at the centre of the table. He sat down. He was a baron. Mrs Weinart had seated her between a baron and a baroness, elderly and frail, but aristocrats nonetheless. She smiled and nodded at the other people at her table, most of them the age of her parents. There was only one young couple, the woman's hand firmly on the man's arm.

Two waiters appeared, one with white wine, the second with water. She thanked them. The baroness coughed lightly and raised an oyster in her left hand, a three-pronged fork in her right. She speared the fish and lifted it to her mouth. Katharina was about to do the same until the baron lifted a shell with his right hand and tipped its contents into his mouth. A light sweat broke out on her palms. She feigned a cough, buying time, unsure whether there was a male and a female way of eating oysters. She decided to copy the baroness, and cold, salty fish slipped down her throat. She thought she would vomit, but ate the remaining three nonetheless, relieved when the next course was warm carrot soup.

'Where is your husband, Mrs Faber?'

It was the baron.

'He is at Stalingrad.'

'An officer?'

'No. Infantry.'

'So, how did you come to be here?'

'My father works with Dr Weinart.'

'Is he a doctor, too?'

'Oh goodness, no,' laughed Katharina. 'He works with him on other matters. He was in Russia with him in the autumn. Protecting the harvest.'

'I see. And you?'

'I look after my son, but I used to work in a bank. As a typist. Then helping customers.'

'Germany is a changed place, Mrs Faber.'

'Indeed, Baron. We must hope that this war ends soon and we can return to normal.'

'I am not sure that I know what normal is any more.'

There was an explosion of clapping from the downstairs rooms.

'The main course has arrived,' said the baron.

'But not yet for us peasants upstairs,' said the baroness.

'I'm sure it will be here soon,' said Katharina.

She checked her hair, ensuring that no strands or rhinestone pins had come loose.

'Do you live in Berlin, Baroness?' she asked.

'We used to, but we prefer to live now on our estate. We understand things there.'

Five waiters came into the room, each carrying a silver platter of roast goose and sugared, syrupy oranges, the fat and juice swirling one into the other as it was set down on the table. Katharina clapped furiously, determined that her appreciation should carry down the stairs. The baron and baroness' hands remained in their laps, their palms together.

She cut into the large roast potato on her plate, its skin crisp and golden, its flesh soft and crumbling. As she waited for the steam to escape, she dipped her fork into the puree of carrot and parsnip. It was sweet but not watery, and the goose was perfect, moist but thoroughly cooked.

'Your jewellery is very fine, Mrs Faber,' said the baroness.

'Thank you, Baroness. It was a gift from my father.'

'It must have cost him a lot of money.'

'I'm not sure it did.'

She took a little of all the desserts, lemon tart, raspberry sorbet and chocolate mousse with slices

251

of candied orange. Coffee followed, served down-stairs with handmade chocolates. She joined her mother and the doctor's wife by the fireplace. Both women were laughing. They stopped but did not explain.

'How did you find the Baroness, Katharina?' said Mrs Weinart.

'Fine.'

'For some people change is very difficult.'

'She says she prefers to live on their estate.'

'So she can remember things as they were. When she was in charge. When she didn't have to mix with ordinary people.'

Katharina sipped her coffee.

'I adore your dress, Mrs Weinart.'

'Do you? Thank you.'

'Where is it from?'

'I got it in Paris.'

'Is it Chanel?'

'Oh no, dear, no. I wore Chanel when we took Paris. This is from Ardanse, a quaint little house run by a petty Russian aristocrat and her sister. It seemed more appropriate than anything French.'

Katharina and her mother stayed until most other people had left. At three, they climbed into a taxi, Mr Spinell between them, his arms round their shoulders.

'Ladies, you were splendid tonight. Both of you. Tremendous ambassadors.'

'For what?' said Mrs Spinell.

'This family, Esther.'

She removed his arm from her shoulder.

'This isn't a family any more, Günther.'

Katharina babbled on about the dresses, the food, the decorations. But her mother's eyes were closed, her face shut tight. She was silent. She climbed the stairs to the apartment, leaning on the bannisters, went to her room and shut the door. Her father, silent too, went to his. Katharina looked at her son, asleep on his back, his arms outstretched. She bent over and kissed him, wobbling only a little.

'It will all be worth it, Johannes.'

CHAPTER 45

Faber inhaled and passed the cigarette to Faustmann.
'Is there a moon?'
'I don't know.'
Faustmann brought the smoke deep into his lungs. Still holding his breath, he inhaled a second time. Faber snatched the cigarette from his mouth.
'It's my turn.'
Faber inhaled, once, twice and the cigarette went out. They were in darkness. Kraus was beside them, asleep, his head buried under his blanket.
'And what day is it?'
'I don't know that either.'
'Tomorrow is New Year's Day.'
'So I gather.'
'What day was Christmas?'
'Shut the fuck up, Faber. It's a day. Another day. What difference does its name make?'
'It's important for me to know.'
'Why? Why is it important?'
'So I know where I am.'
'You're in a hole in the ground, starving to death.'
'In time. Where I am in time.'

254

'You're close to death.'

'Fuck off, Faustmann. Something will happen.'

'Yes, you'll surrender to the Russians.'

'I'd never do that.'

'You will.'

'Hand myself over to those Bolshevik bastards? They treat people like shit.'

'I know. We're much kinder.'

Faber buried his head in his knees.

'It's freezing. It's impossible to stay down here, Faustmann.'

'It's better down here than out there. When the shelling stops, we'll see if we can find somewhere else.'

They fell silent, listening to Kraus' breathing.

'It wasn't supposed to be like this, Faustmann.'

'What wasn't?'

'The war. The Russian front.'

'How was it supposed to be?'

Faber knocked his boot against the barrel once used for fires, spilling the cold cinders.

'Simple. Quick. Like France. Belgium. Roll over and let us in.'

'My grandmother's stubborn. Always was.'

'What? We're fighting a nation of grandmothers?'

'It feels like that.'

'Does it bother you?'

'What?'

'Fighting Russia?'

'I don't see the point. Never have.'

'Because of your grandmother?'

'No. We should have consolidated our hold on the West first. Taken England.'

'We have control of all that.'

'Do we?'

'You just don't want to fight against your own people, Faustmann.'

'Whether I fight or not makes no difference.'

'So why are you doing it?'

'Because they'll shoot me if I don't.'

'That's hardly a noble cause.'

'I can think of none more noble. Why are you fighting, Faber?'

'To protect my wife and child. To secure their future.'

'Bullshit. You didn't have them when the war started. I need a real reason.'

'That is a real reason.'

'That's a bullshit reason.'

Faber stared at him, but saw nothing in the darkness.

'It's the only one I have.'

'Is that why you married? So that you had an excuse to kill?'

'I married because I wanted leave.'

'You stab your leg to get leave. Not marry.'

'I married because I married.'

'Most soldiers fight for a leader, for country or for God. But you chose a wife and then a child. Why?'

'Jesus, I married a woman. I had a child. It happens to most men.'

'You needed a reason, didn't you? Something outside yourself. Exactly what Kraft needed.'

'And?'

'It wrecks your head a little less, doesn't it, when you say that you're killing a man to protect your wife, that you're evicting a child so yours can stay home?'

'Does it? I hadn't noticed.'

'You stare at those pictures of your wife and child, Faber, as though your life depended on them. They give you purpose. And an excuse. That's all.'

'And what excuse do you have, Faustmann?'

'That's the trouble. I don't have any. I have no illusions. I know exactly why I'm here.'

'Why are you here?'

'Cannon fodder for that lot in Berlin.'

'Not that again.'

'It's all there is. You can hide behind your wife and child, kill all around you for your wife and child, but you're really not doing it for them. You're doing it for the fat bastards in Berlin.'

'I'm doing it for our future.'

'So, Fuchs, Weiss and Kraft all died for your future? For the future of your wife and child?'

Faber pressed his hands against his ears.

'I can't listen to any more of your bullshit, Faustmann.'

'No. Nor can I, Faber.'

CHAPTER 46

Berlin, January 3rd, 1943

My darling Peter,

I have just this minute received your letter wishing me a Merry Christmas and of course, of course, I will wait for you. Forgive me for my past few letters, I have just been a little strained by home life.

We are all thinking of you, imagining how frightened you are as you wait to be rescued. But it will happen. My father tells me that intense preparations are under way to take you all out of there. I understand that planes and soldiers are being commandeered from across Europe. Those Russians will be very shocked when they feel the full force of German might across their backs.

Your son is well and awaiting your return. He is, at last, sleeping a little more easily at night, although I see no sign of any teeth so I am not sure if that is what had been troubling him. No matter, he is well now.

Mother, Father and I attended the most marvellous Christmas party at the Weinarts.

They have been so good to us all, and I am very excited to see what job Dr Weinart finds for you on your return to Berlin. I am sure that it will be a splendid one, as they think so highly of my father and the work that you did while here with me.

I am sorry for suggesting that you were having affairs with other women when you were obviously fighting so hard against our hateful Bolshevik enemy. I do know how much you love me and I promise that I will wait for you, right here, in this house, in Berlin.

I have enclosed some more chocolate, and some sausage that I hope will still be fresh by the time it reaches you in Stalingrad. Or maybe you'll be home before it arrives and those Russian peasants can eat it with my compliments.

I am so looking forward to seeing you.

Yours in love,

Katharina

CHAPTER 47

They crawled to the rear and found Gunkel in the schoolyard, an emaciated horse tethered beside him.

'He's a scrawny fucker, boys. I'll get off him what I can.'

'Many left?' said Faustmann.

'One more after this lad.'

Gunkel dug into his pocket and pulled out a handful of boiled sweets. He gave them to the men. Faber sucked on two sweets at once, the sugar rushing into his blood.

'Now let me do my job,' said Gunkel. 'Before this creature gets any skinnier.'

He shot the animal and set to work before it had finished twitching and kicking, before the hide froze to the flesh. An older soldier stood by the horse's head, a gun in his hand, gesturing intermittently at the crowd that appeared, a vulturous circle fixed first on Gunkel, then on the old soldier as a mound of meat grew at his feet. Gunkel put away his knives. The men surged forward, Faber and Faustmann among them. Gunkel took out his pistol.

'Line up boys,' he said.

They did, their bandaged, gloved, frostbitten hands cupped and begging as they moved up the queue. He gave a piece of meat to each man. Two to Faber and Faustmann.

'The kitchen is closed, lads,' said Gunkel. 'You may fend for yourselves.'

'Where's Stockhoff?' said Faber.

'Shot himself in the leg and got on a plane.'

'Bastard,' said Faber.

They hunkered down in the snow, against the school wall, and built fires from scraps of a tree. They boiled water and threw in the meat, sucking on sweets as they waited.

'What about the other men working back here, the cobbler, the tailor?' said Faustmann.

'Sent up front. Old and fat. They hadn't a chance.'

Faber peered into the pot, watching as each bubble wound its way to the surface, turning the meat from red to grey. He poked at it with his spoon, as though that might hurry the process.

'Where's Kraus?' said Gunkel.

'Back in the bunker.'

'Is he all right?'

'Don't know,' said Faustmann. 'He's sweating and shivering.'

'Any infection?'

'On his hand where he has a cut. A bit of frostbite too.'

'So, he's done for.'

Faber scooped the meat out of the pot and began

to eat, burning his mouth but unable to wait any longer. It was chewy and dull, but it was food. He began to shiver. His stomach cramped.

'It'll settle, Faber,' said Gunkel.

He slept then, in the schoolhouse, beside a fire set in a punctured artillery shell, glad of the warmth and the company of other men. The following day, it was too cold to go outside. They kept the fire burning and looked out the window, at the last horse, shivering.

'We should bring him in,' said Faustmann.

'No point,' said Gunkel. 'Not enough on him.'

'But there's something,' said Faber.

'You'd use more trying to get him in here.'

They watched the horse, its legs locked, paralyzed by the cold that spread through its body until it was frozen, until a gust of wind tipped it to the ground.

'We're fucked,' said Faustmann.

'So it seems,' said Faber.

The bombardment began in the early morning darkness, while they were still asleep, most of it from the west; thousands and thousands of guns and rockets pounded them for almost an hour. Faber curled himself up, the blanket over his head, and sobbed. He wanted to go home. To kiss his wife and hold his child. Faustmann and Gunkel dragged him to his feet.

'We can't stay here,' said Faustmann.

'But where is there to go?' said Faber.

'I don't know.'

They staggered out of the school and stumbled towards the centre of the city, across the wasteland, past bunkers blasted open, heads severed from torsos, thighs wrenched from hips, the snow stained by blood. The three men ran faster, scrambling over what had once been streets, until they found an opening into the basement of a department store, its darkness alleviated by candles and oil lamps. Hundreds of emaciated men lay in neat rows, their faces gaunt, their eyes elsewhere.

'Is it a morgue?' said Faber.

He could hear their breathing. Just. And pick out the orange, red hair and mottled skin of the starving, of those closest to death. The room stank of faeces and contagion, of gangrenous flesh.

'We can't stay here,' he said.

'There's nowhere else,' said Faustmann.

'Be grateful,' said Gunkel. 'You're not as dead as they are.'

Faber picked a space between two sleeping men, one of them stick thin and lying on a mattress with the price tag still on, the second difficult to identify under a scattering of children's clothes. He unfolded his tent, flattened the edges and lay down, his blanket over him. Gunkel was right. He wasn't as dead as they were. Not yet, anyway.

He slept but woke in the thinning darkness to the sound of the man on the mattress, groaning as he soiled himself in a spurt of shit.

'Are you all right?' said Faber.

There was no response, but the man on the other side spoke.

'It's what happens at the end. You shit out your insides.'

Faber squeezed his eyes tight, curled his legs and lay still, focused on his breath, its movement in and out through his nose, over the stubble and across the filth of his face, drifting close to sleep until the man shit himself again. Faber sat up. Gunkel was heading for the door. Faber followed.

'I'm coming too. It's disgusting in here.'

They pulled scarves over their mouths and noses and went out into the grey dawn light. Faber inhaled, relieved at his relative strength.

'They're in a bad way in there, Gunkel.'

'They haven't had me to look after them, Faber.'

They slipped down towards the river, hunting for an animal looking for water. The Russians slept on because the Germans were dying anyway.

'There's nothing to hunt, Gunkel.'

'We'll find something.'

'Let's at least wait till the sun rises a bit more. Until it's warmer.'

'Then somebody else might eat it.'

Faber crouched as he walked, hiding from the sleeping Russians, his lungs and limbs struggling for energy, his back bent over. Gunkel was almost upright.

'The further down you go, Faber, the harder it is to get back up.'

'Fuck off, Gunkel.'

'Stay positive, Faber.'

'About what?'

'Life.'

'This isn't life, Gunkel. It's death. Death on legs.'

'As long as you're breathing, it's life.'

They reached the river.

'This is ridiculous,' said Faber. 'There's nothing alive out here.'

'Except us.'

'We're half-dead, Gunkel.'

'Or half-alive, Faber.'

In a yard close to the river, under a tree that had no leaves, they found a pony, shivering, its ribs protruding through its sagging skin. It didn't move as they approached. Gunkel walked up to the barely conscious animal, held it by the ear and shot it through the temple.

'Put it out of its misery,' he said.

'Cut it, Gunkel. Cut it up.'

'There's nothing on it, Faber. The poor bastard was hungrier than we are.'

He walked on and Faber followed, picking his way through frozen corpses. Gunkel whistled.

'Be quiet.'

'There's nobody up. They're hung over, celebrating their victory.'

'How the fuck can you whistle?'

'What else should I do, Faber? Weep?'

Gunkel spotted a dog, thin but alive, and more alert than the horse.

'I'll try him,' he said.

265

Gunkel shot the animal and rushed over, his knife and steel already out as he fell to his knees beside it. He started to cut, furiously, still whistling, but the blood froze faster than he could cut. He fell silent, and still. Faber tugged at his sleeve.

'Come on, Gunkel. We should go.'

'It's my job to feed you, Faber. It's what I do.'

'Get up. They'll be awake soon.'

'I can't feed you any more.'

Faber led Gunkel back up the bank, aware of their vulnerability as the sun stretched its light across the snow. In about an hour, the smell of stewing beef would waft across the river, stirring the senses of those still able to feel hunger.

'Would you take it, Gunkel?'

'What?'

'Their soup.'

'I like our soup.'

'We don't have any soup.'

'We'll be rescued soon, Faber.'

'You can't seriously believe that.'

'They can't just leave us here.'

'They already have.'

Gunkel fell back.

'Go on,' he said. 'I want to piss.'

Faber took a couple of steps and stopped. He turned.

'How can you piss? You haven't drunk.'

Gunkel's pistol was raised to his head. He pulled the trigger and crumpled at the knees. Faber ran back and fell into the snow beside him, rifling his

266

pockets as he twitched and jerked his way to stillness. Faber found two boiled sweets. He stuffed one into his mouth and fled.

He sat on a stone, his back against a fragment of wall, and stared at the sky, at the white clouds travelling west. He put the second sweet in his mouth and took off his hats, his scarves. He wanted Russia to freeze his brain, to cauterize it so that he could no longer think. No longer feel. He wanted only numbness.

They had started cooking. He could smell the beef frying on pans and the bread baking in ovens just beyond his reach. He looked over the wall. He could see the Russians winding up gramophones, pouring drinks for themselves, shouting invitations at them in broken German to come over, to join them.

They banged on pots, shouting that soup was ready. His stomach cramped. He put his hats and scarves back on. He was emaciated. The muscles in his arms and legs were disappearing. His skin was dry and flaking; his lips bleeding. Much longer and he would be like the man on the mattress. He stood up and went back to the basement. He would tell Faustmann. About Gunkel.

'They won't give you any, Faber,' said Faustmann. 'Even if you go.'

'How do you know?'

'They won't.'

'But they're offering.'

'You won't get it.'

'How can you be so sure, Faustmann?'

'They starve their own people, Faber.'

'But we're German. They wouldn't starve us.'

'What are they doing now?'

He slept again but not for long; hunger woke him. He lay still, his legs tucked into his chest, his eyes staring at the dying man's shit-stained trousers.

Others had already gone over. He had seen them walking across the river to the cheering Russians. He rubbed his fingers over his hand. His skin was itchy. And quick to bleed. More hospitable for the lice. And other infections, lethal ones. He could desert, wait for the war to end and then go home. Be a father to his son. A husband to his wife.

But would she want him like that? A man who had surrendered. Would she forgive him and explain it fairly to their son? Tell him that his father had been starving to death in the Russian snow, abandoned. That nobody was coming. No Führer. No general. His chest tightened and he dug his hand under his tunic to massage the skin over his heart, in light circles, his fingers dipping between each rib, tears running from his eyes. After all he had done. His shoulders heaved in the flickering darkness.

He slept for a while, woke, and went outside. He took off his hats again, his scarves. Freezing his head. Freezing his thoughts. Everything white. No blame. No guilt. A bright white nothingness. No past. No future. He pulled on his hats, went back inside and sat beside Faustmann.

'I'm going to get some soup.'

'I see.'

'Are you coming?'

'No.'

'We're dying here.'

'I know that.'

'And you hate this war. This regime.'

'I hate that one too.'

'But you're a communist.'

'Wrong again, Faber.'

'So what are you?'

'Like you said. Dying.'

'But politically?'

'What's the point, Faber? There is no point.'

Faber started to cry.

'I have to. For my wife and son.'

'You fought for them, and now you'll surrender for them. They're lucky to have you.'

'I want to be a father.'

'Good luck, then. Just don't expect soup.'

'They said they've got soup for us.'

'That's what Hitler said, and you believed him too.'

'You're a very cynical man.'

'I'm a dying man, Faber.'

'You can save yourself.'

'Run along, Faber. I'm better off here.'

'Why?'

'They'll shoot me.'

'They won't.'

'To them, I'm Russian in a German uniform.'

'They'll find a use for you.'

'A traitor's bullet, Faber.'

'Maybe not. Come with me, Faustmann.'

'I'll wait here. It seems appropriate.'

'How can any of this be appropriate?'

'I can't be a Russian in Germany any more, or a German in Russia. Here is as good a place as any other. A bit of Russia owned by Germany.'

'But what are you waiting for? You'll die, Faustmann.'

'And you won't, Faber?'

'I might not.'

'You'll wish you had.'

Faber wiped his eyes and pulled his knees to his chest.

'Do you feel guilt, Faustmann?'

'For what?'

'For turning on your own people.'

'Which are my own people, Faber?'

'I feel guilt.'

'The self-indulgence of the loser. You never felt guilt when you were winning.'

'I didn't have time.'

'But you start to lose and you feel sentimental.'

'Is that all guilt is, Faustmann? Sentimentality?'

'No, not for you, Faber. It's worse for you. You want the guilt to absolve you. Just like you want your wife and child to absolve you. Once absolved, you can kill or take soup.'

'That's not true.'

'Isn't it?'

'No.'

'Then what is?'

'I don't know.'

'You'd better go. Get that soup.'

Faber reached his hand out to Faustmann. They shook.

'Goodbye, Faustmann. Good luck.'

'Good luck, Faber. I hope they give you soup.'

'You do?'

'Just find a way to survive without it.'

Faber wore all the blankets and coats he could find, even those covered in shit, and left, his back close to straight as he moved through the rubble to the river, to a walkway of branches frozen into the ice. His feet slipped, threatening to tumble him, but he remained upright, the air crisp and clean, purged of death and decay.

He realized that there were men on either side of him, shuffling, heads down, staring at the ice, refusing to look at each other, to observe each other's surrender. A shot cut through the air. The man on Faber's right fell forward, blood gushing from the back of his head. Faber stopped, registered the direction of the bullet, and ran, forcing the stiffness from his limbs as he fled east, tears streaming down his face. He wanted soup. That was all. And to see his son. To hold his wife. He ran faster, away from them, towards the laughing Russians banging spoons against metal bowls, cheering him on. He laughed too and reached his arms higher into the air, smiling in response to their smiles as he approached a large, black cooking pot. They beckoned him forward. He looked in. Chunks of meat and vegetables were simmering at the surface. He dropped his arms and cupped his hands, begging for their food. They laughed even harder, gold teeth flashing in the afternoon sun, and took his belts and wristwatch. He let them, and begged again. They put a gun to his back and steered him away from the pot, away from the smell of simmering beef. Away from the soup.

CHAPTER 48

They pushed him to a post and barbed-wire pen erected on an open plain of snow. The guards rolled back a section of the fence. He hesitated. They pressed guns against his back, and he moved forward, staring at the snow covering his boots, declining to look at the other Germans, the huddle of frosted eyelashes, stooped shoulders and sunken faces encased in fraying army blankets, each appearing more like a woman at the end of her life than a man at the beginning of his.

He stood apart, detached, certain that his reason for surrender, his wife and child, was more valid than theirs, almost heroic rather than cowardly, maintaining a distance from them until the snow and wind arrived, until he needed their warmth.

He wormed his way into the huddle and remained there for several hours, motionless, almost indifferent to death or salvation but wishing for one or the other to silence the noise in his head, the terrible realization that Faustmann had been right.

He wanted to cry, but decided that required too much energy and fell asleep instead, on his feet, until the prisoners shuffled, slowly at first, then frantically, rushing at the fence, at the guard who banged his gun against a metal bucket, shouting 'bread, bread'. It was dark, but the camp light illuminated the arc of his arm as he catapulted the bread over the fence, a pig farmer doling out the scraps from his table. Faber surged forward and threw himself on top of the other men, punched and kicked as hard as they did, bit too, and secured four pieces, one of them quite large, all of them hard. He stuffed them into his pockets and scurried, rat-like, to a quiet part of the pen to spit saliva on the crust, to suck and soften, ignoring the pain in his teeth, his cramping stomach, the sobbing of men left without any, relishing instead the surge of heat through his blood that made him sleepy and giddy until his temperature plummeted and he shivered, suddenly furiously hungry, desperate for something hot, the promised soup, anything to push away the cold and hunger, to push away the moans of the dying, the bodies of the already dead, to push away the realization that he was next, that he was standing in that grey space between death and life.

When morning came, he was surprised that he was still alive. Frozen and stiff, too numb even to shiver, but alive. The guards opened the pen and he joined a line that led to bread and sausage, silent and orderly. He ate and slipped again into the queue, pleased when they gave him more. And grateful.

They herded the men together, shot some of them and marched the rest further east, away from Stalingrad, their ignominy captured by a newspaper man with a camera perched in the snow, its bulb flashing.

CHAPTER 49

She didn't need food, but she went anyway, joining the early morning queue, dressed, like the other women, in black, her eyes, like theirs, red and swollen, her hair, unlike theirs, fashionably styled and her face freshly made-up.

They didn't talk to her, and she no longer expected them to. She just wanted to be among them, ordinary women with ordinary sons and husbands, the women of the infantry. Elizabeth, Mrs Weinart and all her new friends were married to officers, their husbands either still in Berlin or in places safer than Stalingrad.

The women in the queue whispered to each other, and passed around sheets of folded newspaper that carried thousands and thousands of names and black crosses. They pointed out the names of their loved ones, quietly sobbing, muffling their grief as they were supposed to be proud of the men's sacrifice.

Katharina had already pored over every newspaper until her hands were black with ink, but had found no trace of him. Nothing. His mother had replied, a short letter, to say that she too had heard nothing. He had disappeared.

She bought sausage and went home.

Her father was on the sofa, holding Johannes, tickling his toes. Katharina put the sausage in the fridge and told Natasha to make coffee. She sat down beside them.

'Any news, Father?'

'About what?'

'Stalingrad, Father. Is there anything else?'

'It's over, Katharina. Time to move on.'

She took her son from him.

'As you did with Johannes, Father. You moved on quickly. From your own son.'

'I get enough of that from your mother, Katharina.'

Natasha placed the coffee on the table in front of them. Katharina poured.

'Your husband is a hero, Katharina.'

'How can you be a hero when you lose? They lost, Father. We lost.'

'They sacrificed themselves for the greater good. That is heroism.'

'Where's the greater good in losing?'

'It has given us time to regroup, Katharina. To take Moscow.'

'And then what? They encircle us there too?'

'That's defeatist talk, Katharina.'

'How much do we have to give, Father? First my brother, then my husband.'

'Germany is bigger than you, Katharina. Bigger than all of us.'

'A monster that we feed with our men? Is that what it is, Father, this Germany of yours?'

'That's dangerous talk, Katharina. Talk that will land you into trouble. Are you quite well?'

'I'm fine, Father.'

'You have to get over Peter. Accept that he's not coming back.'

'Why?'

'Because you're a mother.'

'And a wife. And a sister.'

'We need good, sensible mothers, Katharina. For our future.'

'A future that has obliterated its past. Its present.'

'It'll be worth it, you'll see. For Johannes.'

'Growing up without a father. It'll be worth that?'

'We will be the most powerful country in the world.'

'Filled with children without fathers. Wives without husbands. Is that it? The great plan?'

'Just wait. It'll work out.'

'No, no, it won't. It already hasn't.'

Faber would not look at the Russians standing on the banks of snow on the edge of the road. They spat at him and scanned the prisoners for the weakest soldier, the one next to fall, the one whose boots, blanket and coat, whose tin cup and bowl might atone for his presence there. Faber pulled his scarves further up his face, and stared down at his feet shuffling through the snow, his lips mumbling that they would never get him. That he had done no wrong.

He walked until dusk, stepping around the dying,

stumbling over the dead, muttering, cursing, swearing, weeping, his head so cold that he was uncertain as night came whether he was even alive, whether the breath in and out of his scarf was real or remembered. They corralled him into a huge barn with wooden doors that shut out the wind, enveloping him in the sweet, musky smell of stored wheat. He fell to the floor and scrambled for kernels, but the shed was empty, swept clean by rats. He slept where he had fallen, kicked awake by men surging forward for soup, meatless and watery but littered with chunks of potato that he could scoop up with his fingers and shovel into his mouth. He got two portions.

The following day there was no food, the day after that only bread and sausage, but still his wiry frame persisted. They reached the railway track that had no beginning and no end, no station, no platform, nothing to mark why they should be standing at that particular spot. He felt the sun's warmth on his face for seconds, minutes or hours; he again lost any sense of time until a rifle butt pushed him towards a train that he had neither seen nor heard arriving. He hauled himself into a carriage, panting from the effort, his head spinning, and lay exhausted on the loose-fitting wooden slats smeared in cow dung. The dung was frozen until the space was packed with emaciated men, the little heat they produced thawing it to release a suffocating stench that lasted until the train moved off, until the wind cut through the gaps and refroze the dung.

Faber found a place against a wall that backed onto the carriage in front, sheltering him from the worst of the wind and giving him a full view of the other men, their hollowed eyes and cheeks, their filth and feebleness. He shut his eyes and rested his head against the wood, relieved to be sitting, to be out of the snow, to be moving somewhere, anywhere, away from Stalingrad. He began to shiver, his teeth, arms and legs jerking in a confusion of cold and relief.

Katharina folded the newspaper, her hands again covered in ink.

'Still nothing, Father. Maybe he surrendered.'

'Let's hope not.'

'How can you say that?'

'He's better off, Katharina, to have died as a hero than surrendered as a coward.'

'As a hero, he's dead. Surrendered, he might still be alive.'

'Not in his soul, Katharina.'

Natasha brought them coffee and cake, the sponge lighter than it used to be, her improvement in baking a source of pleasure to the Spinells. Katharina gave some cake to Johannes. The boy smacked his lips and waved his hands for more.

'You're better off without that kind of husband, Katharina.'

'What kind of husband should I have, Father?'

'A brave one. One who can look after you.'

'I had that.'

'If he surrendered, he wasn't brave. Not the man you thought.'

'He is the man I think he is, Father. The man I want him to be.'

'You need to build a new life for yourself and your son, Katharina. Find a new husband.'

'I can't do that. I can't think like that.'

'You have to, I'm afraid.'

'But the generals surrendered and are still alive. Peter might be among them.'

'Then he is as cowardly as they are and unworthy of you.'

Her father stood up, walked once around the sofa and sat down again beside his daughter, his arm on hers.

'Listen to me, Katharina. Stop all this talk of surrender. Act as though he is dead, as he most likely is, even if he surrendered. They're up to their necks in snow.'

'He's stronger than he looks.'

'If he has surrendered and is alive, there will be no pension.'

'I don't want a pension. I want Peter.'

'Your mother was right. You should have married the doctor's son. You wouldn't care whether he was dead or alive.'

'That's unfair.'

'You have a child. You have to take care of him. You need that pension. That was your deal with Peter, remember. His death. His pension.'

She lifted Johannes, burying her nose in his hair, breathing in his softness.

'But what if he's alive?'

'He's not, Katharina. He can't be.'

The train stopped, the door was dragged open and they were ordered off. Faber got down, slowly, clumsily, to stand in the middle of nowhere – nothing to see but a train on a track surrounded by snow. He stuck close to the carriage, suddenly attached to its squalor, and watched as the Russians climbed in and kicked at the men still inside, their legs bent at the knee, frozen grasshoppers. They picked up the bodies and threw them off the train, the bones cracking in the winter air. Faber decided not to urinate with the other men. He was frightened of frostbite and anyway enjoyed the momentary warmth of piss running down his leg.

The men were fed – saltfish and water – and the train moved off again, a low hubbub in the carriage as their little surge of energy enabled them to consider what might happen next, even though they already knew.

He lost track of the days, of the number of portions of saltfish and water, knowing only that it got colder with each day and that he never seemed able to slake his thirst. And then it ended. He was ordered off the train. But he did not move, his body attached to the rhythm and routine because as long as he was travelling there was a chance of turning west, of going home. He remained motionless on the cow dung, as indifferent to the Russian guns and shouts as those already dead beside him.

'You should get out. The journey is over.'

It was a man in Russian uniform, speaking German.

'You're German?' said Faber.

'Yes.'

'Does that make you a traitor?'

'And what are you? Get out.'

Faber followed the German to a cluster of long, low wooden huts surrounded by barbed wire. A huge sign loomed in front of him, over the entrance, its script incomprehensible, its meaning clear. He shoved the hair from his face and tried to straighten his twisted, frozen spine.

'I am not a traitor,' said Faber.

'The sooner you lose that kind of sentimentality, the easier it is.'

'You seem to be doing well enough.'

'Better than you, anyway. My name is Schultz.'

Faber walked to a hut constructed out of sawn trees, the bark still on. He joined the end of the queue and waited, his right leg buckling intermittently. He struggled to climb the three steps and entered a room of desks and stifling heat. A log fire burned at each end of the hut, warming the men behind the desks, but suffocating Faber, unable to acclimatize to the heat. He bent over, coughing so hard that he retched, grateful that he had nothing to vomit. Schultz stood in front of the fire, his hands behind him, shouting the same thing, over and over.

'Write your name, age, rank and unit. Hand over all documents.'

Faber went to a desk where a younger man watched as he took off several layers of gloves and material from his hands and began to write, slowly, his fingers cramping from the strain of the fine, forgotten movement. He dropped the pen. The Russian, slight with glasses, put out his hand. Faber picked up the pen and put it in the man's hand. The man pushed it away and shouted. Faber repeated the action. The response was louder and angrier. Faber shook, unable to absorb the shock. Schultz yelled across the room, still by the fire.

'Your papers. He wants your papers.'

Faber dug into his tunic, fingered the paybook in his inside pocket and pulled at it, harder than anticipated, scattering the photographs of Johannes and Katharina to the floor. He handed the paybook to the Russian and bent down to retrieve his wife and child. Katharina kept smiling as the Russian's heavy black boot rose in the air and stamped on Faber's hand. He howled and the guard laughed, as did Schultz, his hands still being warmed by the flames.

Faber was photographed, front and profile, and then ordered out into the camp, onto paths being cleared of snow and ice by men in shapeless black suits, vacant creatures bent low by the weight of their shovels and barrows. Matchstick men. He looked at the sky and inhaled.

He was directed to another hut, one more roughly

built than the first. Inside were rows of tables each bearing a bucket, the water freshly poured but already icing over. Beside each bucket was a scrap of soap and a cloth, rough and dirty, already used. He decided against washing. A guard gesticulated at him, with his head, then with his gun. Faber began to undress, peeling off his blankets, his hats, his coats, the sodden material disintegrating as he tugged and dropped it to the floor in a filthy stinking heap, lice falling from the fabric.

He stood at a bucket, naked, and rested his hands on the bench, his eyes straight ahead, his body motionless. He didn't want to look down. He could already smell himself, the thaw of his frozen stench. That was enough. He didn't need to see as well.

He felt a hand across his head. A slap.

'Wash, you stinking bastard.'

It was Schultz, walking up and down, stamping on the lice.

He wetted the cloth and rubbed it with soap, drawing it first along his arm, then under his armpit and over his chest, tears slipping from his eyes as he moved from the ridge of each rib to the next, folds of sagging skin hanging between each one. His stomach had disappeared so he moved onto his hips, running the cloth over the contours of the bone, covered by a layer of skin, but no flesh. His penis was covered in thick, white discharge; the inside of his legs with dry, itchy red skin; and four of his toes were gone, the smaller ones on each foot dead black sponge.

They shaved him then, scraping his body with a blunt blade, depriving the lice of their hiding places, but nicking him so often, drawing so much blood, that they remained anyway. His legs buckled beneath him. They wrenched him to his feet and continued shaving, his head, his legs, his arms, his pubic hair, exposing him entirely.

CHAPTER 50

Katharina pushed open the door of the cake shop. It was quiet, without a queue, and smelled of sweet richness.

'Good afternoon, Madam.'

The woman behind the counter had bowed slightly as she spoke, tipping her white cap towards Katharina. She dipped her head in acknowledgement, but said nothing.

'Can I be of any help to you?'

'I have come to collect my son's birthday cake. Mrs Weinart placed my order.'

'Ah, yes. Little Johannes.'

The woman disappeared into a back room and Katharina looked at herself in the mirror, at her straight back, her shining, healthy hair and her silk summer dress. She looked well. Better than she used to. She stopped looking when the woman returned, a large cake lying in the palms of her hands. Chocolate. Her son's name perfectly formed in blue lettering.

'It's divine,' she said.

She took her purse from her bag.

'Mrs Weinart said to put it on her account,' said the woman.

'That's very kind of her.'

She watched the woman wrap the cake in clean white cardboard, refusing to allow herself to chat as she used to. She had stopped bantering with ordinary people. She thanked the woman, took the box and walked back along the street, crossing into the shadows, for the sun was hot, and into the path of pale women and children carrying dirty cardboard signs scrawled with potted histories of bombed houses and missed meals. They wanted her money and sympathy. She hurried on, stepping around them and their mewling, suddenly fretting that she had a lot to do, although everything was already done. The apartment was clean, the food was ready and the clown was booked to arrive half an hour before the guests.

It would be the first time she had hosted Mrs Weinart and her children. Elizabeth and other women were coming too, but it was the Weinarts she worried over, fearing that they would be bored, cramped by the apartment's small space, disappointed by the gifts she had bought for them to take home.

In the courtyard, she set down the cake and picked up a hoe to hack again at the weeds between the paving stones. The caretaker had fled to his mountain cousins. Her father had shouted after him, calling him a coward, a traitor, but he went anyway. Mr Spinell threw his possessions into the street, clearing the way for a new caretaker. But none came. The weeds grew flowers and the herbs bolted, all of it ignored unless there were visitors. She banged the hoe a couple of times more and retreated upstairs. She kissed her son on the head and checked on Natasha, making sure that she was dressed, as ordered, in a black skirt and white shirt.

Her mother's room was in darkness, the shutters and curtains still closed; a tiny intermittent glow of orange came from the bed where she lay, her head and shoulders propped up against pillows, just high enough for her to draw on her cigarette. It was already after noon.

'Are you coming to the party?'

'I don't know. Am I?'

'It would be nice if you did.'

Katharina turned and pulled the door behind her, holding it firmly until she was sure it was tightly shut.

Her room was hot despite the breeze through the open window, but calm and clean, restful without the child in his cot. She closed her eyes, but the bright summer light filtered through her bronze-powdered lids, failing to shut her into the darkness she craved. She hovered in refracted light, in a space where everything was broken – fragments of white, yellow, of her brother's face and her husband's smile floating and drifting in front of her. Tears fell down her face. She knew that she was no longer a sister, but needed somebody to tell her whether she was a widow or a wife, somebody to end the uncertainty of floating through a fragmented world. She got up and started to dress. She put on a belted navy dress, its sobriety quietly undermined by flashes of white material hidden under the skirt's pleats. She had navy and white shoes to match, and a navy outfit for her son: shoes, shorts and a jacket laid out on the dining table, ready for him to wear just before the guests arrived.

But he was already dressed. And Natasha had brushed his hair, sweeping back his blond curls.

'I was going to do that.'

She took the child and began to tickle him. He giggled, but went back to Natasha, wanting her to brush his hair again. She did so.

'He's fine, Natasha. I'll take him.'

Katharina walked around the room with the boy, holding his hands, spending the last few minutes seeing whether he might walk by himself. She let go of his hands, but he fell and cried. She comforted him, then surrounded him with the toys she had bought him for his birthday.

'You take him, Natasha. I'll make coffee.'

All but one of Mrs Weinart's children had walked by their first birthday.

At three, the doorbell rang. Katharina straightened her skirt and opened the door. Mrs Weinart and her five children, dressed in pale pinks and blues, hair pinned off their faces by slides and wax, entered with a large box.

'You are very kind to have us all,' said Mrs Weinart. 'The children are very excited.'

They presented their gift to Johannes, but he buried his head in Natasha's chest, his right ear turned to her mouth, to her whisperings, her Russian words a balm for his nerves. Instead Katharina took the gift and showed Mrs Weinart to the sofa. She sat down in the middle, in front of the coffee and cake. Elizabeth and the other mothers arrived and happily lingered for the afternoon, smiling as the children laughed at the funny man in bright colours, grateful for the distraction.

'We need to find you a new husband, Katharina,' said Mrs Weinart. 'A handsome one this time.'

Katharina looked down at her cup, at its matching saucer. She said nothing, but the other women agreed.

'An officer,' said Elizabeth. 'One who works in Berlin, away from all that frontline business.'

She watched, without listening, as their mouths moved, coming up with a long list of potential suitors so quickly that they had obviously discussed the possibilities many times before. She knew some of the men, all low-ranking but officers nonetheless, and listened, leaning back into her chair to await their conclusion on whom she should marry next, her period of mourning evidently over, shorter than it would have been if her husband had been an officer or hero, or if she had been a widow with small breasts and narrow hips.

She nodded at their suggestions, and the

conversation returned to its usual topics, their Russian domestics, the discomfort of war, the long hours worked by their husbands. She mentioned her father instead of her husband, and they liked that, liked her acceptance that she was a daughter again, no longer a wife, all of them pleased that she no longer hankered after one of the Stalingrad soldiers, the men best forgotten.

They sang to her son and went home, seemingly content. She took Johannes to the park and let Natasha clean the apartment. She sat again on the bench she had shared with her husband, while their son slept, worn out by celebrations he did not understand.

She remained there until dusk, staring at the children using long sticks to poke at a duck dead at the edge of the water. She was about to be married again, paired up with another unknown, a second husband, when she was not even sure that she had lost the first. Nor was she sure that she wanted the first any more, because even if he came back he was a coward, a failed soldier. They would not give him work in Berlin, or a promotion in Darmstadt. She would live as a schoolteacher's wife, as his mother lived, frugally, the wedding presents still in careful use, the furniture protected by thirty years of darkened rooms.

Her father was in the apartment when she returned, eating the chocolate cake.

'It's good cake,' he said.

'The Führer's baker. Is there any left?'

'No.'

'I've probably had enough, anyway.'

He moved the empty plate to one side.

'They have landed in Sicily,' he said.

'Who have?'

'The Americans, Katharina. The British.'

'Is it serious?'

'No. We just need to get our troops there as fast as we can.'

'From where?'

'Russia. France. Northern Italy. All over. We have enough.'

'That's good. Mrs Weinart thinks I should get married again.'

'That's a fine plan.'

'An officer this time.'

'You're moving up in the world, Katharina Spinell.'

CHAPTER 51

The restaurant was almost empty, each table set nonetheless, cloths and napkins ironed and starched. She was early. She left again and walked the streets, fingering her hair, dampening down her eyebrows, her nerves.

She had seen him once at the Weinarts, but had never spoken to him. He had spent most of his time smoking and talking earnestly with the men. He had paid her no attention. Nor any other woman.

She returned a couple of minutes after eight and he was there, waiting, smoking, looking at the door, at her as she came in. He smiled, stood up, saluted, held back her chair and offered her a drink.

'A martini. Thank you. But no olive. I don't like olives.'

'That's funny. Nor do I. Overrated, I think.'

He smiled again, and she liked his smile, the way it consumed his face.

'I ordered dinner, already. I hope you like lamb.'

'I do. Thank you.'

'Actually, there was no choice. Supplies seem a little restricted.'

'Even for you?'

He smiled.

'Even for me, Mrs Faber.'

She looked around the room.

'It's very quiet.'

'I think people prefer to be at home with their families these nights.'

'But not you?'

'I don't have a family, Mrs Faber. But I believe you have a son. Mrs Weinart enjoyed his first birthday party. She told me the clown was particularly entertaining.'

'I'm glad.'

'You should be. She's a hard woman to please.'

'She thinks highly of you, Mr Meyer.'

'And she thinks highly of you, Mrs Faber.'

'Then we travel in the same compartment, Mr Meyer.'

She drank from her glass as he lit a cigarette, smoking through the opposite side of his mouth from her husband. Her former husband. Her more than likely dead husband. His eyes were very blue and his hair still as blond as a child's.

'You are surely the only young man left in Berlin,' she said.

'And you get to have dinner with me, Mrs Faber.'

'I must be very honoured.'

The food arrived. And two bottles of wine.

'Why is that you are not on a front, Mr Meyer? I thought all young men were obliged.'

'The Führer finds me useful.'

'Why? What do you do?'

'I make him happy.'

'That, I gather, is quite a skill.'

'One I am good at.'

'You are fortunate then. More fortunate than my husband or brother.'

'You make your own luck in this life, Mrs Faber.'

'I suppose you do, Mr Meyer.'

She went every Thursday at six to a room over the restaurant, the sheets as starched and pressed as the napkins downstairs. He was always there, lying on the bed, smoking, waiting, his cheeks blanched from a life spent indoors. And he was chubby. Almost fat.

'I have a present for you,' he said.

He gave her a box with Paris written on it. She opened it and took out a silk robe, blue, red and yellow tropical birds woven into its fabric.

'It's beautiful. Stunning. Thank you.'

'I have chocolate too,' he said.

'May I have some?'

'In a minute.'

He stubbed out his cigarette and clicked his tongue at her.

She took off her coat, her shoes and her dress, standing away from him at the end of the bed. Then her stockings, her underwear. She was naked in front of him, her arms hanging by her sides.

'And your hair.'

She pulled at the pins and turned towards him

so that he could see it fall the length of her back. She wrapped her arms across her chest. She was shivering.

'It's cold in here.'

He undressed, stretched her along the bed, fucked her, and then gave her the chocolate. She ate it immediately.

'Aren't you going to keep some for your son?'

'He's fine. And my mother would eat it anyway.'

In the dining room it was busier than usual, the men pristine in uniform and medals, the women upright, furs across their shoulders to ward off the October chill. She moved with him from table to table, her arm in his, exchanging pleasantries and warm intentions, smiling still when she reached her own seat at the curtained window, a draught swirling at her feet. He sat down, looked around the room, then at her.

'You need one of those furs. Do you have one?'

'A stole, no.'

'I'll have to buy one for you.'

'That's most kind, Joachim.'

The waiter brought them martinis, both without olives, and listed the evening's menu – rabbit or Norwegian salmon. She laughed.

'Fish! That's why it's so busy. You never said anything.'

'I thought it should be a surprise. Would you like wine too?'

She nodded, he ordered and they fell silent until

the fish came, pan fried, its exterior crisped, its interior moist and firm, a perfect salmon pink.

'It makes me want to live by the sea,' said Katharina.

'Have you been?'

'Twice to the North Sea coast.'

'The Mediterranean?'

'Never.'

'I'll take you when this is over.'

He refilled her wine glass and she ate more fish. She considered saving some for Johannes, for her mother, but ate it all.

The chocolate cherry cake for dessert arrived as the sirens started. Katharina stood up. He told her to sit down again.

'They're not capable. Never will be.'

She looked around the room, at the waiters and generals continuing as they were, and sat back down. He ordered more wine.

'How can you be so confident?'

'We're German. They're not.'

'Is that all? Is that all we need to win?'

'It's a cloudy night, Katharina. And there are gunners on the roof.'

She let the waiter refill her glass.

CHAPTER 52

The sirens blared.

'It's an air raid, Mother.'

'I'm aware of that, Katharina.'

'Come on then, up. Get out of bed.'

'I'm sick of air-raid shelters. Of threats that come to nothing.'

'Come on, Mother.'

'I'm not going.'

'Fine.'

She pulled on her coat, lifted Johannes from his cot and wrapped him in blankets, all the while kissing his still baby soft skin. He cried, but calmed when she held him under her coat, to her heart, his eyes suspended between sleep and wakefulness. Her father ushered them through the door and closed it. They were halfway down the stairs when it opened again. It was her mother.

'All right, I'll come with you.'

'Fine,' said Katharina.

'It's just so tedious. And pointless.'

'They're sometimes lucky, Mother.'

She moved swiftly, rushing ahead of her parents

and then stopping to wait for them, to hurry them along.

'I need to find a cot,' she said.

'Go on,' said her father. 'We'll catch up.'

'He'll be intolerable if I don't.'

'Go on, Katharina.'

The queue moved as calmly as it usually did; they all knew what to expect, the children's former excitement drained by habit. She climbed the stairs until she found a cot, made of rope, with a pillow and two neatly folded blankets. She set the boy down, stroked his hair and stood over him, shielding him from the shadows and movement, stepping away when she was certain he had fallen back to sleep. She went towards the staircase to look for her parents but was forced back by the crowd, by a city on the move. She sat down instead, close to Johannes, irritated that her father had her bag with her book and sewing, the suitcase with the blankets and cushions. It would be a cold, dull few hours.

She closed her eyes and tried to sleep, but listened instead to the noises outside. She was never sure which she heard first, the planes or the flak guns, or whether it was just a simultaneous explosion of noise that lasted until the bombs ran out. She listened to the rattle of the guns, pitying the men on the roofs, but envying them too, heroes showered the morning after with gratitude, flowers and sometimes chocolate. Their wives too. Thanked and lauded. Women married to success. Not to the Stalingrad men who brought silent awkwardness and a swift change of subject to something less embarrassing. She had learned no longer to talk of Peter, to act as though he was dead, although she had yet to receive the widow's pension. She had no papers to prove he was dead. Or alive.

Fragments of concrete fell into her hair. She brushed them off. The bombing was close. Closer than usual. The children whimpered and huddled into their mothers' whispers. Johannes slept on. She closed her eyes and leaned her head against the wall. It could be tolerated. Like Meyer's fleshy hands. Everything had only to be tolerated.

She opened her eyes again and raised them to the sky she could not see. The sound had changed. The drone was gone; its predictable hum displaced by the acceleration of engines. They were coming down from the sky, diving, lunging at the city, so close that she imagined she could see the pilots, their long, skinny faces, their eyes hidden behind round, wire glasses. She screamed and threw herself to the floor, terrified men and women falling on top of her, pinning Katharina to the dust as the planes came down, a furious, indignant swarm, bomb after bomb falling, the thud of each explosion penetrating the walls and ceiling, sucking the air from her lungs, the emptiness filling with dry, suffocating panic until the air returned in a rush; a see-saw of breath and asphyxiation, of deafening screams and deafened silence; the English pilots growing balder and fatter with each bomb they dropped, their heads back, laughing as they drew on thick, dark cigars. She was sobbing. She could hear her son crying in his cot, but she could not reach him, could not get out from under the mound of bodies on top of her. She clawed at the floor, at the fluorescence painted onto the cement, ordering her mind to survive what her brother's had not.

They went back up into the sky, and it ended. Slowly, the people over her got to their feet and returned to their places. She sat up and rested momentarily on her knees, her hair and neck wet with other people's saliva and tears. She wiped them away, straightened her hair and her clothes, and went to her son. He was falling asleep again, but she picked him up anyway, his body leaden, and carried him to her seat, opening her coat so that his right ear was against her heart, her lips and right hand on his head, stroking, kissing, whispering, rocking.

'Your father will be home soon, my love. He'll stop all this.'

The all-clear came and they filed quietly out of the bunker, into a city on fire, a carnival of red and orange flames, of explosions and chaos. She started to run, hearing nothing of her neighbours' wails or the screams of ambulances, nothing but the sound of her own heavy breath along the cratered streets, over the mounds of rubble and fallen lime trees. She refused to see the vanished houses. She didn't want to know. She wanted only to be home.

Her house was intact. Not a blemish. She raced

up the stairs, put Johannes in his cot, fell to her knees and thrust her arms into the back of her wardrobe. Into the sheets. She buried her face in them, smelling him, smelling them, rocking back and forth, sobbing into the fabric, wanting it all to be over, wanting him home and everything to be normal again. Although she didn't know what normal was any more. She had forgotten. Lost all trace of it.

She stood up, opened a drawer and pulled out her gift for him, his name still on the clip, waiting to be claimed. She lay on her bed, still in her clothes, holding the sheets and the pen, waiting for her parents, but fell asleep and woke the following morning to the sound of her son. He was demanding food. She called to Natasha.

'She's gone,' said her father. 'The basement's empty.'

'It must have been terrifying for her.'

'No backbone, that's all. Typical Russian.'

'It was horrendous, Father.'

'They got lucky, that's all.'

'Have you slept?'

'Not yet. It was a long night.'

'I can imagine.'

She lit a fire, made coffee and fed Johannes. Her mother slept on, leaving Katharina to pick up Natasha's routine. She was glad of it. It gave her a reason to go out and see the city.

The butcher's shop was gone, pulverized, but still women queued outside. Katharina joined them, unsure why. Nobody told her and she never asked. She waited half an hour, concluded that nothing would happen and abandoned the queue, a loud cheer rising as she walked away. The butcher had arrived and was setting up a stall on the street. She rushed to retrieve her place, shoving at their ankles with her pram. Nobody looked at her, nobody moved. They would not let her in. She adjusted her fur hat and left.

She headed towards the city centre where she found carrots, bread, some apples, but no meat. At the pawnshop, she chose a dress suitable for the Weinart party. Grass-green velvet. He agreed to hold it for her.

'I need to think about it.'

'We all do, Mrs Faber.'

The city's soldiers and its older men were sifting through the rubble as she went home, looking for those who had survived and those who hadn't. Fires were still burning in parts of buildings too high to reach.

She stoked the cinders and fed lunch to her son. Her mother was still in bed, but awake. Smoking.

'Are you all right, Mother?'

'Fine.'

'It was horrible, wasn't it?'

'It was worse for Johannes.'

Her father returned, covered in dust, without any meat. They had bread and vegetable soup, eating in silence. Katharina put Johannes to bed and packed a suitcase with her papers, Peter's letters, his pen and their sheets. She added food, clothes and nappies for her son and put the case by the hall door, ready for the next air raid.

'You won't need all that, Katharina.'

'I believe I will, Father.'

CHAPTER 53

She put on the green velvet dress and waited for Meyer to arrive to take her to the Weinarts' Christmas party. Her parents had already left, and Johannes had been at the house since mid-afternoon, playing with their children and nanny.

She looked in the mirror and traced her fingers across the lines dug into her brow, over the large purple circles under her eyes, showing through the make-up, seemingly permanent, indelible, a lifelong reminder of terror. Even Johannes had dark shadows, though he was not yet two, and little worry lines etched between his eyes.

The doorbell rang. She opened it wide, and smiled at Meyer. He was holding flowers, an assortment of carnations and roses, and a small box of milk chocolates. She kissed him and thanked him. She invited him in, and poured him some whisky. He stood with his back to the fire.

'It's a lovely place, Katharina.'

'We like it.'

'Maybe we can find somewhere else for your parents, and we could live here.'

'Maybe. Do you want ice?'

306

'Please.'

She moved to the kitchen, the underskirts rustling, the velvet silent. She spooned ice into his glass.

'You look lovely, Katharina.'

'Thank you.'

She set the drink on the table.

'Where's Johannes?'

'Already there. If there's a raid, I want him with me.'

'That was clever thinking.'

'It was Mrs Weinart's idea.'

'She's a clever woman.'

'She's very fond of him. And he adores her children.'

'Everybody's happy then.'

'So it seems.'

He put down his glass, took her arms and began to kiss her neck.

'We should go,' she said. 'They're starting earlier, remember.'

'I want you. Now. Here.'

'Not here. Not until we're married.'

'I can't wait that long, Katharina.'

She slipped out from under him and moved towards the door.

'You'll just have to.'

She picked up her suitcase.

'Why are you taking that?'

'It's for Johannes. In case there's a raid. The things I need for him.'

'Let me carry it for you.'

'It's fine. It's light.'

'It doesn't suit your dress.'

'It's only to the car.'

'You're a funny woman, Katharina Spinell.'

'Faber.'

'Meyer.'

At the party, she and Meyer were seated on the first floor, at the same table as Elizabeth, her husband and other men in black uniform and their wives, who wore large diamonds around their necks and on their fingers. Her parents remained upstairs, in the same room as the previous year. There was no sign of the baron or baroness.

To start, there were prawns and pink champagne. Katharina took a prawn, pulled off the head and yanked apart the shell. She glanced down at Meyer's watch and at the sandbags packed against the windows. It was half past six and already dark; the bombers had never come this early. She tried to slow her eating, to still her nerves, but she swallowed the prawn, and quickly started a second. Elizabeth was on her third, her head bent, obscuring the diamonds at her throat. Katharina drank the champagne and leaned towards her.

'How are the children?'

'They're at home and I'm here.'

'It's not far, Elizabeth.'

'I know and so far we've escaped. We've been lucky.'

'So have we.'

'Where's Johannes?'

'Here, in the house. Preparing for bed, I hope.'

'That helps.'

'A little, yes.'

'It's been awful, Katharina. I find it terrifying. Night after night. Last night was horrible.'

Elizabeth's husband whispered, briefly but forcefully. She nodded.

'Your dress is very beautiful, Katharina. I like the green. Did you find it locally?'

'I did,' she said. 'It's hard to go anywhere else these days.'

Elizabeth looked at her husband. He looked at his watch.

The soup came and went; the applause for the goose was muted, as though they were afraid of drawing the bombers' attention. Katharina chewed the meat, sitting on the edge of the chair, her feet flat on the floor, puzzling over the best way to reach her son, the fastest way to lift him from his cot and run with him for shelter. The Weinarts had a bunker in their basement but she preferred the strength of the concrete shelters on the street. Cellars collapsed, with people still inside. She preferred to be above ground.

She started the chocolate mousse and raspberry dessert, and turned to Meyer.

'I'm ready to go now, Joachim,' she said. 'To collect Johannes and go home.'

'It's too early, Katharina. Too rude.'

'I can't concentrate. I'm too nervous.'

'One hour more and it'll be too late for them. Have some more champagne.'

She did and the hour passed. They partied until dawn, drinking, dancing, and she had sex with Meyer at the top of a staircase, her dress rucked up around her hips. She went home, slept, and collected Johannes before the Weinarts sat down to lunch with their children.

'It was a marvellous night, Mrs Weinart. Even better than last year.'

'You seemed to enjoy it, Katharina.'

'It was kind of you to have Johannes.'

'He's a darling. Like one of my own.'

CHAPTER 54

It was bitterly cold the night they lost the apartment. The wind cut through their coats as they walked back east towards their previous home, outside the reach of the English bombers. Her father still had the key and the lock turned as it used to. She switched on the light in the hall and walked down the windowless corridor into the kitchen. Everything was as it had been, as though they had never left. She put Johannes to sleep in the bed she had shared with Peter, settled her mother into Johannes' bedroom and her father into hers, then sat at the kitchen table until dawn, until her son woke looking for food, for comfort, for an end to the chaos.

She fed him from the food she kept in the suitcase, tucked between the sheets: crackers, tinned meat and dried milk. She changed and washed his nappy. She now had only three. The rest had been in the old apartment, and new ones were hard to come by. Pins impossible. She boiled some water and drank it hot, waiting for her father to wake.

'We'll go the Weinarts and see if they can help us,' he said.

'I need some clothes. So does Johannes.'

She opened and closed each cupboard.

'We have no food, Father. We have nothing. Absolutely nothing.'

'We'll sort something out.'

She went to the bathroom. The water was surprisingly hot.

'Could you look after Johannes?'

He nodded and took the child on his lap. She closed the door, filled the bath and began to undress, the city's dust falling to the floor. She stepped into the hot water and submerged her head, relieved to be away from the noise, the chaos, the explosions. Their whole side of the street had gone. Vanished. Their lives lost in a mound of rubble, curtains, bedposts, wardrobe doors and books. Everything was gone. Their piano, bed linen and silks, the bust of Wagner, all pounded to nothing. She sat up. Everything had only to be tolerated. But it was all intolerable. Meyer's fleshy hands and the voices of the women making plans for the rest of her life. She had a husband. She didn't need another one. She got out of the bath, dried herself quickly with a towel she did not recognize and dressed again in the same clothes.

Her son whimpered. She took him from her father.

'He's hungry.'

'It's a bit early for the Weinarts'.'

'Maybe Mrs Sachs has something.'

'You can't go to her, Katharina.'

'Why not?'

'It's not a good idea. To become dependent on her.'

'But we are dependents, Father.'

'Not on her.'

'Why not on her?'

'She'd enjoy it too much. Our being back here.'

'Back where we started.'

'Something like that.'

'So tell me now, Father, that it was all worth it.'

'One step forward, two steps back. That's how it goes sometimes, Katharina.'

'My husband's child is hungry. I'm going to Mrs Sachs.'

She knocked on the door, lightly, Johannes in her arms. Mrs Sachs was in her dressing gown.

'I thought I heard noise last night,' she said.

'Our apartment was hit.'

'And your old one happened to be empty.'

'Yes.'

'And your father knew about it.'

'I suppose he did. Johannes is hungry and we have no food.'

'I'll see what I can find. But only for him.'

'I understand. Thank you.'

She disappeared down the corridor, windowless too, and returned with some porridge flakes and milk.

'That should be enough for him.'

'Thank you.'

'None of this is his fault. I won't take it out on him.'

'Thank you.'

She went back upstairs, warmed the milk and dropped in the porridge flakes. Her father was smoking and staring out the window.

'How did you know this place was empty, Father?'

'I just did.'

'But how? And where did the people go?'

'They were scum, Katharina. They should never have been given a place as fine as this to begin with.'

'This place is not fine. It's a dump. That's why we left, remember?'

'It's the best we have for the moment. We'll go the Weinarts' after Johannes has eaten.'

The Weinarts' house remained undamaged. Not a crack in a window or a sill knocked out of place. Her father pressed the white ceramic doorbell and a maid asked them to wait in the hall. Mrs Weinart arrived, running down the stairs towards them, her arms, eyes and mouth open wide. Katharina began to cry, burying her head in Johannes' hair as her father explained. Mrs Weinart took them downstairs to the kitchen.

'We'll give you everything you need, Katharina. Everything to start again.'

They drank hot coffee, ate bread, cheese, salami and packed up a picnic for her mother. Mrs Weinart put her arm around Katharina's shoulders.

'We'll come through this, Katharina,' she said. 'Wait and see. They can't defeat us.'

The nanny took Johannes to find clothes that the Weinart children had grown out of, while the butler went in search of suits for Mr Spinell.

'We'll find you another couple of uniforms too, Günther.'

'Thank you, Mrs Weinart.'

'Katharina, you and I will sort out something for you and your mother.'

Katharina followed her up the stairs, to a part of the house she hadn't seen before, where the carpets were softer, thicker, paler in colour.

'You have been very kind to us, Mrs Weinart.'

'Your father has worked hard for my husband, Katharina. We admire that.'

Mrs Weinart opened several wardrobe doors.

'I can only assume that you have nothing, Katharina.'

'Nothing.'

'You had collected some beautiful pieces recently. Things that fitted you perfectly. High quality, too.'

'It has been a good time to find quality, Mrs Weinart.'

'You did well. I admire that too.'

She trawled through the rails, holding things up, putting them back, muttering until she had assembled a pile.

'Take these to my bathroom. Try them on. They might fit.'

Katharina carried them into the room with two sinks, a bidet, bath and shower and placed the clothes on the floor of clean, bright white tiles. As she closed the door, she saw a silk robe hanging from a hook, identical to her own. She went back into the bedroom.

'I have the same robe as you. Joachim gave it to me.'

'You do? Oh, yes, of course you do.'

The Weinarts' chauffeur took them back to the east side of the city, the car loaded with a cot, blankets, clothes and food. Katharina met Mrs Sachs in the hall, pulling on her gloves.

'You're being looked after.'

'We are, Mrs Sachs.'

'You won't need me, then.'

'I suppose not, but thank you for this morning.'

She put the food into the cupboards, scrubbed the floors, sinks, toilet and bath, and made her bed, using the sheets she had shared with Peter. Johannes scurried up and down the corridor, delighted with the slip and glide of the linoleum under his knees. She made dinner, vegetable soup with chunks of meat and grey bread, and called her parents to the table.

Her father came first. He sat in his usual place. Her mother followed, still in her nightdress. She stared at the table, at her grandson sitting in the place once occupied by her son.

'Move him from there, Katharina. Put him in your place.'

Katharina moved her son. Her mother sat down and lit a cigarette.

316

'I'm not hungry.'

'You have to eat, Mother. There might be nothing tomorrow.'

She finished her cigarette, and lifted her spoon.

'So what was it all for, Günther? We end up back here anyway.'

'We'll find somewhere else soon, Esther.'

Katharina broke some bread and dipped it into her soup.

'I won't be moving again,' she said. 'I'm staying this time.'

'Why?' said her father. 'The apartment is a hovel and the area is riddled with communists. They'll despise you.'

'Maybe they'd be right.'

'It's ridiculous to be here any longer than you have to, Katharina.'

'I'm staying. It's out of reach of the bombers.'

'We'll find somewhere nicer outside their range. You'll be hated here, Katharina.'

'I promised Peter that I would wait for him, and this is where I'll wait.'

'My God, Katharina.'

Her mother lit another cigarette.

'And what about Mr Meyer?' she said.

'What about him?'

'You were going to marry him.'

'I'm already married. To Peter.'

Her mother slapped her hand against the table. Johannes startled, but didn't cry.

'You're a stupid girl, Katharina. Meyer is the

317

only one who can get you out of here. Who can get us all out.'

'You do what you have to do, Mother. I am staying.'

'And your son?' said Mr Spinell.

'My son needs his father.'

'His father is useless to you. Find him another.'

'He will only have one father.'

Her mother stood up.

'You're impossible, Katharina. Life is not the fairy tale you want it to be.'

'I'm quite aware of that, Mother.'

CHAPTER 55

The Weinarts sent him a car for his second birthday, a small red one, but there was no birthday party or cake, just Katharina and her son in the park, his feet paddling in the water, his mother holding on to him, ruffling his hair with her kisses.

CHAPTER 56

Berlin, October 24th, 1944

My darling Peter,

Aachen surrendered today, my love. That beautiful cathedral in the hands of our enemies. I once spent a day in that warren of streets, and now it's theirs. The people who want to destroy us. Humiliate us.

How must it have been, my darling, to know the Americans were coming, to sit waiting, knowing your troops were doing their best, but watching them flee, your protectors, fleeing in the face of the enemy?

I suppose that I shall find out. My father refuses to tell me anything about the Russians, but I know it is imminent. The whole city knows it.

I spend most of my days alone with our son, with barely any adult to talk to. Mrs Weinart seldom invites us to visit any more, maybe once a month, or every six weeks. She is not as sociable as she used to be, or else I am no longer welcome. Truth is hard to find these days.

I wonder who will reach us first? The Russians or the English and Americans? I think about fleeing; all day I consider my options. The truth is, my love, I have none. I have nowhere to go. No one who would want to house me and our son. The roads are already clogged and my father refuses to leave anyway. He insists that Berlin will be safe. I don't know why he thinks that. Nowhere else is.

I squirrel away what food I can, hiding it even from my parents. I need to keep our son alive, so that you will meet him one day. Whenever that will be, I don't know, but it will be because I know that you are alive. I know that you would not die on me. I know that, so I will keep waiting for you. Here. In this house. Where we first made love. Where we made our son.

My God, I love you. You and Johannes are all I have.

Katharina

PS I will store this letter and keep it for you. So that you know how much I missed you. How much I needed you.

CHAPTER 57

He vomited as she lifted him out of his chair. She cleaned him up and laid him in his cot in fresh clothes, watching as he fell asleep. She lay down too, uncertain why she was so reluctant to leave him. He had vomited before. Eventually, she fell asleep, lightly enough to hear him yelp, to be beside him as he vomited a second time, his face flushed, his eyes glazed. She picked him up. He was limp, in some state other than sleep. She washed and dressed him, pulled on their coats and ran down onto the street and across the city, stumbling under the child's weight because trains and taxis could no longer function. She carried him in her arms, on one hip, then on the other, wishing she had her old pram, with its excellent suspension. She ran again, but then walked, exhausted by his weight. His leadenness. She reached the doctor's door and knocked. Mrs Weinart opened it.

'Thank God you're home, Mrs Weinart. It's Johannes. He seems really sick.'

'I'll fetch my husband.'

They followed him to his study where he undressed

her son, removing his coat, his sweater, his shirt and vest, revealing skin covered in a red rash. He examined the child's eyes, listened to his breathing, and moved his neck backwards and forwards. The doctor sighed. He put the boy's vest back on, buttoned his shirt and trousers. He handed Katharina the child and his sweater.

'Katharina, it's not good news.'

'What do you mean?'

'Johannes has meningitis.'

'Thank God I brought him to you.'

'He needs antibiotics.'

She breathed into his hair.

'That's fine. He can have them.'

'I don't have enough.'

'Enough?'

'No.'

'What do you mean?'

'I don't have enough to give him any, Katharina.'

'But you have some? You could give him some and make him at least a little better?'

'Supply is very limited, Katharina. Restricted.'

'I really don't understand, Dr Weinart.'

'I need it for other children.'

'Other children?'

'The children of senior party members. I have to keep it for them.'

'They're not sick. My son is sick.'

'They might become sick and need it.'

She felt her legs sag. Mrs Weinart guided her to a chair, so soft that she could barely feel its leather.

'You can't do this, Dr Weinart.'

'I'm afraid that I have to.'

She looked at the doctor, at his wife.

'But you said he was like one of your own.'

'He is, Katharina,' said Dr Weinart.

'So, give him the medicine. As you would give it to one of yours.'

'I can't, Katharina.'

'Who would know?'

'I would.'

'So lie to yourself.'

He laughed.

'I can't do that, Katharina. I am too honest a man.'

'So who are you saving it for, Dr Weinart? The Führer doesn't have any children.'

'At this stage, all my paediatric medicines are for the children of senior party members.'

'Like Joachim?'

'Yes, like Joachim.'

She stroked her child's hand. His cheek.

'And the women with the blue crosses?'

'In all likelihood, yes.'

'But I don't qualify?'

'No, Katharina, you do not.'

'What more should I have done?'

'There's no point in going into that now, Katharina.'

'Now seems as good a time as any other.'

Mrs Weinart put a hand on Katharina's shoulder.

'You're upset, Katharina,' she said. 'Maybe you should go home.'

Katharina nodded and began to dress her son in his sweater and coat.

'I remember that coat,' said Mrs Weinart. 'It's adorable on him.'

Katharina picked up her bag and stood up.

'So what happens to my son, Dr Weinart?'

'He'll go into a coma, Katharina, and not come out of it.'

'And that's it?'

'I'm afraid so.'

'Was my brother not enough for you, Dr Weinart?'

'I'm sorry, Mrs Faber?'

'Not enough of a sacrifice?'

He screwed the cap back onto his pen.

'I think you should leave now, Mrs Faber.'

'First my brother, now my son. Possibly my husband too. For the great cause.'

'You're upset, Katharina.'

'I am, Mrs Weinart. I am upset.'

'It's understandable.'

'When is it your turn, Dr Weinart? Your turn to sacrifice? Your wife, first? One of your children?'

'You should go now, Mrs Faber.'

He took her arm and steered her through his study door to the hall.

'One day you will see that this is better for your son, Mrs Faber.'

'Better?'

'His father failed his country. It is hard for a child to live with that legacy.'

He led Katharina to the front door.

'And these things can have a genetic component, Katharina.'

'What things? Meningitis?'

'No, no. Bravery, courage.'

She stared at him, her child against her chest.

'Choose more carefully next time, Katharina.'

She went to a hospital to show them her son. They sympathized, but had nothing. Nor did the next hospital. He had a seizure in the third hospital. Still they had nothing.

She returned home at dawn and crawled into their sheets, their child cradled in her arms. She took off his hat and kissed him on the forehead, on the lips and cheeks, over and over. She brushed back his hair and sang to him, a lullaby, soothing him, holding him, rocking him, as though he were asleep.

CHAPTER 58

He saw them at the head of the queue. Three of them, laughing. One of them holding a knife. He tucked his bowl into his chest and looked down, pretending not to see them, focusing on a small yellow flower shutting down for the day. The end of the first day of April.

He could see them moving down the line, their guards' boots stopping intermittently. They stopped at him. They were drunk and shouting in broken German. One of them shoved him. He remained upright. They moved on and stopped at the next German. They pushed him. He fell and they yanked him from the line, to a place where everybody could see. They kicked him in the head, the back, the belly, and stamped on him, snapping bones, all the time shouting victory to Russia. And then there was the knife, stabbed in and out of flesh, blood spurting. Screams. Shouts. Russia would fuck Germany's women. Faber stared at the flower, its yellow almost hidden by green sepals.

He moved up the queue, collected soup and bread and sat down. They gathered around him, jackets wet with blood. He was the only German left. They had shot Schultz, and the others had died, leaving him with a handful of Austrians, Romanians and Hungarians. The other prisoners were Russian, sent north for theft, murder and dissent.

He carried on eating, pretending everything was normal. Just another moment to be endured. The soup tasted of nothing. Of worse than nothing. Of spit. Of urine. Of their hatred. Of all the things to be avenged now that Germany had lost. The other prisoners were staring at him, their spoons suspended, their bodies leaning away. He tipped the soup into his mouth. A man can survive anything when his wife is faithful to him. That's what the Russians say. He dipped the spoon back into the bowl and lifted it towards his mouth. They seized him, dragged him from the bench, splinters digging into the underside of his emaciated thighs, and pulled him across the yard, past the dead German, to the box. A space too low to stand up in, too narrow to lie down in. They closed the door and bolted it. No bench. No pot. The only light and air from gaps in the slats of wood. He buried his face in his hands. His bowl would be gone. His spoon too. He'd never get them back.

He touched the wood, its coarse planks and rusting nails. He had probably built it himself, one of dozens of watch-towers, sheds and huts thrown together over the years as they moved from one camp to the next, remaining only long enough to cut down all the trees within a ten-mile radius.

He tried to stretch his legs, to get comfortable, but it was impossible. He sat on his heels, a bird perched in a small cage.

He heard the other prisoners at evening chores, their feet shuffling over dried mud as they swept paths, filled in holes and chopped wood, their breath heavy and laboured, their matchsitck bodies throwing shadows as they passed the box.

It was strange to be apart from the other prisoners and the guards. He had not been on his own since Stalingrad. It was pleasant in a way, to escape the tedium of chores, the stench of the shed packed with wooden slatted cots piled on top of each other, layer upon layer of filth, grime and disease. He was always on a bottom bunk, always vulnerable to the drip of men pissing in their sleep, too exhausted or sick to visit the pot. He leaned his head against the side of the hut. He should rest. Sleep. He had been through worse. He had slept in smaller, tighter foxholes. He'd be fine.

He woke when it was dark. He needed to urinate. He unfastened his trousers and projected as far as he could, but it splashed him anyway, wetting his feet, his knees. He stretched a leg, lost his balance, unfolded the other, toppled again and returned to his initial position, his only possible position. He started to shiver. It was cold.

In the morning, he listened as the men lined up for breakfast, his ears straining for conversation. He heard nothing but intermittent coughing, the near

329

silence broken by the guards' shouts, the barrage of orders and commands that would last the whole day. He had thought that only he had withdrawn from conversation. But all the prisoners had, silence being easier to bear than contact with men who would die or disappear in the night. He had had no energy anyway. No energy to do anything but breathe and work.

They opened the door and shoved a bowl of gruel at him. Water too. But no spoon. He scooped it up with his hand and swallowed. It would keep him alive but it wouldn't repair his stripped muscles, frostbitten toes, dry skin and loose hair. He had no vitamins, no nutrients, none of the good things he had told his pupils of in their lessons. The importance of fruit. An apple. It would hurt now to eat one. To bite into one with his red, damaged gums.

He tried to stretch his limbs, his back, but it was hopeless. He listened to the morning roll call. His name was left out. Gone from its usual position between two Russian names. He knew neither of them. He knew nobody. He didn't want to know anybody. His bowl and spoon were gone. So now he had nothing. The photographs of Katharina and Johannes were gone too. Sold to somebody who had no wife or child, or just lost or shredded. Was that what they meant by communism? Owning nothing? Every man equal in deprivation?

On Sundays, he attended classes on the merits of communism, the instruction given by prison guards doubling as teachers. The room was warm and he was given a hot drink. Sometimes chocolate, or a biscuit. He sat near the fire, even in summer when the grate was empty so that he retained his place, feigning interest in their ranting, their insistence on one philosophy over another. He understood much of what they said, because they said the same thing over and over in Russian and pidgin German, underscoring their points with newspaper pictures of a shattered Berlin, shouting that they would prevail because they were right. He never sought an argument. Only warmth and extra food.

He heard the other men moving out of the yard to begin their slow walk to the forest, to resume the cutting of the day before. Fir and pine trees. He preferred cutting rowan, oak and spruce because it was warmer where they grew, and the animals were less threatening – foxes, deer and squirrels rather than wolves and bears. It was brighter too, the light able to penetrate the leaves, to reach the forest floor. For he hated the dark. Men went mad in the darkness, walking naked through the snow, Russian and German alike; they were left behind when the camp moved on, abandoned, feral.

His legs began to cramp. He banged at the shed door, but nobody came. It was silent. He could not even hear the guards. Maybe they had gone, moved to a new camp. It never took long to leave; they had nothing to carry except a few tools for chopping and cooking. The men he loathed had left him. He banged harder. Somebody banged back, the butt of a gun pounding the roof.

'Shut up, you German bastard. Stalin will never let you out.'

They could do what they liked now. There would be no retaliation.

He slept until he heard the prisoners return, legs heavy with fatigue. They would wash, cursorily, and queue for food. Suddenly the door was opened, and he reached towards the light, the fresh air, but it was shut off again, a bowl of soup and cup of water at his feet. It had potato and traces of some fowl, probably turkey. The prisoners again started their evening duties, indifferent to his light taps against the wood, his yearning for contact.

What had he done? He was a soldier fighting in a war. It was his duty. He had done only what was asked of him. He had done nothing wrong, but they would leave him locked in a box, dying of hunger and thirst, leave him until only his bones remained, until nobody could tell it was him, nobody could tell Katharina how hard he had tried to live for her.

He started to shout, demanding to be let out. They banged on the box with their guns and fired bullets. He crouched and fell silent. He had been through worse. Stalingrad was worse.

When it was dark, they gathered around the shed and pounded on the roof. Dozens of them. Laughing. Shaking the box. Rattling it.

They left and he fell asleep until they returned to taunt him again. Three more times during the night, and again at dawn, whispering through the cracks in broken German.

'We'll fuck your wife, Faber.'

Faber shouted at them, screamed.

'Leave my wife alone.'

Again they banged their guns against the shed and laughed.

'It's our turn now, Faber. Our turn with your women.'

'I never went near your women. Never touched them.'

They shouted at him again, something he didn't understand, and left. There was silence. It was the hour when the wolves retreat and the birds emerge. He was sobbing, at the pain in his back, his hips, his knees, at the injustice. He had never raped, never even touched a Russian woman. He was a married man.

He slept then, waking when he heard the men at breakfast. He started shaking, his body a knot of pain, fatigue, hunger and loneliness. He banged at the door.

'Leave my wife alone.'

Nobody came near him. He rested his forehead on his knees and cradled his legs. A child in a broom cupboard. He passed the laurel hedge and went into his parents' living room. He sat on the sofa. His mother came in, drew back the curtains and set down a cup of tea for him, a matching cup and saucer, and a side plate from the same service, with freshly baked biscuits.

'Thank you, Mother.'

She kissed his head.

'You're welcome, darling.'

He drank and ate and gazed at the shelves, at the books lined up alphabetically and the ornaments still clean from their weekly dusting: the ballerina, pink, dainty porcelain in a house with no girls; the carriage clock as old as the marriage; the plates on display; and his gifts to her from his youth movement trips: a little blue bus from Bonn, a red ceramic train from Dusseldorf; she kept everything, every gift he had given her was dusted every Tuesday. He wondered what day it was. Was it Tuesday? Was she dusting? Would they bring him breakfast?

They didn't. He screamed at them, screamed for food. A guard came, banged on the shed, and walked away.

Faber crawled back onto the sofa and picked up the blue bus. He rocked back and forth. Toe to heel, heel to toe. The blue bus had always been his favourite. Hers too. He started to cry, calling for his mother. They hammered at the shed again. He screamed. They battered the wood, splinters flying at his face. He screamed louder. They fired a shot into the hut, over his head. He fell silent. They walked away. He buried his head in his hands. He wanted Faustmann. Faustmann would know what to do, how to help him through. Or Weiss.

334

Or Fuchs. Even Kraus. They'd keep him straight. A boot in front to focus on, a path to follow. But he had no one. He was alone, dependent on himself, with only splinters of daylight to break the darkness.

He rocked harder, heel to toe, toe to heel. He buried his face in Katharina's hair. Shutting his eyes harder, shutting out Weiss' spilling stomach, Kraft's shit, his shit, everybody's shit. He didn't want it any more. Any of it. All he wanted was his wife. A man can survive anything when his wife is faithful to him. That's what the Russians say. He would survive if she was faithful, if she was waiting for him.

They brought him soup and water. He wolfed both, but didn't ask for more. He fell into a deep sleep. They let him out the following morning, in time for breakfast, in time for the march to the forest.

CHAPTER 59

Her father knocked, pushing open her bedroom door. She was still in her nightclothes, smoking.

'We should leave, Katharina.'

'Why?'

'One day, two days at most, and they'll be in the city.'

'What about those barricades you built, Father? Won't they stop them?'

'Don't, Katharina.'

'Kitchen tables and sofas. That should do it.'

'You're being rude. Get dressed.'

'I'm not going.'

'You're as bad as your mother.'

'I'm staying here. I keep telling you that.'

'I'm not leaving without you.'

'Of course you are.'

She lit another cigarette, from the one still burning.

'Where will you go, Father?'

'West. Try to cross the bridge.'

She closed her eyes. He left. She went to sleep. When she woke, she heard a banging, but not the sound of shelling. She walked down the hall. Her mother was in the kitchen. Banging the cupboard doors.

'There's nothing to eat, Katharina.'

'Not for some time, Mother.'

'And to drink?'

'I'll heat some water.'

The two of them, the mothers of dead sons, sat at the kitchen table, with cups of hot water and cigarettes.

'What will happen, Katharina?'

'We'll run out of cigarettes.'

'And then?'

'Do you care, Mother?'

'Not a lot, no.'

'Well then, why bother asking?'

'It hasn't gone very well for us, has it, Katharina?'

'No.'

'I wonder how it might have been if you had married the doctor's son?'

Katharina went back to her room. She closed the door and sat at the window, looking down at the street, at the woman draped across the kerb, her body beginning to bloat. The buildings opposite were gone, and the row of houses beyond them had been flattened too. Their side of the street, however, remained untouched.

She was still awake at four in the morning, smoking, drinking hot water, when her father returned.

'I've got food,' he said. 'Wake your mother.'

They watched as he unwrapped the newspaper, showing off his four pieces of grey meat, long and narrow, each one about half the width of a chicken breast. Katharina poked at them with her finger.

'What is it, Father?'

'Meat.'

'It's rat, isn't it?'

'It's food. Take it or leave it.'

The gas still worked in their house. He fried the meat and she ate.

'Why did you come back, Father?'

'I couldn't cross.'

'That's a surprise.'

'I'll try again in a few hours.'

'Does it matter? West or east, we've lost.'

'The Russians are bastards, Katharina.'

'And we're not?'

In the morning, they moved into the cellar. The other neighbours were already there, Mrs Sachs among them. Katharina sat on the floor, a blanket over her legs, staring as Mrs Sachs poured coffee and handed a cupful to her husband with a chunk of still-warm bread. Katharina swallowed her saliva.

'Where did you find that, Mrs Sachs?'

'I have connections, Katharina. Ones more reliable than yours.'

'So it seems.'

'You're better off without anyway, Katharina.'

'I'm sorry?'

'Help you lose a little weight. Those Russians like a bit of fat around the bottom, women used to cream cakes and chocolate. Like yourself, Katharina.'

She curled under a blanket to wait, to listen,

although she was uncertain for what she was waiting or listening. She had seen the women arriving from the east, terrorized. They talked feverishly or not at all; their eyes staring straight ahead, looking at nothing, seeing everything.

'It'll be a relief, won't it, Mother?'

'What will be, Katharina?'

'When they're here and we can just get on with things again.'

'We're being invaded, Katharina.'

'But at least it'll soon be over. Waiting is worse.'

'We'll see.'

'She has a point, Mrs Spinell,' said Mrs Sachs. 'Waiting is always the hardest part. It won't be as bad as we think.'

'Your communist friends will be here at last, Mrs Sachs,' said Mr Spinell.

'Where are your friends, Mr Spinell?'

They fell silent, cramped into the small cellar, its door under the stairs fortified by three chairs and a desk. Their toilet was in the darkest corner, a bucket tucked behind a scrap of curtain, its contents emptied during lulls in the shelling, piss, shit and crumpled newspaper scattered over the street.

They were there all of a sudden, as though a dam had broken, thousands of them hammering the streets with their feet. She looked at them through the tiny window. At their big, clumping, filthy boots. The tanks, grinding at the tarmacadam. Half-tanks and jeeps. Heavy guns pulled by horses, ponies and American trucks. Animal dung all over the pavements. She sat down again and buried her head under the blanket, pressing the wool against her ears. But she could still hear the triumphant rattle of the machine guns and the bellicose singing, the victorious, drunken swagger of them all. She had not expected so much aggression. She had expected soldiers like her husband and brother, gentle men carrying out their duties. But these men were angry and terrifying. And they wanted revenge. She stuffed the blanket into her mouth and screamed. She wanted her husband.

They barely moved for two days, sipping water and nibbling crackers, accepting Mrs Sachs' offerings of dried sausage, her father's gratitude muted. They heard them on the stairs, hard to tell how many, charging from one apartment to the next, smashing down doors, shouting at each other, running along hallways until they crashed through the cellar door, unperturbed by the barricade, torchlight swinging from one side of the room to the other. The soldiers staggered, laughing, looking first at Mrs Sachs, then at Katharina; their beams focused on her as she pressed into her mother. Mrs Spinell moved away from her daughter. Katharina leaned towards her father. He moved away too. The soldiers shouted at her and gestured with their torches towards the door. She was still. One of them hit her across the head with his torch, the beam careering across the room. She looked at her mother, at her father. They looked at their feet.

She held onto her father's sleeve but he jutted his chin towards the door.

'Good girl, Katharina.'

She stood up and they slapped her bottom. She climbed the steps to the entrance hall where dark was settling. They knocked her to the floor, but she scrambled away from them, on her hands and knees to the bottom of the stairs. They grabbed her legs and flipped her over, a flat fish on the pan.

One of them slapped her face, ripped her knickers and pulled apart her legs. The first. Pushing at her. His fist in her face when she tried to stop him, to close herself down so he couldn't enter. Then a searing, ripping pain. His weight on her chest, suffocating her, his cloying, acrid stench; drink, horse manure, campfire smoke and sweat. She turned her face away from him, towards the stairs, staring at the fraying linoleum, the wood worn smooth by her childhood feet running up and down the steps, to and from school, and later, when she was older, to and from work. And then Peter. His feet on those steps. She felt a final thrust. He fell on top of her, belched into her face. She closed her eyes. He pulled out and spat at her. At her face, her eyes. She rubbed his spit away and tried to sit up. The second pushed her back down and ripped her blouse, her bra. Reeking of cigarettes, he pinned her shoulders to the floor. And then she saw her son's little feet, up and down. Crawling, then walking, his little hands gripping one bannister, then the next as he hauled his way up. The third. Rougher than the others. The fourth. More gentle, or was she so numbed? Then the first again. More hitting. More spitting. More of him when she wanted none of him. The second. Or was it the third? The smell of cigarettes. The fourth only once. The first insisting that he could go a third time, his fists against her face when he failed. He stood and pissed on her, the others laughing as they hauled up their trousers, picked up their guns and left, the hall door open so that she could see the street, the horse and human dung smeared one into the other by wheels and tracks, the city no longer hers, no longer German; the grocer's shop shuttered, the shop empty – Mr Ewald had fled to the Black Forest. She was waiting for Peter. She had promised she would.

She reached out to pick at a fraying thread, but it was too far away. Her hand fell to the floor. Why had she bothered going up and down those stairs? What had been the point? Her son and brother were dead. Her husband might be dead too. Was she as good as dead? Would she ever be known as anything other than the woman given away by her father, by her mother? She whispered to Peter, begging him to be alive. He was all she had.

It was dark when she woke, blood crusted on her face, legs and clothes, their fluids mixed with hers. She pulled herself upright and, using the bannisters, dragged herself up the stairs. The door was open, the flat ransacked, but the bed was intact, the sheets still on. She crawled under the covers and went to sleep, waking to find Mrs Sachs beside her, a basin of water and cloths on her lap.

'I'll wash you, Katharina.'

She struggled to open her eyes, her mouth. Her voice rose only to a whisper.

'Where's my mother?'

'In the cellar. She's not able, Katharina.'

'She was able when it was Johannes.'

'It was a different time, Katharina.'

'I'll do it myself.'

'It's a big job, Katharina. You'll need some help.'

'I needed help earlier, Mrs Sachs. Not now.'

Mrs Sachs left. Katharina fell back to sleep. When she woke again it was daylight. Mrs Sachs was again beside her.

'Do you think Peter did that? He was a soldier.'

'A German soldier, Katharina. Properly behaved. A good man.'

'He hated being a soldier. I didn't understand then, Mrs Sachs. But I do now.'

'What, Katharina?'

'That they mould them to be like each other. As mad as each other. As vicious. That's what armies do.'

'Not the German army, Katharina.'

'Pillagers. Rapists. That's what all armies are, Mrs Sachs. What they become.'

'You don't know that.'

'Those Russians hated me.'

'Come on, let's clean you up, Katharina.'

Mrs Sachs helped her sit up and began to wash her face, her body, the water cold, the tears streaming quietly from Katharina's eyes, both women silent. Three of her teeth were broken, and her nose, eyes and lips were badly bruised. Her vagina was torn, her breasts and stomach covered in deep purple bruising. Mrs Sachs handed her some hot tea with a little sugar and covered the worst of her wounds with home-made poultices, the herbs older than they should have been.

'Thankfully you don't appear to need antibiotics.'

Katharina sobbed then.

'What am I going to tell Peter, Mrs Sachs?'

'I doubt, Katharina, that you will ever have to explain anything to him.'

'But what if he comes back? What do I tell him?'

Mrs Sachs leaned into her.

'You tell him nothing, Katharina. You tell nobody about this.'

'Won't people find out?'

'We won't tell them. You've been through enough already.'

'What if there's a child, Mrs Sachs? How will I explain that?'

'We'll deal with that when it arises.'

'You know somebody.'

'I do, Katharina. He's good. And safe.'

'Thank you.'

Her parents stayed in the cellar until the Russians

stopped drinking and began serving soup to those still in the city. They took the soup and moved back into their bedrooms.

'You'll feel better soon, Katharina.'

'Will I, Father?'

'I'm sure of it.'

She went to her bedroom and locked the door. She looked at herself in the mirror, at her bruises and her broken teeth. She lifted her scissors and cut her hair. Piece after piece falling down her back, to the floor.

CHAPTER 60

The other men in the carriage had written. He had decided against it.

He stared through the window, silently watching the landscape change and shift, relieved when the enormous forests fell out of view.

He looked for Katharina at the station, even though he knew she would not be there. The women who were, wives and mothers, sobbed when they saw their men, running fingers over hollowed cheeks, setting their heads against the men's bony chests. He moved away from them, towards the back of the station, through a horde of old men and women pushing photographs into his face, pictures of strong-shouldered sons, clean uniforms and smiling faces. He shook his head. Over and over. No, he knew none of them.

He went to a clinic where they washed and fed him, and treated him for lice, gum infection and scabies. They let him sleep for several days and, when he wanted to go, dressed him in a second-hand suit. They gave him money too, and a brown paper parcel that he could tuck under his arm.

'I'm going to see my wife and child,' he said.

'Good luck, Mr Faber.'

'Thank you.'

He pressed the doorbell and stepped back onto the pavement. He nodded at the grocer stacking his stall with bright, red tomatoes. Nobody came to the door. Faber went into the shop, paid for a tomato and ate it, licking at the juice dribbling down his chin, his mouth thrilling at its sweetness.

'You enjoyed that, Sir,' said the grocer.

'Are the Spinells still living here?'

'I've only just opened. I don't know the neighbours yet.'

'Do you have any dark chocolate? Any white flowers?'

'No Sir, those things are still hard to come by.'

'Thank you.'

Faber pushed at the door. It was unlocked. He went into the dark hallway and up the staircase, covered still in fraying linoleum. He stopped outside the door and listened, but heard nothing. He knocked. Lightly. A second time, with a little more force. She opened the door as he turned to leave. Spoke to him. Whispered.

'Peter.'

She reached out her hand, and he took it, wrapping it in both of his.

'You're still here, Katharina. You waited for me.'

She nodded, her lips and eyes closing. He stepped towards her. She buried her head in his chest. He kissed the top of her head.

'But your hair?'

'It's more practical this way, Peter.'

'I liked it long.'

'It's short now.'

A door opened. It was Mrs Spinell, her grey hair long and unkempt.

'Johannes?'

'No, Mother. It's Peter.'

The old woman closed the door again.

'Come in,' said Katharina.

He bowed his head, and stepped inside.

'I tried you first at the other address.'

'We moved back here a long time ago.'

'There is nothing of the house. Nothing left.'

'No. Nothing. Would you like coffee?'

'Please.'

She started to walk down the corridor. He pulled her back to him.

'It's good to see you again, Katharina.'

'And you, Peter. Come on, I'll make coffee.'

She turned to go, but he held her still.

'What happened to your teeth, Katharina?'

She hesitated.

'I fell,' she said. 'During an air raid. In the dark.'

'We can fix them.'

'I've learned to live with them as they are.'

He let her go and followed her down the hall, staring at the shortness of her hair, the narrowness of her hips. Her shoulders were bent forward, rounding her spine. She was different. But then so was he.

'Are you all right, Katharina?'

'I'm all right. And you?'

'Yes, I think so.'

He went into the kitchen, condensation still shimmering on the walls. A child was sitting at the table, his schoolbooks in front of him. Faber hunkered down beside the chair and touched the boy's arm.

'Johannes.'

'Hello. I'm doing my homework.'

'So I see.'

'I'm not supposed to talk. I'm supposed to concentrate.'

Faber smiled and stood up again, stemming his tears.

'Oh, I'm sorry. I'll let you get on. We can talk when you're finished.'

The child nodded.

'It's good to see you, Johannes. To meet you at last.'

'Thank you,' said the boy.

He returned to his homework.

Katharina had her back to them, slowly taking cups from the cupboard.

'We'll go to another room,' she said. 'Are you hungry?'

'Probably. I have learned not to be.'

She cut two pieces of bread and spread them with honey. She slid them onto a plate and poured coffee into the cups. There were no saucers. She led him to the room at the end of the hall, her bedroom.

'I remember this so well, Katharina.'

'You smell better this time.'

He smiled, briefly. She set down the cups and plate. He wrapped his arms around her, kissed her on the cheek and left his lips there, his eyes closed.

'It's so damn good to be here, Katharina.'

'How hard was it, Peter?'

'Terrible, but another time. Not now.'

She ran her hands over his face, her fingers lingering in the crevices.

'You're so thin.'

'I thought you liked me skinny.'

'Not like this. We'll have to feed you up.'

'I find it hard to eat a lot.'

'We'll go gently.'

'Thank you.'

'Eat now. The bread.'

He sat down on the end of the bed. She stayed by the window, sipping her coffee, looking down at the street, at a German man stepping off the pavement as Russian soldiers approached him.

Faber finished eating and lay down on the bed. She lay beside him and drew a blanket over both of them. He kissed her, on the lips.

'I missed you, Katharina.'

'How did you get through it?'

'I don't know. I had you and Johannes. That helped. Enormously.'

She kissed his lips, his cheeks.

'And how was it here, Katharina?'

'Awful. But you're here now. I knew you would be. One day.'

He ran his fingers over her lips, over her thinner face, and kissed her. She was crying, tears quietly sliding down her face.

'Why did you cut your hair?'

'I wanted to, Peter.'

'Will you grow it again? For me?'

'No.'

'But I like it long. It's how I think of you.'

'You'll have to think of me differently, Peter.'

He removed the blanket and sat up. He lit a cigarette. She took it. He lit a second.

'The room looks the same,' he said.

'I share it with Johannes.'

'He's a fine boy, Katharina.'

'He's a good child.'

'I lived to see him, you know. To hold him.'

She stood and looked again down at the street, at the Russians surrounding a woman, checking her papers.

'He's not yours, Peter.'

'Who isn't?'

'The boy. In the kitchen. He's not your son.'

'Of course he is.'

'No. He's not. Our son died. Of meningitis. When he was two.'

Faber stretched his bony hands across his thighs.

'So who is he? The child in the kitchen?'

'His actual name is Peter Johannes. But we call him Johannes. It's easier for us all.'

351

'No, Katharina, who is he? Who is his father?'

'I don't know.'

'You don't know?'

'Russian.'

'You went with those bastards?'

She drank the last of her coffee.

'I was raped, Peter.'

He closed his eyes, his lips moving in an almost silent whisper.

'No, Katharina. No. Not that.'

He was silent then. She sat beside him and held his hand, stroking his skin.

'When, Katharina? When did it happen?'

'April. When they won. Eight years ago.'

Tears fell down his face, and he took his hand from hers.

'That's too hard for me, Katharina.'

'It was terrible, Peter.'

He was nodding.

'No. It's too hard.'

He wiped his eyes and lifted his plate and cup. He handed them to her.

'Is there any more?'

'What?'

'Is there any more food?'

'Yes. Of course. I'll fetch you some.'

She poured coffee and cut two more slices of bread. Her son wanted some too.

'You'll be having dinner soon, darling.'

'But I'm hungry.'

She cut another slice for the child, and spread

it too with honey, a little more than she had given to Faber.

'Who is that man, Mummy?'

'An old friend.'

'He looks strange.'

'He's been away a long time. Now, back to your homework.'

She returned to the bedroom and he took the plate and cup.

'Why didn't you pretend that he was mine, Katharina? Make it easier for me.'

'No more lies, Peter. Only the truth.'

'I've had enough of truth.'

He ate and drank. Slowly.

'How could you go with them, Katharina? Have you any idea how they treated me?'

'I had no choice.'

'We all have choices, Katharina.'

'Do we?'

'You could have hidden from them.'

She looked again down at the street. The Russians let the woman go.

'There were four of them, Peter.'

He sucked on the bread, as chewing hurt too much.

'Mrs Sachs advised me never to tell you.'

'So why are you telling me?'

'You need to know the truth.'

'Why do I need to know the truth?'

'Because I need you to know the truth.'

He lit two more cigarettes. She took the one he offered her.

'Why did you keep him?'

'I had nothing left. He gave me something to live for.'

'You had me to live for. I told you I would be back.'

'I didn't know, Peter. I couldn't be sure.'

He stared at her.

'You gave up on me, Katharina.'

'I didn't, Peter. I waited here for you, as I promised.'

'You gave up on me, and had somebody else's child.'

She shook her head and stared back at him, her arms tight across her chest.

'I was raped, Peter, because I stayed in Berlin waiting for you.'

'So it's my fault that you were raped?'

'No, that's not what I said, Peter.'

'So what did you say? What are you saying?'

'I need you to accept me as I am, my son as he is.'

'No. I can't do that. I want you to be the way you were, the mother of my son.'

'That can't be, Peter.'

He ran his fingers through his hair.

'Maybe we can start again, Katharina? Have another child?'

'A sibling for Johannes?'

'No. Not him. Just us. Starting again.'

She wiped her eyes with her sleeve and straightened her skirt.

'How are your parents, Peter?'

'I don't know. I'll go there next.'

'Are you staying for dinner?'

'If you have enough.'

'Father will bring something back.'

'How is he?'

'Fine, though he has some arthritis.'

'And your mother?'

'She lives in her room. Johannes' old room.'

He pressed his fingertips into his temples.

'What did you expect of me, Katharina?'

'I don't know.'

'Did you expect me to want him?'

'He's a good child, Peter.'

'He's a Russian bastard.'

She walked to the door.

'Are you here for dinner, Peter?'

'You asked me that already.'

'I'm asking again.'

'I don't know whether I want dinner.'

Peter looked at her, at her short, cropped hair, at her broken teeth. He walked to the window and saw the Russians.

'How can you live here, Katharina? With them everywhere?'

'Where should I go, Peter?'

'To the west. The Americans, the British, even the French would be better than this.'

'They've been good to us, Peter. They give enough food. Medicine when we need it. And Father has some work with them.'

'He works for the Russians?'

'Didn't you?'

'I had no choice, Katharina.'

'We all have choices, don't we Peter?'

'He can choose not to.'

'You work for the Russians or for the Americans, that's your choice.'

'The Americans are better people.'

'Are they? The Russians fed us before the Americans. The Russians gave me antibiotics when mother had pneumonia. No one else did.'

He lit another cigarette. Only one.

'I can't stay here,' he said. 'With them. After all they have done.'

'We did it first, Peter.'

'We're not as bad as they are.'

'Aren't we?'

'You should move, Katharina. Get away.'

'My son is half Russian, Peter. It's easier here. And there are other women like me here.'

He drew heavily on the cigarette.

'So where will you go, Peter?'

'Away.'

'Will you stay in Germany?'

'No. Somewhere different.'

'Like where?'

'Somewhere there was no war. Ireland maybe.'

'It's supposed to be very beautiful.'

'There are no forests, and it might be a good place to think.'

'About what?'

'About nothing, Katharina. I want to think about nothing.'

They fell silent.

'Will you come with me, Katharina? We could start again.'

'With my son?'

'No. By yourself.'

'Then no.'

'You're my wife. He's not my son.'

She touched the door handle.

'I promised you that I would wait for you, Peter. I have done that.'

'And that's it? That's all it was? A promise? An undertaking?'

'So it seems.'

'I still want to be with you.'

'No, you don't.'

'I pledged myself to you, Katharina.'

'We pledged ourselves to a lot of things, Peter.'

He offered her another cigarette. She took it and sat on the end of the bed beside him, a gap between them.

'How do you think it will be living in Ireland?' she said.

'Easier than here.'

'I wonder if it is,' she said.

'What do you mean?'

'Germany is so hated, Peter. It must be horrible to be German in another country.'

'I don't know. I suppose I'll find out.'

'Would you like some food to take with you?'

'If you have any to spare, yes, that would be very kind.'

They returned to the kitchen and she crouched beside her son, to help him with his homework. Faber looked away, staring out the kitchen window at the fading afternoon, at the grocer stacking wooden crates. He saw Mr Spinell come down the hall, leaning heavily on a stick. The old man put a bag on the table and they shook hands.

'You're a strong man to have survived that. What work did they have you do?'

'Felling trees.'

'That explains how it's such a powerful country. Forcing its prisoners to do something useful. Something for the country. We should have done that instead.'

'I hate the place.'

'It's the future, Peter. I've started to learn the language.'

Mr Spinell sat down, slowly.

'There's meat, bread and vegetables. Lovely tomatoes.'

Katharina began to prepare a sandwich, quizzing her son's spelling as she chopped the tomatoes. Faber picked up his brown paper parcel.

'Actually, don't worry about food for me. I should be on my way.'

He shook Mr Spinell's hand.

'Send my regards to your wife, Mr Spinell.'

She opened the hall door for him. He kissed her on the cheek.

'Goodbye, Katharina.'

'Goodbye, Peter.'

She closed her eyes, shutting him out.

'I'm sorry, Katharina. I thought it would have been different. I imagined it differently.'

'We all did, Peter.'

She closed the door and he went slowly down the stairs, into the street. The wind whipped at his legs and neck, but he was used to colder weather, so he walked on, away, towards the train station, his shadow stretching in front of him.